ARSENIC AND OLD LIES

BENEDICT BROWN

Storm
PUBLISHING

This is a work of fiction. Names, characters, businesses, places, events and incidents are either the products of the author's imagination or used in a fictitious manner. Any resemblance to actual persons, living or dead, or actual events is purely coincidental.

Copyright © Benedict Brown, 2025

The moral right of the author has been asserted.

All rights reserved. No part of this book may be reproduced or used in any manner without the prior written permission of the copyright owner. This prohibition includes, but is not limited to, any reproduction or use for the purpose of training artificial intelligence technologies or systems.

To request permissions, contact the publisher at rights@stormpublishing.co

Ebook ISBN: 978-1-80508-827-1
Paperback ISBN: 978-1-80508-829-5

Cover design: Rose Cooper
Cover images: Shutterstock, Rhinefield House Hotel

Published by Storm Publishing.
For further information, visit:
www.stormpublishing.co

ALSO BY BENEDICT BROWN

The Marius Quin Mysteries
Murder at Everham Hall
The Hurtwood Village Murders
The Castleton Affair
A Body at the Grand Hotel

Lord Edgington Investigates…
Murder at the Spring Ball
A Body at a Boarding School
Death on a Summer's Day
The Mystery of Mistletoe Hall
The Tangled Treasure Trail
The Curious Case of the Templeton-Swifts
The Crimes of Clearwell Castle
The Snows of Weston Moor
What the Vicar Saw
Blood on the Banisters
A Killer in the Wings
The Christmas Bell Mystery
The Puzzle of Parham House
Death at Silent Pool
The Christmas Candle Murders
Murder in an Italian Castle

The Izzy Palmer Mysteries

A Corpse Called Bob

A Corpse in the Country

A Corpse on the Beach

A Corpse in London

A Corpse for Christmas

A Corpse in a Locked Room

A Corpse in a Quaint English Village

A Corpse at a Wedding

A Corpse at A School Reunion

A Corpse from the Past

*To my wife Marion and our incredible children,
Amelie and Osian.
You make the hard work worthwhile.*

ONE

I don't know if a dead body has ever inexplicably turned up in your home, but I wouldn't wish it on anyone. When I first found Gilbert Baines in my writing room, my breath caught in my throat, and I struggled to think as my world fell to pieces around me. I felt as if there'd been an earthquake, and the ground might crumble away at any second. I can't honestly say that I'd liked the man who was slumped over my desk, but that didn't mean I wanted him dead, and I was already imagining the impact his murder would have on those I love.

Beside the door there was a calling card belonging to Lucien Pike, a man who had apparently taken it upon himself to terrorise me. What I couldn't decide was whether he had killed Gilbert to get me in trouble or for some other dark reason I was yet to consider.

My detective's instincts fired up, and I found myself examining the scene of the crime. Aside from the paper rectangle, which would seem to explain who was responsible for the crime, I found no threads from the killer's clothes or unusual tread marks that would help identify him. And the stillness within this room – not to mention the thick red ring around

Gilbert's neck where the garotte had cut into him – had a more intense, visceral effect on me than any of the murders I'd investigated.

I heard my mother approaching from the rear of the flat and called for her to remain where she was. Perhaps it was my desire to protect her from such violence that spurred me into life, but I immediately went to the hall to telephone the police. With this done, I remained in the doorway to await their arrival, like a soldier on guard duty.

A dispatch of constables finally appeared, and I watched as one officer after another endured his own stark moment of horror at the sight of the dead man. If Chief Inspector Darrington looked worried as he stepped into the hall and wordlessly sidled past me to take in the scene, he was positively green when he returned a minute later.

"It's shocking," was all he would say at first.

The orderly and precise officer is a man of no little experience. I've always found his judgement to be top-notch, and I was surprised by this reaction. It felt wrong to interrupt him, though, so I waited for him to explain his thinking.

"It's truly unsettling." He glanced down at his hands as he spoke. "He looks so out of place there, sitting in a window that faces a road where hundreds of people pass every day. I'd say he can only have been dead an hour. I don't know what to make of it."

"I believe he must have used the spare key under the mat to come inside," I explained without being asked. "He'd certainly seen me use it on occasion, but then the killer may have watched me and witnessed this same thing. What I can't say is what either of them were doing here in the first place." I was well aware that, with no other solution apparent, my ex-sweetheart's fiancé's death could be laid at my door, and I decided to acknowledge the possibility. "I must tell you I had nothing to do with this. I hope you know that."

He frowned before answering and deep lines formed on his forehead. "That may be, but my officers will still need to interview you, Marius."

"I didn't kill him," I said, echoing countless suspects on the cases Lady Bella and I had investigated – that would be the Lady Bella who still didn't know that her fiancé was now dead in my writing room.

Darrington didn't reply. He peered past me once more at poor Gilbert Baines.

"I've been away with Bella and my family. We were investigating a murder." Why I thought this was an argument against my involvement in the crime, I cannot tell you. "What I'm trying to say is that Gilbert was already here when we got back. My mother will tell you the same thing."

He turned to look at me, and his eyebrows rose optimistically. "She was with you when you found the body?"

I swallowed then as I realised that this seemingly perfect alibi wasn't so perfect after all. "Sadly not. She walked straight to the back of the house, and when I realised what had happened, I made her stay in the kitchen while I telephoned the police."

All he offered in reply was a muffled "Oh" and I noticed that a passing constable gave his superior an uncomfortable look which seemed to say, *It's not looking good for him, is it, guv?*

My previously safe, comfortable reality continued to slip away from me. "You don't really think that I arranged to meet Gilbert here, and then quietly killed him whilst my mother was in the flat?"

"I haven't had time to think anything. You keep putting words in my mouth." Darrington's brow was still ruffled. Perhaps it was paranoia, but I felt that he was taking a mental note of the very scenario I had described. He at least tried to set my mind at ease. "It sounds quite improbable, but you will be treated just like any other suspect. Innocent until proven guilty and all that. The only thing that works against you is that—"

"My former love's fiancé is dead at my desk." I sighed as the truth of this settled in my mind.

He bit his lip, and I realised I'd made another faux pas.

"No, Marius, I wasn't going to say that, because I hadn't imagined you'd ever been in love with his fiancée. I didn't even know he had a fiancée. I was only going to say that a jury might think that a mystery novelist like you would concoct an improbable situation like this one if you wished to kill someone and get away with it."

The panic that was surging through me had finally peaked, and we both fell silent to gaze at the dead man.

"Assuming that you are not to blame for his death—"

"Which I'm not."

"Assuming you are not to blame, do you have any sense of why someone would want to kill him?"

"He wasn't killed by just anyone. He was killed by a man so arrogant that he left a calling card on the floor for me to find before I saw the body."

"Then perhaps you should have started with that rather than blathering about the victim's fiancée." He showed a rare spark of anger, but it soon subsided as I pointed to the card I had found.

It was on the telephone table where I'd left it, and it read, COURTESY OF LUCIEN PIKE.

"I see." I had thought that this might interest him, but he only looked more doubtful. "You may be worried about what will happen to you, Marius, but look at it from my perspective. I have to leave here this morning and tell my superiors that a well-respected London banker was found murdered in the St James's home of a sensational novelist. Meanwhile, the ostensible culprit is Lucien Pike: a shadowy figure linked to various unsolved crimes who may or may not be part of an international syndicate of criminals. I'll be laughed out of the Metropolitan Police."

"Well I would hardly invent such a story." Even as I said these words, I could tell that he was thinking back to the imaginary jury and what the prosecution would say when laying out the evidence against me. It was all too much, and I groaned in frustration. "I should have written romantic novels. This would never have been an issue if I'd only written romances."

Before I could further lament my fate, a cheery figure appeared at the door, and there was my friend Detective Inspector Valentine Lovebrook. "Sorry I took so long to get here," he called down the hallway as he wiped his feet on the mat. "It wasn't until I got back to my house that I received the message from—"

Before he could say another word, his superior leaned around me to make his presence known. "I'm glad you're here, Inspector. Now get to work and find out why this man was killed." He was already leaving. "I have to report back to Scotland Yard, but I expect you to keep me informed of any progress."

He pointed his underling to Pike's calling card and, looking just as perplexed as when he'd arrived, marched off towards his car.

"Lucien Pike," Lovebrook said brightly once we were alone. "I don't suppose you can tell me why he killed your ex-girlfriend's new love in your home?"

I turned to bang my head against the wall.

Lovebrook tried to console me. "I obviously don't think you're to blame, Marius, but what has Pike got to do with Gilbert?"

The dull pain to my forehead did not make me feel any better, but I continued banging it all the same.

"In which case, how about a cup of tea?"

Rather than answering immediately, I turned to walk to the

kitchen where my mother was handing out hot drinks to a line of appreciative officers. When they saw how unimpressed the suddenly serious inspector was, they soon bustled off to do their jobs – each snatching a biscuit on their way. My basset hound, Percy, sat by the door, watching them pass in the hope that he might be allowed a few crumbs of his own.

"Mother, are you quite all right?" Although she hadn't seen the body, I was worried what effect a murder in our home would have on her.

She put a hand to her curly, shoulder-length hair to check that she was tidy. "Perfectly, thank you, Marius. Can I make you both a drink?" She didn't sound like herself but set about making another pot of tea for our benefit.

Making tea to stay busy when there are bad things of which you do not wish to think is a common technique in our family. Since my father went missing, Mother has boiled enough of the stuff to quench the thirst of the nation.

Lovebrook took the last biscuit, which I thought a little unsympathetic of him. "Come along, Marius. Don't leave me in suspense."

I practically collapsed into a seat at the small dining table. "There are some things I should probably not reveal, so if Darrington asks how you know so much, tell him you forced it out of me." I took a deep breath and considered what the overbearing chief inspector might do if I fell afoul of him. "Lucien Pike was the minor criminal whom my solicitor-father was representing when he disappeared a decade ago. He turned up on my doorstep back in May claiming to be a government operative in need of a private detective. He wasn't, of course. He'd actually hired us to rescue one of his cronies from the intelligence services, and after an at times torturous ordeal – during which Bella and I just about managed to avoid sparking a war between Britain and France – the man who gave us our mission vanished like the ghost that he is. Is that clear enough?"

For a moment, Lovebrook looked puzzled. "No, not at all." He never goes long without smiling. "Luckily for you, Darrington has had me searching for Pike off and on for the last six months, so I know something of his game."

I had never imagined the inspector getting caught up in the world of spies and traitors into which Bella and I had briefly (and unsuccessfully) dipped our toes. I had to hope he was better at espionage than we'd been.

"Anyway," he soon continued, "I wasn't asking who this fellow is. I was wondering how Gilbert was connected to him. Do you have any idea?"

"I can't begin to fathom it." My voice had grown more insistent again. "I don't even know why either of them would be in my house."

"Of course, it would be a clever stratagem to place this phantom's card at the scene of the crime if you wished to bump off a rival."

I was considering bashing my head against the wall again when Mother came to my defence. "There's no way that Marius could have killed someone with me here. It would have required the poor man in the writing room to stay perfectly silent when I entered the house and again when he was choked to death. I would have heard him otherwise."

Valentine Lovebrook was such an affable character that he almost succeeded in charming my mother even as he accused her only son of a terrible crime. "I do accept that, madam. However, if what we all suspect but no one dares utter is true, and Marius is in love with Lady Bella, he may have gained more from Gilbert's death than anyone else."

"How did you—" I began, but they just talked over me.

"Point taken." Much like my father, who possessed an excellent legal mind, Mother was a capable debater and took up the case once more. "Still, Inspector, you are wrong on one count. With Gilbert out of the way, Marius might make a life with

Bella, and *I* would be the person to gain most from the murder." Her eyes were two of the twinkliest around, and they positively sparkled just then. "Never underestimate an old lady's desire for grandchildren."

Although there was more than a touch of what the Germans call gallows humour in what she'd said, she delivered her response in a suitably sombre tone.

"I didn't kill Gilbert," I felt the need to repeat once more. "And I didn't place the calling card on the carpet to throw suspicion on a man with whom I have learnt not to trifle. But perhaps the best defence I have is that, within a minute of entering the house, I warned my mother about the body. Aside from everything else, I simply didn't have time to kill him."

Lovebrook was munching on his Rich Tea and had to swallow a mouthful of crumbs before replying. "That's good enough for me. The question now is how do we go about finding a culprit who has evaded all attempts at capture and identification?"

I looked across the dining table at the inspector. He looked back at me just as blankly and it would fall to my mother to break the deadlock.

"Surely the first thing you must do is find out why anyone would have wanted to murder Gilbert in the first place."

I nodded with quiet respect, whereas Lovebrook mumbled something vague that I couldn't decipher.

"That is definitely near the top of the list, Mother," I told her, still unable to fathom how strait-laced Gilbert was connected to a vicious criminal. "But our first task is to tell Bella that her fiancé is dead."

TWO

The telephone is a wonderful invention. I don't know where the world would be without it. It brings people together over hundreds and, increasingly, even thousands of miles. It facilitates rapid communication, which has no doubt already saved countless lives. In fact, it has turned humanity into a great network, with each person a fount of knowledge that, much like an entry within an encyclopaedia, can be accessed and studied at whim.

That notwithstanding, there are some tasks for which even this modern marvel was not designed. You wouldn't want to ask your sweetheart to marry you over the telephone – unless she were in prison and there was no other way of your speaking to her (although, if that is the case, I would question whether she is the right girl for you). Proposals are best made in person, much like medical examinations, but there is one task more than any other which should only ever be conducted face to face.

I took the inspector and Percy in my car, and we drove out of the capital towards the place where I was born. I decided that it was worth bringing my dog, as he and Bella were terribly fond of one another, and he could sit looking confused as she hugged him. I must admit that, try as I might, the dear hound is still better than I am at empathy and that sort of thing.

I wouldn't be stopping in the village where I'd grown up, or becoming reacquainted with any old friends still living there. The last time I'd done that, things had become rather complicated. Instead, I drove my red, no-longer-quite-so-shiny-as-it-once-had-been Invicta 3 Litre up the hill to the gates of Hurtwood House. The usual old fellow wasn't on duty, but a dour-faced guard waved us through when Lovebrook showed his credentials.

The view of Bella's family home had never before struck such fear in me. A sight that I had often found awe-inspiring had become severe and frightening. I doubt it was the mock-Jacobean architecture that did it. It was the repeating memory of what had happened to prompt our visit.

The image of Gilbert's vacant stare flashed in my mind. The way his hand stretched out over my desk, as if he were reaching for help, caused a knot to form in my stomach, which I wouldn't be able to untangle for days. Baines and I hadn't been friends, but I had come to see that he wasn't all bad. I felt awful for what had happened to him, but even worse for the fiancée he left behind.

My poor, kind-hearted Bella. The very thought of the heartache we were about to spark was too horrible to imagine, and so I looked at the elaborate gardens around the house and tried to push the horror back down.

I could only think that my companion was doing the same thing. Lovebrook stroked my lump of a hound and muttered, "It really is an impressive place, don't you think?"

"That's just the word for it," was my nonchalant reply, but we'd almost reached the stable where Bella's family keep their automobiles, and there was no longer any need for conversation.

By the time we reached the front door, we must already

have been spotted by a member of staff, as it swung open and there stood the butler.

"Ah, Mr Marius and your officer friend," Pullman chanted in that melodic voice of his. "Lady Bella has not been home long herself. Is she expecting you?" The upright fellow smiled amiably and awaited my response.

I wasn't sure how to answer even this simple question. "No, this was not in any way planned."

"Very good, sir. I've no doubt she'll be happy to see you. If you'd like to follow me to the day room, though I'm sure you still remember the way." He looked a little mischievous for a moment, and I managed to produce approximately a quarter of a smile.

It felt wrong. It all felt wrong. It was unfair that Lovebrook and I were forced to smuggle this terrible secret in there with us. There should have been a warning system – perhaps a series of alarms – to tell everyone to behave sombrely in our presence. Pullman could have bowed his head as he saw us through the gloomy old building, instead of whistling a jolly tune. Maybe then, when we reached the long, bright room that gave onto the woodland at the side of the house, Bella wouldn't have made a joke as soon as she saw us.

"You simply can't live without me, can you, gentlemen?" Standing in a long red dress, in the middle of the sunlit room, she was positively beaming. "Tell me we don't have another case to investigate! I'm all for adventure, but I'd like the odd day off in between."

"Bella..." I tried, but my voice wavered, and I came to an unexpected stop. I thought for a moment that Lovebrook would take up the task, but he stayed silent, and I was about to speak again when Bella did.

"What is it, Marius? Why do you look as though—" She didn't finish this sentence; she must have realised that we had not come to pay a social call. We were not the bearers of good tidings, and anything she said could only make the situation worse.

"It's Gilbert." I breathed out these two words at once. It sounded as if I was choking on them. "My dear friend, I don't know how to tell you this, but..." I gave a half-second pause. That's all it was, but that was enough for her to catch my meaning. She made a sound that was so short and so sudden that it almost didn't reach me. "He's dead, Bella. He was murdered in my flat."

I'd expected a cry of anguish, but instead she froze. The muscles in her body appeared to have come loose from their usual contacts, and the signals no longer got through. She didn't even blink for the count of ten, but then she fell into the wicker armchair behind her, which screeched on the tiled floor as it scraped backwards a few inches.

"There's no question about it," Lovebrook was quick to reassure her. "We will find whoever was responsible. There's a good chance that Lucien Pike was involved, so we'll triple our efforts to locate him. You needn't fear on that account."

I believe that even the ever-positive inspector must have known that any such promises amounted to very little; he breathed out heavily at the end of this short speech and looked almost as bleak as I felt.

Bella could not muster a reply. She turned on her side in the chair and pulled her legs in to make herself smaller and harder, as the world had just become. I wanted to run over to her. I wanted to put my hand on her cheek and tell her that I would do whatever she needed, but I just froze where I stood.

Lovebrook waited a suitable length of time before asking any questions but, when he did, he moved to the chair next to hers and put one hand on her shoulder, as I should have.

"I wish I didn't have to say anything more," he began. "And I can't imagine the grief that you are feeling at this very moment, but time is of the essence."

Until this point, Percy had been standing beside me, watching the odd scene unfold. I do sometimes wonder what dogs make of the humans they have to put up with, but he was clever enough to realise that his dear friend Bella was unhappy, and so he waddled over to her and put his head on the edge of the chair. Her eyes were closed, and she opened them just a fraction to look at him. Still she said nothing, and so I finally broke from my inertia and went to sit on the other side of her.

"It won't take long, Bella, but if we don't help the inspector, the killer could go unpunished."

I don't know whether this meant more coming from me, or she realised how necessary her help was, but she silently nodded.

"Thank you," Lovebrook said, then paused to find the composure to continue. I'd seen him interview several different witnesses, but it was clearly more difficult this time. "All I can really ask is for you to think back over this last year and tell me whether there was anything different about Gilbert that could explain what happened to him." Nothing came back but quiet sobs, so he persisted. "Had he made any new acquaintances? Had his habits changed in any way? Have you any reason to believe he is connected to Pike?"

Bella's breathing was loud and rasping, and she had to tame it before she could speak. "He's had a lot of work at the bank recently. He had some very large investments to handle, which meant that he stayed late more often than before."

"What about his charity work, Bella?" I asked. Apart from his fiancée and his work, this was his only interest of which I knew.

"What about it?" Her voice trembled as she spoke. "He wasn't helping ex-convicts. He volunteered in the new orphanage in Whitechapel."

"Still," Lovebrook replied a little more positively, "one of the staff there might have seen someone loitering nearby. If Pike is the killer, and a card that was left at the scene would seem to suggest that is the case, he may have followed Gilbert this weekend or come into contact with someone he knows."

"Lucien Pike?" Bella muttered, as the news that Lovebrook had already shared two minutes prior finally reached her. "Why would he hurt Gilbert?"

Lovebrook smiled in that awkward but charming way of his. "We were hoping you might be able to tell us."

Bella looked off across the room as more tears fell. It was hard to say whether she was hearing much more than half of what we were telling her, and so I tried to be clear and precise.

"Did he have any family in London?"

Bella's hands were on Percy's long, soft ears, and she stared into his soulful eyes as she answered. "His parents died when he was barely an adult, and he had no siblings. I believe that was why he was so interested in helping children who were born without the advantages that my family..."

This relatively coherent response broke down as the memory of her fiancé came back to her. She reached over to a small side table where a block of paper and an elegant fountain pen sat. Sobbing the whole time and occasionally having to stop when the emotion got too much for her or the tears splashed onto the paper, she scribbled down the address of the orphanage and handed it to the inspector with her eyes once more closed.

"You have my promise that I will do all I can to see that justice is done." Lovebrook rose to standing. "If anything important should come to mind, you can contact me through Scotland Yard."

I didn't know what to say after this. We'd driven all that way for a three-minute conversation, and I didn't want to abandon her. I wanted to make everything better, but I couldn't imagine how. But as silence filled the gap between us, she pulled Percy up onto the chair and I realised that there was one thing I could do for her.

"If it's not too much to ask, you would be doing me a great favour if you were to look after this creature for a few days. He requires constant affection, and I really don't know whether I have the time. Of course, my aunt and uncle are in the village if he makes a nuisance of himself, and you want them to collect him."

If anything, this made her sadder. I'm not the best at talking to the heartbroken or bereaved, but I had hoped that the loan of a soppy dog might be a nice gesture.

When her parents appeared in the doorway, and I was about to turn away, she opened her eyes once more and fixed them on me. "Marius, you didn't have to come here." She paused then and, for a moment, I thought I'd made a terrible mistake. "Thank you."

I smiled for her sake, but her father's deep voice echoed about the room then, and I knew that my role had run its course.

"Dear boys," the Duke of Hurtwood said in a teasing tone, "what have you—"

The Duchess must have realised that this was not the time for quips, as she stopped pushing his wheelchair and looked across at their daughter in concern.

Bella hugged Percy, and her sorrow rose to the surface again. I imagined the pain she was suffering as a cyclone turning within her. There were moments when it might fall calm, or go spinning off in different directions but, before long, it would return to wreak more havoc and destruction.

Her mother looked at us as she pushed her husband past, and I doubt I'd ever felt so guilty in my life.

THREE

Pullman was waiting at the door with a message for Lovebrook.

"I have a message for you from Chief Inspector Darrington. He requests that you telephone him before you leave."

Lovebrook was whisked away to do just this, and I lingered in the hallway as various maids looked disapprovingly at me. I had forgotten just how quickly news travels in a big house like Hurtwood. They must have all thought that I'd broken Bella's heart... again.

When the inspector returned, he didn't look at me directly but motioned for me to follow him outside.

"I've been thinking," I said as we walked around the side of the house together. "There's a good chance that Gilbert was an innocent bystander in all of this. Lucien Pike may have come there to kill me and found the wrong person."

"I suppose it's possible." Lovebrook turned to watch a coal wagon roll past. "Or perhaps he wished to incriminate you for the killing but picked a poor time to do so? Think about it like this: you foiled an elaborate scheme he hatched, and he must be furious about it."

I placed both hands on the bonnet of my car as I tried to fit the pieces together. "No, I don't see it that way. If he wished to make it look as if I had murdered my love rival, then why leave his card in my house?"

Lovebrook winced. "I concede that it is not a habit of murderous criminals to sign their work."

"Where do we go from here?" I asked, gripping the car far more tightly than I'd intended. "Pike was already a ghost. The fact he has now murdered an unremarkable banker is unlikely to flush him out into the open."

The inspector had been hesitant ever since we left the house but had now fallen silent.

"Lovebrook, what's the matter?"

He sighed, and I felt sorry for him without knowing why. "Chief Inspector Darrington doesn't want you to investigate the case. He says your involvement would only hamper a conviction should Pike ever make it to trial."

"That's ridiculous," I replied without considering the truth of the statement.

"Is it? I'm inclined to think that you will struggle to treat any evidence we accumulate with the neutrality that a good detective needs. Either way, Darrington has made it clear that, should you ignore this friendly advice, there will be severe repercussions, so I would recommend doing as he says. He brought me to book once when I first moved to London, and I still have bad dreams about it."

It was rare for him to be so stern, and it took me aback a little. "So that's it then? Case concluded. The killer goes unpunished?"

"No, of course not, Marius. I and a team of experienced officers will do all we can to ensure that Pike gets his comeuppance. Modern policemen are not the bumbling halfwits that mystery novels often portray."

He opened the door to the Invicta and climbed inside as I seethed. I might well have remained in this silent state all the way back to London, but Lovebrook wouldn't allow any such thing.

"We will look into every aspect of Gilbert's life, from his work to his love affairs and his involvement at the orphanage. If I'm really lucky, I'll get very close to Pike before the higher-ups decide that he is too much of a risk to British society, and the case is assigned to someone whose name I am not allowed to know."

I couldn't decide whether to laugh or scream, so I did the former. "That's very reassuring."

I started the engine, and he smiled back at me in that slightly vague, innocent manner of his. "I promise you, Marius. We will do all we can."

As we drove back through Surrey, I did my best to formulate a plan to solve Gilbert's murder before the police could. By the time that I arrived at home, I had reluctantly accepted that this would be quite impossible.

It wasn't just that I knew little about Gilbert and would have struggled to find out anything about him without Darrington knowing what I was up to. I'd already spent months failing to find the shadowy criminal responsible for his death. There was no reason to think that anything would be different this time.

I dropped Lovebrook by his car on St James's Square and parked in front of the East India Club. My flat was terribly quiet. Gilbert's body had been removed, and the place tidied up somewhat, but I rather wished that a few of the constables had remained so that it wasn't quite so empty. Mother had an appointment to see friends, Percy was off doing important work, and I hadn't felt so lonely in months. All I could think about was Bella and the tempest of emotions she was suffering.

If the truth be told, there was more than a dash of guilt mixed in with my melancholy. From the moment I'd met my former love's new love, I'd wished that he didn't exist. Now, all of a sudden, he didn't, and I couldn't have felt worse about it. To distract myself, I returned to the novel I'd been half-heartedly writing for some weeks. My original plan for my third book had ended up being quite preposterous, so I'd abandoned it entirely, whereas the replacement was so generic and dull – or a guaranteed money-maker, as my editor claimed – that I could summon little excitement for it.

"Does the world really need another mystery set in a grand old house with six suspects all harbouring secrets that prevent them from ruling out their involvement in a murder?" I asked my dog, before remembering that he was thirty miles away. I doubt he would have offered much by way of a response anyway.

I tried to be logical and consider the fact that, whether I did any work or not, Gilbert would still be dead, and I would be none the wiser as to why. At the same time, if I didn't manage to write anything, I would still have my editor calling every week to complain that I'd only released two books in who knows how many years and my public were baying for another.

My editor is a persistent and manipulative man of whom I am very fond; I couldn't take the added pressure of Bertie's begging, and so I sat in my bedroom – as far from the scene of the crime as I could get – and I wrote.

I wrote a scene in which a grand chandelier falls on the chief suspect in the murder of Lord Oglesby just as the police are about to arrest her. I thought this violent method of dispatch added a real punch to an already puzzling enigma, but every word I wrote sounded just awful in my head.

The famous man sat in the red chair, I scribbled before having second thoughts and crumpling the paper. "Who writes nonsense like that?"

There was still no one there to answer me, but I gave it a second try.

Inspector L'Estrange was famed throughout Britain for his brilliance. Every person on the Duke of Bartram's estate knew of the complex cases L'Estrange had solved, and yet none of them could have imagined what he was about to say...

"What was he about to say?" I put my pen down to ask, then spent the next quarter of an hour staring at the wall.

"On coming here to Pemblewick Manor, I never imagined that I would assemble you here to declare that the Duchess of Bartram herself was responsible for the death of—"

Before the inspector could say anything more, there was an alarming sound from above their heads. This was swiftly followed by an unbearable high-pitched whir as the immense crystal chandelier came hurtling down. Several of the suspects dived out of the way in time but, standing in the centre of the group, the Duchess could do nothing but raise her hands ineffectually as the ornate lamp crashed down on top of her.

Silence filled the room for fifteen long seconds before Lord Chigley stepped forward to declare...

"What?" I tapped my pen on the pile of paper that was supposed to turn into a book. "What would someone say in such an instance? *She's dead* sounds terribly trite, but what else is there?"

Night had fallen across the city, and so I stared out into the dark garden at the back of my house for a seemingly infinite stretch before giving up altogether.

Not wishing to be alone with Gilbert's ghost any longer, I put on my khaki officer's coat and went outside. The air was cold, and the wind buffeted me, but at least it wasn't raining... at first. Before I knew it, the skies had opened, and my hair was soaked. I had lived through far worse during the war, of course, and my coat had saved me often enough then. It was a fitting end to a horrible day, and I struggled to accept that, a little less than twenty-four hours earlier, I'd been living the life of Riley at a luxurious hotel on the English Riviera, preparing to expose a killer. I hungered for such pleasant surrounds, but most of all I wished for company.

I had no particular plan for where to go, but when I turned onto Pall Mall, I knew where I would end up. There is a bar on Villiers Street, owned by a man named "Staff" Gordon, which is as dark and clandestine as any cave. It is the perfect place to drink away one's sorrows with the cheerful hum of conversation as an accompaniment. Like an insect that only emerges after dark, I was drawn towards its dim, appealing light.

I don't know what gave me the idea that someone was following me. It is often said that we have a sixth sense for such things. The streets were too busy with smoothly flowing cars and thunderous buses for me to have heard anything, but as I reached Trafalgar Square, I was certain that my walk across the city was not a solo endeavour. Had I not been so lost in thought, I might well have noticed the fellow some twenty yards behind me as I left my flat.

I crossed Duncannon Street to see if the blighter would follow me, and then panic set in. I had no weapon beyond the pen in my pocket, and the thought that Pike had sent someone after me was a daunting one. There was little of interest on the other side of the road, but my pursuer followed me over. He waited until a bus was passing and then nipped behind it and in front of a disgruntled driver who beeped the horn of his Wolseley ever so peevishly.

I didn't dare turn all the way around in case it was Pike himself, but I caught hazy, side-on glimpses of the hunter as he left the shadows two streetlights behind me. The roads in that part of the city are far too open to lose a tail, and I decided not to run as I didn't want the man to know I'd spotted him. My advantage, if that is what it can be called, was that I am a naturalised Londoner and know the area around Trafalgar Square just as well as I do my village back in Surrey. I know that Duncannon Street leads to the Strand, and that just where the two roads meet is one of London's busiest railway stations.

I was also aware that Charing Cross has multiple entrances, plenty of small spaces into which I could disappear, and long tunnels to shoot along should I need to escape. I didn't even glance over my shoulder as I passed the Eleanor Cross on my way towards the bright beacon of the station. I'd always found it a pleasing building, with its French Renaissance-style hotel towering over the entrance, but it was particularly inviting just then.

I looked at my watch as though afraid I would miss my train, then pelted through the narrow entrance on the western corner of the station and into the main ticket hall where countless black-suited businessmen stood reading their newspapers as they waited for trains to London Bridge or the suburbs beyond. It was tempting to hide amongst them, but my coat was too noticeable for that, and so I sped towards the eastern exit before my shadow could see where I had gone. It was originally my intention to double back on myself towards the street but, by now, I wanted to see who was following me. To this end, I slipped into the cobbler's a few shops along from the exit and sat down in the chair there to have my brogues polished.

The eager middle-aged shoeblack had the bulbous red nose of a wine drinker and quickly set to work with polish and brush, chatting away as he did so. He was such a babbler that I didn't need to contribute a great deal, which suited me perfectly. The chair had its back to the shopfront, but I could watch the walkway behind me by turning my head to one side. I thought my chances of being seen were low, and so I fixed my eyes on the exit and mumbled the odd note of agreement whenever my companion required it.

Sure enough, a few moments after I'd sat down, a young lad in a flat cap and dark clothing hurried past the shop looking worried. I couldn't see his face, of course, but his whole manner – with raised shoulders and quick steps – told me that he knew he'd been outwitted. I don't mind admitting that it gave me a small thrill.

I waited to see what would happen next. It was a good job I did as he turned back along the corridor, and I could see him quite clearly as he stood at the corner of the concourse, peering at the crowd. He had soft features and looked at least a decade younger than me. The cap, which he wore pulled down over his eyes, told me that he didn't want to be noticed, but with his cleft chin and dimples, I felt I would recognise him again if our paths ever crossed. He had no idea that the man for whom he searched was just a yard or so away on the other side of a pane of glass. Showing his frustration with a short, sharp grunt, he moved off through the station, leaving me to pay the cheery cobbler and disappear into the night.

FOUR

The wine that I drank in Gordon's did me no favours, but it made me wonder how famously debauched authors like Coleridge and De Quincey ever managed to finish a paragraph, let alone a poem or paper. I also reflected on the young lad who had followed me. He didn't look the type to hang around with a man like Lucien Pike, and I wondered whether I had acquired an obsessive admirer. I'd heard of writers whose readers took their love for literature a step too far, but my own career up to this point had been so unremarkable, it was hard to imagine myself in such a situation.

I woke up the next morning with a sore head and a feeling of intense guilt but was well aware that I would forget these downsides the next time I crossed paths with a bottle of wine.

I knew my mother would offer no sympathy, and just looking at the pages of my embryonic novel made me feel like a terrible writer, so I decided to go on a grand expedition to the building next door. The London Library had long been my refuge. I visit several times a week, and it was one of the main reasons I bought my excessively well-located flat in the first place.

I adore libraries, perhaps even more than bookshops. The very smell as you enter should be sold as a perfume, though it's a good thing it's not, as, like an overly excited schoolboy, I would fall in love with every woman who wore it. One of my smallest but most pleasant achievements in my time in the capital is the fact that I have spent so long in that worthy establishment that the staff all recognise me. They even help me with my research when I need it. I imagine they get bored with all the distinguished poets and literary lights they have to serve and take some pleasure from helping a hack author like me. I once saw the poet T. S. Eliot there, and he did not receive the attention to which I have become accustomed.

By the time I sat down in the reading room, I had accumulated a pile of newspapers half my height. I rolled my sleeves up, quite literally, and began leafing through them in search of some spark of inspiration. All I needed was one short, intriguing article to set me on the right path – and help me forget that there was a murder I had neither the permission nor the resources to investigate.

I tend to concentrate on papers from the nineteenth century. Perhaps lower standards of reporting back then left room for sensationalism, but I've always thought that the Victorians really knew how to murder one another.

I'm not just talking about the really violent cases of which everyone has read. I am a connoisseur of minor mysteries that have long been forgotten. My first novel, *A Killer in the Wings*, was inspired by the story of a man who had killed not one but two wives, before a third gullible woman agreed to marry him. That gave me the seed of an idea that would grow and develop until I had a whole novel. And in just saying this, I realise why I have no interest in hearing most writers talk at length about their creative process.

The point I'm trying to make is merely that I went to the library in search of something – anything – better than what I had. I was tired of old misers being killed off and rich widows falling prey to charming young rogues. I wanted a new story to tell, and did I find one in my pile of newspapers?

Well, no.

I spent the morning leafing through old broadsheets, and all I found were depressing descriptions of husbands killing wives, accounts of greedy men murdering colleagues to take over their businesses, and fools caught with their hands in the till who thought they could stab, shoot or poison their way to freedom. Admittedly, a narrower range of crimes made it into the newspapers in the Victorian age – and almost all the aggressors were men – but I certainly didn't come across any curious cases that I could novelise to make myself a household name.

I was close to giving up and ringing my editor to see whether he fancied lunch when, of all things that should happen in a library, a fight broke out. I can honestly say that the kerfuffle between two large oiks was more interesting than anything I'd read that morning.

They were really laying into one another and a small crowd soon built up to watch them. I'm not one to dwell on violence, but I was glad of the distraction and went to see them throttling each other between the bookshelves. The usually sedate attendants were suddenly as animated as any audience at the Royal Albert Hall on a Thursday night. If they'd had their wallets with them, I imagine they would have held aloft their money and placed bets. That was, of course, until the combatants made a fatal mistake: they threatened the books.

"You should never have crossed me," the bigger and broader of the two shouted as he grabbed a dictionary-sized tome from the shelf next to him and raised it above his head. I hadn't realised at first how young he was. His immense muscles and thick neck made him look quite mature, but he can't have been more than twenty.

"No, I should never have got caught. There's a difference,"

the other replied and, taking his cue, looked for a leather-bound weapon of his own.

"All right now. We'll have no more of that!" A librarian I had never seen away from her desk before charged over and grabbed them both by the ear. I'd rarely witnessed such a valiant display, and there was a round of polite applause as she marched them from the building.

I found it curious that this scene had flared up so suddenly. There had been no shouting in the build-up, nor much sound as the two men entered the peaceful environment. Even more impressive was just how quickly life returned to normal. As soon as the brutes were off the premises, the previously febrile atmosphere dissipated like a popped bubble, and the usual sense of tranquillity was restored.

Such peace is an undervalued commodity. At the London Library, however, you pay four pounds and two shillings per annum for the privilege, and it is worth every penny. Filled with a sense of calm that had previously been missing, I returned to my desk, determined to complete my task. I took the next *London Chronicle* from the top of the unread pile, and my eyes travelled over the front page like a brush across a canvas. I must admit that I started when I came face to face with the photograph of a woman who looked familiar. I couldn't place her at first, but I had the definite feeling I'd seen her before.

The headline said, MRS RICHARD MORTIMER SET TO STAND TRIAL FOR MURDER, and I didn't question when this had happened or why the case would stand out to me, but I ravenously consumed the article beneath.

It was announced today that suspected poisoner Felicity Mortimer – née Chandler – will stand trial at the Old Bailey for the murder of her husband. Mr Richard Mortimer, the former Lord Lieutenant of the City of London, was twenty-three years her senior. Mortimer had been confined to bed with gastric prob-

lems for some weeks before his condition worsened, and he died on the fifth of September this year. However, it has recently been revealed that a post-mortem on his body found traces of arsenic in his blood, and one witness claims that Mrs Mortimer was seen soaking flypapers in water just days before her husband met his sorry fate.

Defenders of the accused have been quick to explain that Mrs Mortimer's actions were the innocent ministrations of a loving wife. They also say that she never once attended her husband alone in the week he died. Further evidence would appear to undermine the picture of her as a devoted spouse, however, and debate has begun over the question of just how faithful she was to her stricken husband. The truth of the matter will surely come to light in the trial, which is set to start on the second of December.

It was only as I finished reading this meagre and sensational article that I realised why she looked so familiar. I glanced up at the masthead – this case wasn't some ancient affair that had taken place in the time of Dickens and Thackeray. Richard Mortimer had been murdered in my lifetime, and the striking picture of his wife brought back the memory of a time when her name was on everyone's lips. I looked at her once more and tried to imagine that this elegant person captured in monochrome had plotted her husband's death.

Was this enough to inspire a whole novel? I remembered that she'd been found guilty, but that was fifteen years since, and I had no idea what happened to her afterwards. Was she hanged for her crime or still rotting in a cell somewhere? Her situation had caught the attention of the press because of her comely features, but were there enough complexities to the story to make it interesting to my readers today?

I didn't wait to find out but ran to the nearest assistant and asked for help. "John," I said, for I knew his name and he mine, "how can I find more articles on this woman from 1913? I want the whole story from beginning to end."

"I'll tell you how," he said, already turning to walk towards the newspaper archive, deep within the library. "You ask me where to find them, then I pop off, only to reappear a short while later with everything you need."

"You are a gentleman, sir."

"That may be." He stopped to laugh, then dropped his voice lower when a stuffy-looking fellow at the nearest table glanced up contemptuously. "But it certainly helps that I remember this case as if it were yesterday."

Dear John had perfectly round cheeks that reminded me of a beaming baby. He was always happy to help and, with a hand raised in a lazy wave, he wandered off through the labyrinthine complex of buildings. While the façade of the library was narrower and less remarkable than my own next door, it gave access to a vast space that had been pieced together through various property purchases over the years. This illusion of being bigger inside than out was another of the things I liked about it.

While John sought out the papers I needed, I walked across the square to buy him a bottle of something strong to show my appreciation and a ham sandwich for my lunch. I believe that my brain was already alive with ideas for the book I now intended to write. I just had to hope that reality would live up to my expectations. If not, then I would have to give in to the wilder impulses of my imagination and create something new.

In the end, I shouldn't have worried. I spent the rest of that morning immersing myself in the life and perils of Mrs Felicity Mortimer. I learnt about the trial that found her guilty, the outrage that followed her death sentence, and the claims by several highly respected people that her incarceration was a miscarriage of justice. It became a *cause célèbre* for many and led to calls for the Home Secretary, Lord Thomas Verlaine, to commute her punishment.

Shortly after I'd begun my far from exhaustive study, I had another question for my friend.

"John, this case is fascinating. I was only a boy when it happened and there's something I must know."

I'd just given him his brandy and his cheeks had grown even rounder. "I'll do what I can, Mr Quin."

"What happened to her after all this? Was she hanged?"

"Oh, no, sir. She was spared a visit to the hangman, but she's still in prison as far as I know."

I should probably have responded to this, but I looked down at the papers before me and tried to make sense of my thoughts.

"It was a terrible business, and everyone had an opinion on the case. Half of Britain thought she was as innocent as a daisy."

I looked quickly up at him. "And the other half?"

He didn't reply for a moment, though his eyebrows moved one after another like a crashing wave. "They thought she was a devil who escaped the punishment she deserved."

FIVE

What I particularly liked about the case were these markedly different opinions that Felicity Mortimer sparked in people. As John had so neatly summarised, depending on which newspaper one read, she was an angel who had been chained to earth by our callous society or a siren responsible for seducing and murdering her respectable husband.

It certainly didn't dent my interest that the judge and jury in her trial had apparently ignored evidence in Mrs Mortimer's favour. First and foremost was the fact to which the more generous leaders from the time kept returning: Felicity Mortimer did not attend to her husband on her own in the five days before he died. There was always a professional nurse observing her. It was hard for me to get beyond this, especially as, until then, his condition appeared to have been improving.

I don't know at what point I changed from viewing this story as inspiration for a novel and came to think of it as an unsolved crime that needed my attention but, by the time I left the library, I had already chosen my next course of action. I went back to my apartment and telephoned the best-connected man in London. My editor Bertrand Price-Lewis knows every journalist, author, sportsman and socialite in the Great Wen.

"Marius, dear boy!" He received the call with all his usual rambunctiousness. "It's a pleasure to hear from you. How is *Murder at Pemblewick Manor* coming along? Have you got to the scene with the garden shears yet? I am particularly keen on horticulturally influenced murders... in fiction, of course, not real life. You know, there is an interesting correlation between people who enjoy gardening and those who read mystery novels. One day, someone smart will base a whole career around it."

Bertie was a prattle-box, and I knew that he could ramble on if left to do so.

"There are a few things I'd like to discuss with you," I finally managed to interrupt. "Why don't we meet for lunch, and I'll tell you all my news."

"Where are you thinking?" If there is one man who does not need persuading to while the afternoon away in a comfortable restaurant, it is Bertie. Before I could answer, he was reeling off the names of some of the chicest establishments in London. "If you haven't sampled Boulestin in Southampton Street, then you simply haven't lived. Though I'm also partial to the partridge at Simpson's in the Strand. And as I always say, if a place is good enough for Sherlock Holmes, it's good enough for me."

At this moment, my mother appeared from the kitchen holding a pork chop in one hand and a leg of lamb in the other. She mouthed the obvious question down the hallway to me, and I held up my hand to make her wait a moment longer.

"My mother is cooking, so I was thinking of asking you here. But if you're inviting us out at the company's expense, it would be rude to say no."

Mother isn't one for fancy places, but I convinced her to put the meat back in the larder and fetch her best coat. I had once found it strange to be a bachelor whose mother lived in the spare room, but any such reservations were long forgotten. We sallied out like the dear friends that we are. Admittedly, in the unlikely situation that I one day find a wife, we might have to reconsider the arrangement, but for now I am happy to have a companion, a confidante and, yes, a live-in cook.

"Dead?" Bertie asked when we were sitting at a corner table in the dining room at Verrey's on Regent Street. "As in deceased?" The frequently jolly Welshman looked quite astonished, as did my mother, who was peering about the sophisticated restaurant with her mouth agape.

I, meanwhile, was pretending not to be impressed. I'd never eaten there before, but it was the kind of place where the Marquess of Edgington would dine when in town. The ornate ceiling was supported by a run of silver arches, under which green baize panels held one seemingly endless mirror on either side of the room. They reflected back the elegance all around, from the sumptuous dresses of the ladies consuming sole Polignac and *oeufs à la Russe* to the coiffured poodle who cowered beneath his owner's table whenever a lounge-suited waiter came near.

"Are you seriously telling me that Lady Bella's fiancé is dead?" Bertie repeated when neither of us had answered. The fact that he already knew the pair had got engaged did not surprise me.

"I'm afraid so," I replied in a solemn voice, as my head filled with Bella, and I wondered whether she was still suffering so acutely as when I'd left her.

It was his turn to fall speechless. He kept shaking his head and muttering indistinguishable sounds.

"Strangely, however, that isn't why I wanted to see you." I had no wish to appear callous by changing tack so quickly but, for all his influence and diverse acquaintances, I doubted there was anything my editor could do to convince that mule Chief Inspector Darrington to allow me, a hobbyist detective, to interfere in the investigation.

Before I could move the conversation seamlessly onwards, Mother took up the previous topic. "It's a dreadful affair. That man was murdered in our flat. Just think of the sort of people with whom he must have been consorting to end up like that."

I don't mind admitting that I was surprised by her reaction. We were yet to discuss Gilbert's death in any great detail, and it hadn't entered my mind that he could have brought his murder upon himself.

Bertie's eyes glowed a little more. "Turned out he was a wrong 'un, did it? Swindling the bank's money, was he?"

A feeling of immense impatience came over me then, and I had to bite my tongue to stop from being rude. It wasn't my companions' fault that they were interested in the case. And though I told myself that I was desperate to free an innocent woman from a cold and cruel prison, the truth was that I would have done anything not to have to think about Gilbert again. I'd seen corpses before – and even investigated the deaths of people I'd known all my life – but this time it meant more. My guilt at the way I'd treated him was knotted together with the pain I now felt whenever I imagined Bella's plight. It was simply too much to bear.

"Can we please focus on a more important matter?" I found myself demanding, once my mother had taken our friend through her theories on the case – some of which, though I was currently unwilling to think about them, were rather clever.

They looked a little troubled by my interruption, but one of the French brothers who owned the restaurant came to take their regular diner's order, and I didn't have to explain myself just yet.

"We'll have the soufflé of sole fillets *à la* Verrey," Bertie began, translating the French menu so that my mother knew what we would end up with, "a Venetian salad, the chicken Parmentier, quail liver omelette, the entrecôte Olga and a selection of desserts – obviously including your wonderful iced biscuit."

"An excellent choice, monsieur," the heavy-browed Frenchman responded with a small bow.

Bertie clapped his hands together and, with a smile so wide I thought it might split his cheeks, said, "So that's for me. What are you two having?" His rowdy laughter carried across the room and caused disapproving heads to turn in our direction.

Both the restaurant's owner and my mother hesitated for a moment, uncertain whether this was a joke until our friend collected the menus and passed them back. "That will be all. Thank you, Frédéric."

"Of course, monsieur." Bowing once more, the man retreated to his post near the entrance.

"Now, what were you saying before?" he turned to me to ask, and I had to build up the courage to address the thing that I was most keen to discuss.

"There's a woman called Felicity Mortimer." They both drew back as though terrified to even hear such a name.

"Felicity Mortimer the poisoner?" Mother whispered, while pulling at her sleeve.

"Felicity Mortimer, the woman spuriously condemned for murdering her husband," I corrected her. "I read about her case in a host of old newspapers, and I found it curious. From what I've learnt so far, it seems quite unreasonable not only that she was given such a harsh sentence but that she was found guilty in the first place."

I don't know why people come to the conclusion that I can't think for myself. My ever-so-caring mother and my unnecessarily paternal editor acted as though only they knew what was best for me.

"I'm sure it is a fascinating case," Bertie told me, picking his words carefully. "And if you're looking into the matter in order to find inspiration for your book, then I don't see—"

I decided to put him *into* his misery as soon as possible. "It's not for my book... well, it is, but I also wish to discover whether there really was a miscarriage of justice."

His subsequent groan told me that we were about to see the other side of his personality. "For goodness' sake, Marius. Why are you the only author in town who finds the idea of making money so abhorrent? You already have an excellent story to tell. *Pemblewick Manor* has great potential! For all we know, it could become so successful that you pay off the mortgage on your house. Your name could be mentioned in newspapers and literary salons for the next decade or more."

I knew it was wrong to argue back – I'd learnt that from my real father when I was a child – but that didn't mean I was smart enough to avoid doing so. "I'm not interested in *Pemblewick Manor*, or the imaginary murder of the imaginary Duke of imaginary Bartram. Until I find out whether Felicity Mortimer should be rotting in Holloway Prison or walking around England a free woman, I doubt that I'll have the concentration to write another word."

Perhaps unsurprisingly, Bertie continued to focus on his prime motivation as a publisher. "Do you know how much money Carmine Fortescue has made from his Sergeant Stephenson books?"

Bertie knew that if he wanted to get under my skin, he need only mention my rival.

"I don't care how much that blowhard makes from his—"

"Over one hundred thousand pounds! He's richer than a maharaja."

Before I could pretend that this didn't bother me, an apologetic waiter brought three pistachio ices as a culinary shoeing horn. Slowly and quietly, he backed away from the table, as if hoping we hadn't noticed him.

A fragile silence held for a few moments before the poodle across the room started yapping, which spurred my mother into life. "Don't you think it's possible, Marius—"

They weren't going to talk me out of my decision. "I very much doubt it, but please continue."

When she spoke again, her voice was harder than I'd heard it in a long time. "Don't you think it's possible that you're looking for a distressed damsel to save because you know there's nothing you can do for Bella?"

I didn't know what to say to this. Her comment was almost too honest.

When I didn't reply, Bertie continued to lay out the facts as he saw them. "Felicity Mortimer killed her husband. I have no doubt about that. The extra detail you should know, however, is the way in which she brought so many people to her cause. I remember the case well, and I remember the impact it had on close friends of mine who were so convinced of her innocence that they wrote to the Home Secretary on her behalf. One man in particular devoted a year of his life to saving her without success. You see, whoever visited Mrs Mortimer had the same experience. The woman is enchanting, and I mean that in a literal sense; she bends people to her will, and you're best off staying well away from her."

I took the smallest spoon from the top of my plate. It looked like something that a scientist would use for measuring tiny quantities of dangerous chemicals. My miniature helping of pistachio *entremets* was delicious and the perfect thing I needed to help me delay my response.

"I will make a deal with you, Bertrand."

Mother had looked nervous for some minutes by this point. She stopped eating and put her hands together in her lap as she awaited my conditions. For his part, my editor sat back in his chair, evidently looking forward to our negotiation.

"I'll write *The Dull Monstrosity of Pemblewick Manor* as

promised, just as long as you find me a way to visit Mrs Mortimer at the prison where she is being held."

He smiled and tapped the ends of his fingers against one another. "Very well. But you'll have to finish the book before Christmas, without delays or excuses, or you will receive no payment until it is published."

Some part of my brain was aware that I'd come out worse from this agreement than he had, but it didn't feel that way at the time. I leaned across the table to shake his hand. "It's a deal."

In what I could only think was horror, Mother's eyebrows were raised at sharp angles.

Perhaps for her sake, Bertie tried to forget the good bit of business he'd just done and adopted a concerned tone. "Just promise me that you keep a wise head on your shoulders when you enter that prison, Marius. From everything I've heard about your wronged woman, she gobbles up soft-headed men like you for sport."

SIX

Much of what Bertie said about Felicity Mortimer sounded remarkably similar to the scare stories I'd read in the newspapers. After her conviction, any number of her "close acquaintances" burrowed their way out of the woodwork to talk of her duplicitous manner and predatory behaviour around men, which they had previously overlooked. It is just the kind of thing that sells newspapers, so I took it with a pot of salt, but my mother and friend echoing the tone of the articles still had its effect on me.

By the time I made it to Holloway Prison the next day, I'd started to feel concerned about exactly what kind of monster I would meet there. I queued with a glum, grey rabble of unlucky relatives and bored solicitors to be let in to a large space beyond a castle-like gatehouse and several locked doors. There were no chairs or even cups of water provided, and the families there were kept physically apart from their loved ones. One little boy running to see his mother was manhandled away from her and, whenever a reminder was required, a regular *clank, clank, clank* sounded as the warder cracked his baton on the bars that separated us from the bowels of the prison.

"Mr Quin?" the woman I had gone there to see enquired in a soft, somewhat fragile voice, and I admit that I didn't immediately recognise her.

It was hard to say exactly how she had changed. I suppose the best description I can summon is that she looked like a photograph that had faded in the sunlight. Everything about her was toned down by several degrees. She was far thinner, and her face was quite gaunt compared to the pictures from the time of her trial. Her hair had lost its auburn warmth and become a little wiry. And yet, when I looked more carefully, I noticed those same charming features I'd seen in her portrait on the front of the newspaper in the library.

"Yes, that's me," I replied after two long seconds of reflection. I foolishly held my hand out and the *clank, clank, clank* resounded across the internal courtyard. "Thank you so much for agreeing to my visit."

She smiled ever so cautiously. "It's certainly more entertaining than staying in my cell. I know that room very well after fifteen years here."

Before I replied, I found myself freezing again. It was the oddest sensation simply to hold myself in space like that. I don't believe I breathed for a few seconds as the reality of the moment settled in my brain.

"I can imagine." When I did respond, my words felt vague and empty. I like to think that I'm an adaptable sort, but I didn't know how to talk to this person. I immediately realised that, had Bella been alongside me, she would have known what to say. She could have charmed Felicity Mortimer like no one else, and I would have stood marvelling at the ease with which she went about her task.

It soon became apparent that this couldn't continue. She looked at me with something approaching sympathy, which I hadn't been expecting when I arrived at that gloomy edifice and submitted myself to having my person searched by a rough and disdainful guard.

"Mr Quin, would you mind telling me why you decided to visit today?"

My tongue still felt heavy in my mouth, but I forced myself to speak. "Yes, of course. I've come here because I believe that a great injustice has befallen you."

This did not trigger the instant wave of hope which I might have expected. Instead, she looked around at the other spaced-apart groups and the grey brick walls.

"You must call me Felicity," she said in a small, restrained voice.

This was almost enough to suggest that everything negative I'd heard about her was pure fiction. Surely the devil-tongued temptress that the British press had attacked would have uttered this in a seductive manner. Surely she would have tried to ingratiate herself with the man who had come to save her.

"I genuinely believe that your case deserves re-examining, and I would like to help you."

It was her turn to hesitate. Her expression was perplexed, her voice oddly flat. "It is very kind of you to take an interest in the matter."

I was confused by her attitude, even though I recognised the instinct that had produced this response. Whenever a reader compliments my books, I thank them, and yet I'm not sure that their praise registers in my brain. It is a writer's fate to always be his own worst critic.

I hurried to explain myself better. "I'm a private detective. My friend and I have investigated a number of complex cases this year, and I rather hope that, with your co-operation, I might be able to help you, too."

She shook her head, and my heart sank a little. "As I said, Mr Quin, I really am grateful that you would take the time to visit me, but..."

She turned away once more and wouldn't finish that sentence.

"But I'm not the first person to make such a claim. Is that what you're suggesting?"

Her eyes immediately flicked back to me and, for the first time, she regarded me with something approaching curiosity.

"That's exactly right. When I was first arrested, a man I hadn't previously known did all he could to free me. Carleton Hobbes met with Lord Verlaine, wrote letters to the newspapers and convinced any number of influential figures to back his campaign, but none of it made the slightest difference. The one thing he achieved was to spare me my death sentence, though I sometimes wonder whether that would have been preferable to a life spent like this."

I felt the urge to touch the sleeve of her dingy beige dress to show that I cared but remembered just in time that it wasn't allowed. "I understand why you might not believe me, but what harm would it do to try?"

I was about to reason with her once more when she answered the question. "Hope can be more painful than despair, Mr Quin. I have long been resigned to my situation. If it weren't for that, I doubt I would have survived. Your presence today offers a flicker of light that, when it is inevitably snuffed out, will make this hell all the darker."

She never looked at me for more than a minute without turning away again. It was the little boy who had been kept apart from his mother whom she now regarded, and I remembered from my reading that she would have no such visitors of her own. Is that what drew me to the case? The idea that she had been pulled away from her family, just as my father had been ripped from my own life? I couldn't say for certain, but the almost magnetic pull of her case was quite undeniable.

"They were taken away from you, weren't they?" I asked

her. "Your children, I mean. I believe I read that they were given up for adoption."

She nodded silently, but her gaze remained where it was. "Yes, that's the worst part of my punishment. I've never seen them once since I was taken from my home and locked in a cell. My little girl Eva and the twins must think that I killed their father. Or perhaps their new family told them I abandoned them. Perhaps they don't even know I exist."

"Isn't it worth my trying for their sake, if not yours?"

Her hands joined together at her waist, but she did not reply.

"Isn't the faint possibility that you might one day be reunited with them enough to take that risk? I can't promise that I'm anything more than an occasionally lucky detective rather than a genuinely good one. But I think you could do with a little luck. Imagine that I find the evidence that overturns your conviction and that, the next time I come to this prison, it's to see you walk free. Wouldn't that possibility be worth the broken heart that you'll suffer if it comes to nothing?"

She didn't just turn from me but walked away entirely. She stared at the nearest wall as though looking into a mirror and trying to make sense of the face gazing back at her.

I crossed the courtyard, too, but gave her the time she needed to find her words.

"I don't know that I have it in me to believe in anyone again."

"Then I'll just have to temper your expectations." This idea encouraged me somewhat, and I had to hope it would do the same for her. We Britons are nothing if not modest to the point of self-effacement, and I began to list my failings. "When I told you that I am a detective, that wasn't the whole story. By trade, I'm a moderately successful mystery writer – with a grand total of two books now published. In my spare time, I opened a crime-solving agency for the simple reason that I am in love with a young woman who is above me by all conceivable measures."

I had to take a deep breath then, as I believe this was the first time I had admitted this to anyone other than Percy. "And while it is true that Bella and I have so far solved every case we have investigated together, I will be on my own this time. It is quite possible that the only reason I have been able to form any relevant conclusions and interpret tricky evidence as I have is because I was so desperate to impress my fellow detective. Therefore, the chance of my making headway alone is extremely low and you should keep your expectations at a similar level."

The most surprising element of my visit that morning was not the dehumanising stare of the warders on duty – who viewed not just the inmates but their visitors as unruly animals in a zoo. Nor was it the circuit on the dusty ground where the prisoners had evidently been marched around in circles so often that, much as a horse tied to a stake, they'd left behind a well-worn track.

No, the thing that I couldn't have predicted was Felicity Mortimer's laugh. The unexpectedness of it almost forced me back a step, and her subsequent transformation was quite mesmerising. She was as bright and cheerful as her photograph, and the colour instantly returned to her. I knew then that, whatever she might claim, her spirit wasn't entirely broken.

"Very well, you second-rate author, fifth-rate detective. I will tell you what you need to know in order for you to fail to secure my release."

"Wonderful!" I said, and I imagine I looked just as cheerful as she did.

SEVEN

Every good (and second-rate) author knows that it's best to break up long conversations in a book if you wish to stop readers from growing distracted. As we were in a prison, that was impossible, so I continued straight on as we were before.

"Perhaps you should tell me the story from the beginning," I suggested as I moved to stand in front of her beside the wall.

"I imagine you know most of it, and don't forget that dear Carleton inspected every element through a magnifying glass and still couldn't get the government to quash my conviction."

"It doesn't matter. Tell me everything that happened from the time your husband fell ill."

I believe the reality of this task weighed her down then, but she took a deep breath and set about it. "I'll go back even further to when we first met if it helps." Well, there was one more brief pause, but then she went full steam ahead. "I was seventeen when Richard Mortimer came calling. We had met him at a social gathering, and I assumed that he was coming to enquire after Mother's hand in marriage. They were both forty years old, and she was a beautiful, if unlucky, woman who was recently widowed for the second time. We were not rich compared to my future husband, but we were comfortable thanks to the money my stepfather bequeathed us."

Her expression changed with each new part of the story, and a wistful smile now took possession of her features. "I must say that I'd never met anyone like Richard. He was terribly charming and attentive. When my mother realised that I was the one he was after, she was over the moon not to have to go through the same dance again. Within a week, we were engaged. A month later, I was married."

I noted that she employed the singular *I*. It suggested from the beginning that she considered herself alone in the union.

"Richard had a successful watchmaking business, invested the dividends wisely and had high ambitions for himself. He had worked his way up through the Worshipful Company of Clockmakers to become a councilman for the city. In time he was appointed Lord Lieutenant, but it was never enough. He believed that everyone still viewed him as a merchant from Cheapside, born into poverty. He tried to compensate for this by wearing flamboyant clothes and going everywhere on horseback which, by the turn of this century, was already old-fashioned. I imagine he hoped that our marriage would augment his standing, but I was never going to transform his reputation and, if anything, his associates only laughed at him more readily when they learnt of his young bride.

"I don't know whether this disappointment contributed to his poor health, or it was all in his head, but the fact is that, when he wasn't out dining with the great and good of London, he was at home pouring dubious patent medicines down his neck and complaining of pain in his stomach, liver, spleen and anywhere else that occurred to him. He was eventually diagnosed with acute dyspepsia. He was terribly proud of his ability to consume high levels of strychnine to treat his maladies, but I always thought that was what caused his problems in the first place."

"Do you think that his abuse of such substances is what ultimately killed him?"

"It's hard to say." She looked troubled, not so much by the story she had to tell, but her desire to be accurate. "He suffered with his health long before we met, and most doctors were willing to humour him because of the regular bills they would inevitably send. I never had a very clear understanding of what was wrong with him, but we'd had three children together and a thousand arguments before his health restricted him to a bed for any length of time."

She fell quiet, and I had to prompt her to continue. "What caused the arguments?"

For the first time since the conversation began, it was clear that there was something she would rather not share with me.

"Everything and nothing. We simply weren't suited to one another, and neither of us behaved as we should."

I considered raising a sensitive topic but then changed my mind. I soon changed it back again. "The newspapers say you were unfaithful to him."

"It's true." Biting her lip for a moment, she summoned the courage to reveal what had happened. "Not physically, but emotionally, at the very least. I met a man who was kind to me when I had no one else. We saw one another quite often at parties and dinners and I fell in love with him." She shook her head despondently and wouldn't look at me for some time. "Nothing happened outside of the letters we exchanged, but Richard became aware of my feelings. A few short months before he died, he lost his temper in a way I'd never seen before. He became... violent. When the staff intervened to calm him down, I told him that it was quite unreasonable of him to react in such a way when he had fathered children outside of our marriage, but he—"

"I beg your pardon," I had to say to make sense of what I'd just heard. "Do you mean that your husband was conducting affairs with other women, and yet it was the chaste love you felt which the newspapers so hungrily reported? Why didn't they mention the illegitimate children he sired?"

"They didn't know about them," she answered quite simply. "Richard never acknowledged the poor creatures as his own, and the judge ruled such information inadmissible – along with my husband's aggressive behaviour."

I couldn't hide my vexation. "On what possible grounds? Not wishing to speak ill of the dead?"

"All my barrister was allowed to say was that our marriage had not always been a happy one. Of course, the prosecution used that as further evidence of my motive to kill."

"And what did your barrister do about it?" I'm sure that I sounded quite incredulous. I certainly felt it.

For her part, Felicity described the situation as though it were a minor annoyance, rather than the foundations of a great injustice. "Dear Noel was a good man, but he no longer possessed the sharp legal mind he'd once had. He tried his very best for me and was quite heartbroken when we lost. But I'm getting ahead of myself. There wouldn't have been a trial if Richard hadn't died."

I waited for her to take us back in time once more.

She raised her chin just a touch, as though steeling herself for the difficult scenes she had to recall. "When he found out that I cared deeply for someone, he threatened to kill me. He got as drunk as a drowned mouse one morning and wrapped his hands around my neck. Thankfully, he had a coughing fit and grew tired before he could do any damage. I ran from the house and would rarely be alone with him from that day forward."

"But you didn't leave him?" I had to ask, and I hoped that I had taken on something of Bella's interview technique after all.

"No, I didn't. For the sake of the children, we stayed together. It was around then that Richard insisted we leave our home in Chelsea to move to his sister's home. It wasn't just his physical state that was in decline; he had become increasingly paranoid. He claimed that the London air was killing him, so we moved to Rhinefield House in Hampshire. Deirdre had married very well, and her husband owned a fine estate in the New Forest. With her rise to the higher echelons of society, her view of the world became just as distorted as her brother's. She never liked me in the first place, but when we were living in her house, she and her family treated me with such disdain that I was afraid for what might happen.

"My primary concern was not myself but my children, and Deirdre treated them unkindly from the very beginning. I suppose she took out her anger towards me on them, as she wouldn't allow Eva and her brothers to play with their cousins. She used to tease and trouble them just to see how they would react. The twins were sensitive children and would cry and cry when their aunt poked and abused them."

My detective's instincts were ringing bells in my head, and I instantly wondered what part Despicable Deirdre had played in her sister-in-law's imprisonment.

"And yet, when it came to the trial, my in-laws offered to pay for my defence. I received a letter saying that Richard's sister wanted me to have the best barrister that money could buy to ensure I got a fair hearing."

The alarm bells quietened just a little, and I was disappointed that I might not have solved the case so easily after all.

"Still, when we were there at Rhinefield House, she viewed me with suspicion, and I tried my best not to offend her. After a couple of months, with the twins aged two and Eva just a baby, Richard was confined to bed. He was given so many prescriptions by the family doctor that he was unconscious half the time. When he was awake, he was normally reading about some miraculous new cure that he would inevitably try before moving on to another when that didn't work. That was why he asked me to buy him arsenic."

"He sent you to get poison on his behalf?"

She frowned at this. "He believed that it would do him good. He wasn't seeking to end his life, if that's what you're thinking. For right or wrong, arsenic has been used for centuries to treat countless maladies. I myself used it for my complexion when I was younger, and I believe it is still included in certain medicines."

"Then why didn't his doctor give it to him if it was beneficial?" I'd remembered mention of the substance in the newspapers. Perhaps inevitably they neglected to mention that the supposed victim had chosen to consume the stuff himself.

"Because most doctors today don't believe the risk is worth the benefit. In Richard's case, I was inclined to agree. He was already so dyspeptic and in such agony whenever he ate that I couldn't see what good it would do. I only got it for him because he begged me."

"Did you buy it in your own name?" I asked, as I knew that, even before the recent strengthening of the laws around poisons, there would have been a register to sign.

"That's right. And of course, this proved to everyone in court that I was the devilish husband-killer they'd read about in the newspapers. But I handed the bottle to his nurse as soon as I got home from the chemist."

Another detail came back to me. "That wasn't the only access you had to arsenic, though. Isn't that correct?"

She glanced down at the ground again as the sound of our neighbours' conversation peaked and fell once more. "It is indeed. The week before he died, I ran out of my usual lotion and had to make one up myself. I soaked some strips of flypaper to extract the key ingredient and would have mixed it with a special cream, but the Rhinefield House nanny saw me and thought the worst."

"She accused you of trying to murder your husband?" The

case became harder to comprehend with every new detail she revealed.

"She was her mistress's favourite. Deirdre assigned her to look after my children, and Nanny Yapp just loved to report back on everything she thought I'd done wrong. I suppose it's my own fault, really. I wasn't as diplomatic with her as I could have been and soon made an enemy." She sighed and the glimmer of resilience that I'd seen in her faded.

"Was that the only reason that the family suspected you of plotting to kill Richard?"

"No, sadly not. I was a perfect fool and entrusted Nanny with a letter to take to the post office. I'm sure that, as soon as she was out of the house, even as she was looking after my children, she tore open the envelope to discover what I'd written."

There was an important point she was yet to reveal.

"I don't wish to be indiscreet, but would you mind telling me for whom the letter was intended?"

She considered my plea for several seconds and put her hand to her grey ponytail that was tied with a length of string. "Yes, I'm afraid I would. It makes no difference to what has happened to me since, and I wouldn't wish to cause an innocent man any more trouble than I already have."

That very much told me not to pry where I shouldn't. I couldn't resist one further question, though. "To be perfectly clear, could you at least confirm that it was not the man who tried to help you after your conviction?"

She smiled a little, and it made me feel better about my approach. "You mean Carleton Hobbes? No, Carleton was a stranger at the time, though he deserves my love and a whole lot more for the effort he made. I'm sure he'll be willing to share all that he found if you'd like to visit him at his house in Bloomsbury."

"I will be certain to do that, thank you. But please tell me exactly what happened after your husband's family came to suspect you."

She turned so that her back was against that cold, dull wall. As she spoke, her gaze travelled about the scene. "Deirdre made a great spectacle of humiliating me. She gathered the household together and, though they were only tiny, my children had to watch as she told everyone what a brazen woman I was. I swore that I had been a faithful wife to an unfaithful husband, but she wouldn't hear a word against her brother. She told me that I would never attend Richard again without someone else present."

I thought that a tear peeked from one of her eyes at that moment, but it might have been the light shifting over the courtyard. "My dear children had to witness their mother's shame. Their lives were already painful enough without that, and I begged Deirdre to think of her nephews, who were old enough to understand the situation."

I didn't want her to dwell on this painful scene, and so I helped her along to the next point in the story. "And you were never alone with your husband after that day."

"Never, but when Richard became so sick he couldn't keep his food down, they sent off samples to be tested to see whether there were traces of poison."

"And were there?"

"Not enough to kill him. He hadn't used the bottle of arsenic I'd bought him for some time. And I certainly couldn't have given him anything after that point. There was always someone with him."

I clapped my hands in frustration. "Then why on earth were you condemned for his murder? And why did the judge hand down the death penalty when there doesn't appear to have been anything but the lightest, most circumstantial evidence to convict you?"

She really was a fascinating character, and nothing like the *femme fatale* I had been expecting to meet. Despite what my loved ones feared, I was not a fly falling into her web. No, she was more interesting than that. She was a woman who had suffered greatly and, I had to believe, unfairly, but she was still able to look at the world with a modicum of positivity.

She smiled with her eyes as she replied. "I can answer one of those questions."

"Oh, yes?"

"Yes, the judge detested me from the first moment. His summing up before the jury could consider their verdict lasted twelve hours, and much of that was taken up with his thoughts on the wickedness of the modern world and the destructive influence of Jezebels like me." She was able to recount these details without a moment's hesitation, whereas I found myself holding my breath. "Do you know how many times he referred to me by name that day?"

I couldn't answer. I just shook my head.

"Not once. He called me 'the woman' throughout. The last thing he said was that it sent him into an apoplexy to know that a member of the fairer sex could kill her husband simply to indulge in her carnal desires with another man. He presented no doubt or balance in his statement. He made it clear that the only verdict that should be issued was a guilty one. And that is why I am still here today."

EIGHT

I have to wonder whether anyone – barring a released prisoner, of course – had ever left a prison feeling quite so exhilarated. When I'd travelled beyond iron door after iron door and stepped outside, I was entirely convinced that Felicity Mortimer was innocent, and I knew exactly what I needed to do to prove it. But first, I stopped at a phone box beside the railway station to share my impressions with Bertie.

"You were wrong," my voice crackled down the line to him.

"It's lovely to hear from you, too, Marius." He spoke in a tired but accepting voice that suggested that he already knew he wouldn't like what I had to say.

"I'm sorry for the lack of pleasantries, but I've telephoned to tell you that I have confirmed my belief you were mistaken about Felicity Mortimer."

"Oh, was I?"

"She's no devil. She's a perfectly normal woman who wouldn't have risked losing her three children just to get rid of a husband who spent most of his time sick in bed. She certainly wasn't the temptress you made her out to be."

I could hear him shaking his head down the line. "That's all very well, Marius. But have you considered the possibility she is all things to all men? You went there looking for someone reasonable, and that's what she gave you. My friend who took up her case is the romantic sort and fell quickly under her spell."

I ignored his argument as, for one thing, I've always considered myself the romantic sort, but also because... well, because I jolly well didn't agree with it. "I don't suppose your friend's name is Carleton Hobbes?"

"As a matter of fact, it is." I'm sure that he scratched at his bushy white beard just then. He always does that when he's surprised.

"Wonderful. Well I will need you to introduce us before long. For now, I'm off to see Felicity's barrister."

It was really no wonder that he knew who this was. "Noel Carpenter, isn't it?"

"That's right. I suppose the two of you are old friends."

"We've crossed paths on occasion." He cleared his throat softly. It was unlike him to prevaricate. "Though, for a number of reasons, I wouldn't expect you to get very far with him. Most pressingly, his wife may not let you in the house, even if you say you have my blessing: especially if you say you have my blessing."

Smiling at the nerve of the man, I swapped the receiver to my other ear. "Are you suggesting that I give up my quest, old boy?"

"Not at all. I'm suggesting that you buy Millicent Carpenter a bottle of sweet wine if you want any hope of speaking to her husband. Good luck, Marius. You're going to need it."

As the echo of his laughter was still knocking about in my brain, he ended the call, and I went in search of a vintner.

It was not yet midday and there was relatively little traffic as I drove from Holloway to Muswell Hill in the north of the city.

The air was crisp, but I left the top of my Invicta down to breathe more deeply after the conditions I'd experienced in the gaol. I almost felt guilty for my freedom and was fairly certain that I'd done worse in my life than Felicity Mortimer ever had.

I do not have an atlas-like knowledge of the streets of London, but Noel Carpenter lived only a short distance from Alexandra Palace, which I'd been to on several occasions. His house was moderate by the standards of someone like my beloved Bella, but it was a mansion compared to the house in which I'd lived as a child. It was all red brick and looked like many grand Victorian family homes. The only difference was the tall turret on either side of the building. I could only think that they'd been built to show that, for this Englishman at least, his home was his proverbial castle.

"Yes, what do you want?" the woman who answered my chirpy knocking demanded.

She was perhaps in her seventies with short, curly grey hair and similarly coloured eyes. She didn't open the door all the way but peeked through a narrow crack. I'm fairly confident that she had her foot pressed against the bottom in case I turned out to be a lunatic.

"Mrs Carpenter? My name is Marius Quin. I believe that Bertrand Price-Lewis is a mutual acquaintance."

Her initially stern expression softened, and she smiled. "That's one reason for me not to trust you. Bertie is one of the biggest rascals in London."

"You needn't tell me, madam. He's my editor."

She eyed the bottle of sherry that I'd made no effort to hide. "You poor boy. You must come in and have a drink to warm you up." She moved aside, and the door seemed to swing open of its own accord. "I can only imagine what it must be like to have that man as your overlord. He's a tyrant! A lovable Welsh tyrant!"

She pointed me through, and I stepped past her to enter an

expansive entrance hall with a green and white diamond-pattern on the tiled floor. There was no staircase visible, but several doors led off the room in different directions. Something about it reminded me of Alice's arrival in Wonderland, and it gave me pleasure to picture the curious places that could be found beyond each portal.

"I'll take that, thank you, Marius." She winked as she pilfered the bottle from under my arm, but I didn't mind one bit. "If you follow me, I might have something already open."

"It was actually your husband I wished to—"

She didn't wait to hear what I had to say but hurried on slippered feet through the door directly in front of us. I hadn't paid much attention to her clothes before but could confirm that Millicent Carpenter was not dressed as a playing card or talking animal. She wore a smock of some description that appeared to be from the Orient. I know very little about clothes, or the Far East for that matter, but the short, stand-up collar looked a little Chinese to me.

We came to a stop in an incredibly bright room at the back of the house. I swear that there was more light inside than out thanks to a series of mirrors on the wall and a bank of large windows that overlooked a wide lawn. I suppose you might have called this space a conservatory or winter garden, though the roof wasn't made of glass. In terms of its purpose, it was most definitely an artist's studio, and I now noticed flecks of paint on the pale blue material of Mrs Carpenter's clothes.

"You'll find two glasses in the cabinet in the corner," she told me as she picked up a brush and went to stand at her easel.

I took this as a command and poured out two snifters of muscatel wine. It was a mellow reddish-brown colour and smelt like fruit bursting with succulence on the day of the harvest. I gave her a glass, and we were both happy to take a first sip.

"Now that we are suitably in wine, Mr Quin, you can tell me why you have come here."

She had been so accepting of my presence until now that I was alarmed she could change so quickly. Her voice was blunt and uncompromising, and her eyes narrowed as they took in the faint sketch on the canvas before her. Only half of the picture had any colour, and it was largely marked out in pencil, but I could see that it was going to be a landscape of some description. It was not a pastoral view of rolling English fields, however, but a scene of somewhere wild and exotic. There was so much life and verdancy already emerging from the outline that I would have loved to see the finished picture.

"I'm looking into the case of Felicity Mortimer," I told her in as open and obliging a manner as I could muster.

It did nothing to placate her. "In which case, you had better pour me a larger drink. I was rather hoping that Bertie had sent you here to learn about blending watercolours or how to hold a brush."

Her glass was already empty, whereas mine was half full, but I topped them both up and she asked another question.

"Very well, then. What sort of books do you write?"

She was at least a decade older than my mother, but everything about her gave the impression of youth and confidence. I can't honestly say I'd met anyone like her before, and I hurried to answer in case I drew another rebuke. "I'm a mystery writer. I write... mysteries."

Her eyes flicked towards me momentarily. "How mysterious."

"And I must confess that I have a stab at detective work myself from time to time. That's more or less how I ended up hearing of Mrs Mortimer's case. In fact, I've just been to see her in prison."

She held her brush still against the canvas and closed her eyes for a moment. I decided she was picturing the place that she wished to recreate, and it occurred to me that she might have travelled to such interesting climes herself.

"I'm sure Mrs Mortimer had a fascinating story to tell." There was no malice or sarcasm in her voice, but it didn't appear that she would offer anything more, so I asked her what I really needed to know.

"Mrs Carpenter, is your husband currently at home?"

She sighed and put down her glass. "Do you really want to see him?"

We left the conservatory that wasn't a conservatory and walked further along the corridor to a room on the opposite side of the house. I could hear music long before we arrived and, when Mrs Carpenter opened the door, it grew louder. I'm no expert when it comes to classical composers, but it was certainly very bombastic. I had a feeling it might have been by Tchaikovsky, though I could just as well be entirely wrong.

When I peered inside, I found a small, comfortable room, decorated in warm colours with the only splash of white being the hair of a little old man in a rocking chair with a tartan blanket over his knees. Noel Carpenter looked twenty years older than his wife, and I suppose he may have been. Nonetheless, I could tell from the moment I saw him that he had just as much character packed into his tiny frame. He waved his arms about frantically in time with the music and occasionally let out a "boom" or "clash" as the timpani sounded on the spinning disc on his gramophone.

"Noel, my darling," his wife said with a melody to her voice. "Mr Quin is here to see you."

"Quin!" he responded, but he didn't turn to look at us and his movements continued.

Mrs Carpenter nodded to show that I could enter, and then she disappeared back to her work. Feeling like a trespasser, I shuffled inside. One wall of the room was obscured by a shelf of black and gold leather-bound tomes which were arranged by year dating back to the mid-seventeenth century. I could only assume that they were legal annals, the contents of which I couldn't imagine anyone wanting to read unless paid to do so.

When my host didn't look at me, I sat down in a seat opposite and tried to get his attention.

"Mr Carpenter, I've come to see you about Felicity Mortimer."

"Mortimer!"

He raised one hand to make me wait as the music was reaching its crescendo, and he still had some conducting to do. The brass and strings soared, and his hands flew about like two sparrows trapped in a bell jar. When the piece came to its abrupt conclusion, the silence was pronounced.

"As I was saying," I continued in the same neutral tone, "I've come here today because I'd like to talk to you about your work on the Mortimer murder trial of 1913. I'm sure you'll remember it. She was a—"

"Lovely lady," he said, his eyes finally meeting mine. "Yes, lovely lady."

He had the most complex pattern of wrinkles of anyone I'd ever seen, and they grew all the more tangled as a great smile illuminated his face. Felicity had told me that he was a kind man, and I certainly got that impression. If I could have adopted him as my grandfather, I would have done so in an instant. That didn't make it any easier to conduct a conversation with him, though.

"That's right, she is a lovely lady," I said a little patronisingly, before correcting my tone. "And that's why I believe that she has no place being locked up in a cell for a crime she didn't commit. Perhaps with your help, I will be able to make it right."

He nodded as he listened and his small, quick eyes were forever moving.

"From what she told me this morning, there were any number of irregularities in the trial. For one thing, I can't understand how you, as her barrister, were barred from presenting evidence of Richard Mortimer's infidelity and violence. I believe that the judge was prejudiced against her from the very beginning, and I'd like to know what you believe brought about this miscarriage of justice."

Although the music had finished, the thick shellac disc kept turning on the gramophone and Noel Carpenter now sat watching it. I was about to rephrase my question, but he started humming the piece we'd just heard, and I finally realised that he was more than just eccentric.

"Sir, do you remember any of this? Do you remember the trial? It was a national scandal, covered all over the British Isles. Can you recall Mrs Mortimer's sentence?"

He fell quiet and turned to look at me sadly once more. He rolled his shoulders, and the tufts of hair around his head appeared to stick out further. As I peered into his pale blue eyes, I felt as though I were looking into some far-off and unknowable galaxy. There was so much to learn there, but I could already see that I had no way to access it.

"Terrible," was all he would say. "Lovely lady. Terrible situation."

He looked so despondent that I felt guilty for sparking even these limited memories and so, rather than continue on a path that would evidently lead me nowhere, I changed the topic.

"Do you like football, sir? My father used to take me to matches when I was a boy growing up in Surrey. I even played a little."

"Oh, yes, football!" He rubbed his hands together, and I knew I'd chosen well. "Barton!"

"You liked Jimmy Barton, did you? He was marvellous."

He shook his head then in an almost exaggerated manner, as though he were annoyed at himself for not being able to find his words. He put one hand out in front of him, as though seeking to touch the words he required even as they remained just out of reach. The poor man was clearly aware of his limitation and, just when it looked as though he would give up, he let out a low laugh and said, "Athletic."

"Oh, the club? Barton Athletic? I've never seen them myself, but my dad used to talk about their success. He said that he liked the teams better when he was a boy, and that the soul of the game has changed since then."

Mr Carpenter laughed again and then put his fists up to cheer. I wondered if he could see his team playing in front of him and was reliving a moment from earlier days. Whatever happened, I lost him again after that. It appeared that he could only remain lucid for a short time before the veil that obscured his thinking would descend once more. The human brain is more of a mystery than any case I could investigate, and I doubted whether even the best doctors could say what had changed in the short time we'd been talking.

For my sake as much as his, I spouted some inanities for a few minutes longer until Mrs Carpenter returned to collect me.

"Ah, the lovely lady." Her husband beamed when she entered the room.

He looked at her with so much love then that it almost broke my heart. Whatever the condition was that had attacked his once-fine mind, I had to wonder whether it affected his loved ones even more than it did the man himself.

"Marius has to leave now, Noel," she told him, putting one hand on his shoulder and bringing her face down to his level to ensure that he paid attention.

"He's a very nice boy."

I believe that the presence of his wife steadied him somewhat, as his sentences had become a touch more grammatical.

"That's right." Mrs Carpenter laughed and turned to look at me. "He is a very nice boy."

The old man nodded contentedly to himself and, his wiry eyebrows moving in unison, said, "He always has been."

"Goodbye, Noel." I rose from my hard wooden seat. "It has been a real honour to meet you."

Noel cranked the handle of the gramophone, and Millicent selected a new disc for him. As another grand and pompal composition filled the air, we left the room.

"He has his good moments, but I'm afraid he no longer remembers much about his career."

I walked next to her in silence. While my first thought was to ask why she'd let me see him if that was the case, I chose a different question. "What about his files from back then? Would you happen to have anything about the Mortimer trial?"

She nodded as if she were expecting this and took the next door off the corridor. I got the sense that I was not expected to follow, and so I stayed right where I was.

"This is the file you need," she said a couple of minutes later before handing me the bundle of papers. "Noel hoped to write his memoirs when he retired, but his mind wasn't up to it. You might as well take them with you. I can't imagine anyone else wishing to read them."

"Did a man called Carleton Hobbes ever request copies or come to speak to your husband?" I was curious about the lengths to which Felicity's supporters had gone to challenge her sentence.

We had made it to the entrance hall, and she pointed to the door politely. "Not to my knowledge. Reporters would always come begging for interviews, but they soon realised I wouldn't let them anywhere near Noel and gave up."

When we reached the front door, she stopped to answer a question I was too discreet to put to her. "The doctors say he has Alzheimer's disease." She held back any emotion, but I could still feel the weight of her burden. "Some days he seems to disappear within himself, and some days he talks his head off. It's the strangest disease, but he is always so gentle. When we were younger, we would fight like hyenas over the silliest things, but for the last fifteen years and longer, he has been the kindest companion I could imagine. His disease makes some people violent and aggressive, but, in Noel's case, it has served to soften his rough edges."

I held my hand out to her, not just to shake but because I felt that the contact might do us both good. She held it for a moment and, before she could bid me farewell, something she said suddenly fell into place in my brain. "Did you say fifteen years? Your husband's condition was already evident all that time ago?"

She looked a little surprised that the tender moment of solidarity between two practical strangers had been interrupted by an amateur detective's meddling.

"That's right, Noel had retired when he accepted the Mortimer brief. He only took it as a favour to the dead man's family. They'd heard good things about his work and wanted to ensure that Felicity Mortimer had a fair defence."

NINE

I got back into my car and missed my dog for the first time (that morning). I'd never actually wanted a pet. When my uncle bought Percy, he didn't ask me whether a needy puppy would fit in well in my chic central London flat. I wouldn't even describe myself as a dog-lover, but goodness me I miss the persistent mutt when he isn't around. I would say that there is no kind of loneliness like that of a dog owner *sans chien*, but that would be unfair to poor Felicity and her children.

This wasn't the only thing that occurred to me as the Invicta drove me home – well, I was at the wheel, but it always seems as if that finely tuned automobile is leading the way. In contrast, I felt loaded down by my expanding knowledge of the wrong I needed to right.

I intended to drive to see Bertie in Bloomsbury. I'd consulted him so often that he'd come to feel like a client, though he was more likely to pay me to give up the investigation than see it to fruition. In the end, I stopped the car beside St Pancras Gardens and went to sit in the weak sunshine beneath the remarkable tree there. There was a brief (melancholy) period after I first moved to London when I read little but

Thomas Hardy. Back then, I had come to this former graveyard which, as a young architect's apprentice, he had been employed to clear. A mess of displaced gravestones had been wedged into the earth in tight, concentric circles around the tree, and such a moody setting seemed the perfect spot to go through the file I'd been given.

I quickly found transcripts of interviews conducted with various friends who spoke at the trial on Felicity's behalf. There were also summaries of what the witnesses for the prosecution were expected to say – with Deirdre Stradbrooke and her husband predicted to be particularly vicious in their criticism of their sister-in-law. I discovered a copy of the police notes from the time Felicity was first arrested and an account of the inquest into Richard Mortimer's death.

From the summary I read, it was clear that his will would have counted against his wife in court. Everything was left in her name, and there were no provisions made for their children, though, if Felicity was dead or otherwise indisposed, his fortune passed to his sisters.

I moved on to the barrister's notes. Noel Carpenter had once been a thorough man and there were receipts for the services of experts that the defence had paid, along with a summary of the advice that each had given. Despite this, it was sometimes hard to follow the logic of his approach to the case, and I already felt that, had Felicity been represented by a barrister at the top of his game, a clear argument against the prosecution's charge should have been successful.

After an hour spent looking through the pages (and skipping parts that were irrelevant), I had a much better sense of what had happened and what would need to be proven in order to secure Felicity's release. One thing that fascinated me, of which I barely understood a word, were the reports on the state of Richard Mortimer's body and the quantities of arsenic and other chemicals found within him. They might have been written in Egyptian hieroglyphs for all I could make of them, but the fact that they existed gave me hope.

I bundled the papers together once more, now confident of what to say to a man who thought I should stick to writing silly stories, but whose help I very much needed if my work that week was not to be in vain.

"I know you worry about me, Bertie," I told him once his always crotchety secretary had deigned to grant me entrance to his plush office on Russell Square. "But I'm not going to marry the woman. Nor am I planning to lend her any money. She does not have her claws in me and, if you'd met her, you'd know that she isn't the demon the world imagines."

He sat down on the edge of the large desk that dominated the southern side of the room. "I have."

"I beg your pardon?" I understood the words but not their meaning.

"I have met Felicity Mortimer."

"How is that possible?"

"At a party in Knightsbridge a few years before the murder. Of course, you must remember that I was much younger then. A real man about town, in fact."

He was an ever so round fellow, with an ever so jolly air about him, and it was hard to imagine any such thing. Perched where he was, he looked more like Humpty Dumpty than a stylish bohemian gadfly. I didn't tell him that. I just sat down in a spare chair and waited to hear the rest of the story.

"I met her husband first, and he was a terrible buffoon. Based on his clothes and the hint of make-up on his face, he evidently thought he was a seventeenth-century gent. The only thing missing was a powdered wig."

"What about her?" I asked when, instead of continuing, he sat looking pensive.

"She was utterly charming. She couldn't have been more than twenty-three and everybody thought it quite ridiculous that a woman like her should have married that pompous clockmaker. By the end of the evening, I'd heard any number of rumours about her. One man told me he had taken her as a mistress. A woman said that Felicity was the illegitimate daughter of a minor royal. Everyone I spoke to agreed that she knew what she was getting into with Mortimer and must have had an ulterior motive."

I breathed out indignantly. "So what you're saying is that she was a beautiful young girl of whom people became jealous and made up lies. If you're expecting any of this to turn me against her, you can think again."

"I'm not." He pushed himself off his desk, then straightened his tie and went to fetch his jacket. "I just want you to know the sort of attention she attracted. You may well be right. It is conceivable that Felicity Mortimer is innocent, and our cruel society thought the worst of her after her husband died, just as the people at that party thought badly of her because he was a conceited cod's head."

He had reached the door by now and bade me follow him with one bended finger.

"I'm sorry, Bertie," I called across the reception, "but I don't understand where you're going. I haven't even told you why I'm here."

He didn't stop but headed for the stairs and spiralled down them to the ground floor. He was surprisingly swift when he wanted to be and must have reached the front door ten seconds before I did.

"I'm looking for an expert on poisons," I said before he could carry the conversation off towards some no doubt fascinating but entirely different destination. "Would you happen to know one?"

"I do indeed!" he said rather comically, but he was a curious man, and this was perfectly normal for him.

"You see, I somehow managed to charm your friend Millicent Carpenter. She gave me Noel's files from the trial, and I need to understand the relevant toxicological tests that were performed on Mortimer's corpse."

"That shouldn't be a problem. I'll put you in touch with a man who knows all about that sort of thing." There was definitely something mischievous about him then. He clearly wasn't going to explain, so I stopped talking and waited for him to tell me what the point of his story was (and also preferably where he was taking me).

"I didn't know the Mortimers well, but Carleton Hobbes was heavily involved after the trial."

"The man Felicity describes as her great friend and hero."

"That is correct, Marius." For a moment, he sounded like a teacher who is happy with a pupil for understanding a basic lesson. "He never told me how he became involved in the case, but he was a devoted advocate for that woman's innocence, and his experience defending her changed him."

We were headed towards the Imperial Hotel, and I half hoped that, to take my mind off the wickedness of the world, he would treat me to lunch. I would not be so lucky, and we kept walking.

"So who is this chap? All I know about him is that he defended her when she was at her lowest ebb."

"He did more than that. Carleton organised the efforts and resources of all those who wished to help Mrs Mortimer. He devoted himself to overturning her conviction and petitioned many public figures to support her."

We turned left onto a comparatively wide alley to access Queen Square.

"You didn't answer my question," I pointed out. "Aside from his connection to Felicity Mortimer, who is he?"

Bertie's little legs kept motoring us to wherever we were going, and he didn't look at me as we spoke.

"Carleton is one of those people who never quite found his calling. He's brilliant in his own way, but he must have tried twenty different professions without sticking at one. Off the top of my head, I remember that he's been an actor, a landlord, a solicitor in training, and I met him when he decided to become an author. I published a rather worthy novel of his about a poor family from the turn of the century. He might have gone on to have a real career, but he decided that he couldn't afford the literary life and swiftly sought out his next challenge. We stayed friends, nonetheless, which is why I was able to call him up and ask whether he'd mind a visit."

We had reached the long, rectangular garden in the middle of the long, rectangular square. There were a number of bushy horse chestnut trees, almost as tall as the tenement buildings, and so I couldn't see to the other side of the park, but it smelt for a moment as if there were men burning bitumen to lay a new road. As we walked past a group of schoolchildren having an autumnal lesson outdoors, I realised that there was no sign of any works. A moment later, a few shouts of concern went up and I quickened my step. It wasn't until we cut through the metal railings and back onto the street that I saw the smoke.

"My goodness, Marius," Bertie declared in a nervous voice that did not sound like his own. "That's Carleton's building!"

I broke into a run, and I was impressed by just how easily my friend kept pace. I could see no flames, but when we reached the steps up to the front door of the tall, Georgian house, the smoke was billowing from the windows with an intensity that you don't often see. Fold after fold of thick, grey-black smoke escaped into the atmosphere, and I propelled myself forward.

Using the momentum I'd built mounting the steps, I barged

the door with my shoulder. This was not a great idea, as I hurt my shoulder and the door stayed shut.

Without reproaching me for being born with half a brain, Bertie ran his fingers around the rim of a terracotta pot which held a topiarian privet bush. He quickly found the key and unlocked the front door, but all this achieved was to allow a cloud of smoke to surround us, so that we were soon coughing up a lung or three.

I dropped to my knees in the tiled porch and grabbed a handkerchief from my pocket to cover my mouth. This was another perfect opportunity for me to do something without thinking. There was a layer of clear air beneath the smoke, and I could see a man lying halfway along the hallway. Before anyone could tell me otherwise, I did the obvious (admittedly foolish) thing.

"Marius, you lunkhead. Come back here," was the last I heard from Bertie as I crawled inside the burning house.

I could feel the change in temperature immediately, but there were still no flames visible. I got the distinct impression that the conflagration was contained within the room to my right. If I could get to the unfortunate fellow in front of me, I felt we both had a good chance of surviving.

Not that I was weighing up probabilities at that moment; I was scrambling forward on instinct and occasionally had to duck as the smoke ate up the oxygen. For a moment, I was back in France during the war. I'd had to crawl like this through no man's land, with artillery fire and explosions raining down, and nearly lost limbs and my life for the trouble. Something takes over at moments like that and you push on without thinking.

In Hobbes's flat, though I'd like to think the act was somewhat heroic, I must have looked like a manic baby. Bellying along the floor was more difficult than I had hoped, especially as one of my arms was needed to cover my mouth. The handkerchief was no match for the thick particles of smoke that hung in the air, but I finally made it to the man I could only assume was Carleton Hobbes.

Of course, getting back outside would be even harder. I couldn't very well drag him back with me and keep a hand to my face, so there was only one thing for it. I lay next to him, grabbed his collar with my free hand and, snake-like and with no small effort, wriggled to the front door.

"Marius, you wonderful maniac," Bertie called from the garden when I emerged.

A police constable had arrived and rushed up the steps to help me. I had inhaled more smoke than I'd realised and, as soon as the fresh air hit my lungs, I began to cough. The constable tried to help me, but I pointed to the still inert Hobbes, and he carried him to safety.

A crowd had gathered beyond the metal fence at the end of the path, and there was a small cheer when the officer laid the rescued man down on the cobblestones in the garden.

"Poor Carleton," Bertie said, as I sat on the steps, and he examined his friend.

"Was I too late?" I asked between deep, stinging breaths.

"Much." His voice was flat, and he shook his head as the constable stood up from his fruitless task. "His throat has been cut."

TEN

We gave our statements to an ageing inspector with lambchop sideburns and a bowler hat. He didn't seem particularly interested in the case or either of us. He certainly didn't want to know anything about Felicity Mortimer or why her friend might have been killed, though, on that score at least, I was just as much in the dark as he was.

"It doesn't make any sense," Bertie told me once we were sitting on a bench in the park in front of the dead man's house. The London Fire Brigade had managed to limit the damage that the blaze had caused to the downstairs sitting room, which I thankfully hadn't had to enter, but the square would smell of smoke for days.

"I've found that life rarely does."

"No, now listen." He was clearly perturbed by something... beyond the murder of his friend, I mean. "Why would anyone kill him now? From what he told me on the phone, he'd been working as a clerk in his uncle's office for the last two years. The only thing he had of any value was his flat. He wasn't the type to have enemies and in all the time I've known him, the only long-term companion he had was a tortoise called George, who died of old age."

"I hate to say it, dear friend, but I think that you know the likely reason."

I would have told him what this was, but it was obvious enough.

"Very well. If this is all connected to Felicity Mortimer, why now?"

"Because everything that I've discovered about her case makes it seem as if there was a conspiracy to find her guilty. Her in-laws, who apparently hated her, suddenly had a change of heart when Richard Mortimer was murdered and went out of their way to hire Felicity a top-notch barrister. However, as you know, they chose an elderly man who had already retired because of the mental decline that affected his work. It doesn't take a genius to realise that people like that wouldn't want us to find out about their scheming."

I thought this was enough to convince him, but Bertie isn't the kind to settle for simple explanations. "You're missing the point. If that was the case, why kill Carleton? He tried his very best to clear Felicity Mortimer's name and failed. If he had possessed any crucial evidence, he would have been murdered long ago."

I raised one hand to explain away this trifling discrepancy before realising that I didn't know how. "Gosh, you're right."

Bertie dropped his head into his hands and silent sorrow wracked his body. "He was a decent fellow. He didn't deserve this."

To add to my guilt over Gilbert, Bella and Felicity, I now felt terrible for Bertie and his friend. "I'm so sorry, old thing. I truly am."

"You can put it right." Suddenly filled with purpose, he turned to point his finger at me. "You can keep doing whatever it is you do when you're wasting your time with dead bodies instead of writing books for me. I don't give a stuff about Felicity Mortimer and her seductress ways, but I was very fond of Carleton Hobbes. So find out who killed him... and then write the story you promised."

I stood up and offered him my hand by way of a guarantee. "I'll need to meet the expert on poisons that you mentioned."

He blew his white fringe from his eyes. "You'll find him in front of the arch in St John's Square at three. He's there playing chess every afternoon."

"How will I recognise him?"

"Oh, you'll recognise him." He let out a brief, despondent laugh before peering back at the smoke-tinged building.

"He sounds like a curious person."

"In more ways than one." He released a deep breath, and I could tell that the events of that morning had really affected him. When he spoke again, his voice was softer and more forgiving. "Do what you can, Marius. But please know that none of this is your fault. I don't blame you for what's happened. Though I might not be so forgiving if you get yourself killed."

I had to swallow at the thought of it. "I'll do my best, Bertie. You must look after yourself, too."

He blinked away tears as he stood watching the firemen coiling a thick rubber hose. "I have a wife who would never let anything happen to me. I'll go home to see her."

Without another word, he wandered back the way we'd come an hour earlier. I might just as well have followed him, as my car was still parked in front of his office, but I had some thinking to do. I left the smell of burnt carpets and curtains and walked without thinking where I might find myself. This all sounds very romantic, but in the end, the place where I found myself was an establishment in Soho which, Lord Edgington assured me, sold the best sandwiches in England. The monstrosity of meat, cheese, onions and half a loaf of bread was certainly filling, though I can't say it was the kind of eatery that I expected the upstanding marquess to frequent.

The sandwich did me a world of good – providing as it did both energy and a jolt of optimism – and then it was time to head to St John's Square. I would say that stumbling over two murdered individuals in a week was bad luck by anyone's standards but, over the course of the last year, I'd come to accept that I was destined to know as many dead people as living ones.

I drove across London reflecting on the deaths of Gilbert Baines and Carleton Hobbes. I had ignored one case to concentrate on the other, but in the absence of my dog, my mother and my co-detective, I felt as if Gilbert were sitting next to me in the front of the Invicta, evaluating my every act.

"He's only been dead a couple of days," I said aloud to soothe my conscience. "Felicity Mortimer has been rotting in prison for fifteen years. She hasn't spoken a word to her children in that time, and I doubt she's had a single good night's sleep."

This seemed to lay his ghost to rest for the time being, but it did nothing for the invisible weight bearing down upon my shoulders. Bella's absence was almost as strong as her presence whenever I was lucky enough to be in it. I felt a terrible mix of guilt, sadness and longing to see her again. I wanted to know that she was surviving the all-encompassing grief that had fallen upon her, but I accepted that I had no right to trouble her at such a moment. Don't worry, though, I was about to feel a great deal worse.

"You," I said when I'd parked my car and walked to the medieval-looking gatehouse of St John, which was squeezed in between more modern buildings.

"Marius," the oaf at the folding table who was setting up a game of chess responded. "How kind of you stop by."

"Carmine Fortescue," I said, mainly to confirm to myself that the slovenly fellow really was before me. "Bertie sent me. He knew I wouldn't be happy to see you, and so he neglected to mention your name."

As usual, my rival author looked ever so pleased with himself. "Have you come in search of a game?"

I could barely bring myself to answer. "No, Fortescue. I need some advice."

He put the last piece down on the board and clapped his hands together. "Fine. Never wear those shoes with that suit. They don't go together at all well."

"Not that kind of advice, though I'll be sure to consult you the next time I visit my tailor."

I closed my eyes. Gilbert's violent demise still haunted me. Finding a potentially crucial witness with his throat cut was no joy either, but having to maintain a conversation with the man I dislike most in the world was a step too far.

He wiped his nose on the back of the sleeve of his brown woollen suit jacket, and I wondered what right he had to critique my appearance. If there is a rich man in London who dresses as poorly as Carmine Fortescue, I haven't met him. His shabby clothes barely fitted, and yet it was only that week that Bertie had spoken of the fortune his client had made from his tedious novels.

He didn't say anything for a few moments, but his eyes never left me. "You could at least sit down. I feel like I'm the one taking up your time."

I peered about the square, which was quiet after lunch. There were no children playing games or businessmen out for a constitutional. I don't know whether I would have sat down if there had been any witnesses, but that's what I did.

"Now, how can I help you?" Fortescue's huge, round face – which always seemed to have more skin on it than one person required – had rarely looked so contented. It was his greatest desire for everyone on the planet to want something from him so that he could hold it over them.

"I asked Bertie for someone who knows about poisons. He sent me here." I was shaking my head. I couldn't believe that I'd failed to question my editor's motives. He had literally told me that I would recognise the man I was meeting.

"Oh, poisons. How charming." He had a glib, devious manner. Glancing down at the chessboard, he placed one finger on top of his king as he spoke, as if to remind me who had the power in this situation. "You know, there's a funny story behind that. Previously, whenever I killed one of my characters using cyanide or strychnine or what have you, I would consult a doctor I know to ask him about the symptoms and speed with which my chosen venom would dispatch the victim. This went on for so long that he eventually told me, 'Carmine, I can answer your questions, but at this stage I feel you must know far more than me about the toxicology of every lethal substance that exists in the British Isles.'

"I didn't believe it at first, but I soon realised that he was right. I have murdered so many people in so many different ways that I have become quite the expert. Bertie suggested I could even write a book on the topic, though I would fear that some nefarious sort would abuse my knowledge for his own ends."

There was lots not to like about the man, but his insistence on proving just how much more he knew than everyone else was particularly grating. The fact that he really did know more about poisons than I did was harder to swallow than a cyanide and strychnine pancake.

I was in no mood for prattling and got straight to the matter that had brought me there. "There is a woman named Felicity Mortimer. I believe that she was unjustly sentenced for the murder of her husband. I'm looking for evidence to overturn her conviction."

I took the report on the poison that had been in her husband's system when he died and placed it face-up on the free part of the table so that he could make sense of the figures and facts that meant nothing to me.

"I remember this case," he told me noncommittally as his eyes darted back and forth across the page. "She was rather an attractive woman, if I'm not mistaken. I always wondered whether that counted against her in the trial. The judge was particularly critical of her." He wasn't saying anything I didn't already know, but I decided not to rush him.

"Yes, I believe she was at a disadvantage before she even stepped into court."

"I'll make a deal with you." He flicked the manila folder closed with a careless hand. "I'll tell you what you need to know if you play one game of chess against me."

"Do I have to win?"

"I don't expect you to *be able* to win." The jowls under his chin always wobbled whenever he said something rude. "Just sit there and play me, and then I'll tell you something really very interesting that I've noticed in the report."

I was tempted to roll my eyes or at least reply with a dissatisfied huff, but I didn't want to irritate him any more than necessary. "Very well, but only one game. And you can't complain if it doesn't live up to expectations."

He was over the moon that I had accepted his terms. Having adjusted a few of his pieces by a fraction of a fraction of an inch, he most graciously pointed at himself to show that he would start. He pushed one of his pawns forward two squares and then, moving my hand cautiously, I chose a matching piece and shifted it out to meet his.

"Did you know that the word 'checkmate' comes to us from the Arabic phrase, *shāh māt*, which means *the king is dead*?" A flicker of a smile registered on his face as he sent his queen shooting diagonally across the board to be able to attack my pawn, and I did not reply to his trivial comment.

I'm not a total novice at chess, so I moved one of my knights to protect the piece he was threatening. He immediately placed his bishop in the middle of the board and, beginning to sense that I was in some kind of danger, I moved my other knight out from safety to cover his queen.

"My goodness," he replied, his eyes ever so wide, but he didn't take his turn.

"What?"

"I've never seen this happen before. I'm a little amazed." He was biting his lip, his eyes fixed on the game before us.

"Is it good? What's happened?"

Moving ever so slowly, he reached across the board to seize his queen. "Four moves," he whispered and then brought the piece forward once more to take my pawn which was diagonally to the right of my king. "Checkmate in four moves."

"How can... Surely it isn't..." I was lost for words. "You must be some kind of genius!"

"Oh, you know." He was never good at hiding his high opinion of himself. "I wouldn't say I'm a genius. I'm just an exceptionally good amateur."

I was shaking my head by now as I considered the fate of my poor monarch, who was trapped in by Fortescue's pincer movement. Even if the king had executed a vain but glorious mission to kill the enemy queen, that dastardly bishop would have bumped him off. My two poorly positioned knights could do nothing but look on, aware of their own powerlessness.

"Now," my opponent said, still basking in the glow of his success, "about the arsenic that was found in Richard Mortimer's post-mortem." He paused then, much as he had before he'd delivered the fatal move in the game. "There wasn't nearly enough of the stuff to kill a man, especially if, as this report suggests, he was used to taking it as a stimulant and aphrodisiac."

Now I really was taken aback. "How could it be?"

"I mean that people who expose themselves regularly to arsenic build up a tolerance to it. It would have taken a lot more than he had in his system to—"

"Not that." I sounded a touch impatient. "I understand that. I'm asking how a woman was sentenced to hang for his murder if there was barely any poison in his body?"

He turned his head to the other side and blinked rapidly before responding. "I can't possibly say. What I do know is that, if her barrister had presented this information at the time, it seems unlikely she would have been found guilty."

I couldn't think just then, let alone speak. Every single discovery I'd made on the Mortimer case was hard to believe, but this surely topped the lot. "That's where I got this file."

"I beg your pardon?"

"Her barrister. The old man who defended her had this information in his house."

I'd surprised him for the first time. "Now that doesn't make sense."

"It might if you knew all that I do."

He leaned closer over the chessboard. "It sounds as if it would make the basis for a good story."

I crossed my arms and leaned back on the stone bollard on which I was perched. "Don't think about stealing this from me, Fortescue."

He pretended to be offended. "Would I ever?"

"Yes, you would. The very first time we met, I – the wide-eyed ingénue novelist – told you – the established author whom I admired – about a story I had in mind. Four months later, before I could set pen to paper, you'd turned it into a bestseller."

I decided that I had got all I could from him and stood up from my truly uncomfortable seat.

"My boy," he said with that smug grin on his lips, his voice cloyingly patronising, "it is often hard to say from where inspiration comes. My brain is a sponge which absorbs interesting nutrients from here and there and everywhere." The skin on his cheeks wobbled again as he pretended to pluck ideas from the air. "The fact that the plot of my hugely popular novel, *A Noose for the Knave*, resembles something that you mentioned to me in passing does not in any way prove that I stole a story from you."

That blowhard even knew which story he'd pinched!

"Yes, but the fact that you didn't have the good grace to change the names of the characters I'd planned to use certainly did." I turned to leave, but he was just so despicable in every way that I decided to stick the knife in. "You know it was terribly unlikely that I should fall to the scholar's mate in our very first game of chess at a time when I am in a hurry for answers. I wonder what the chances were of my losing so swiftly."

All of a sudden, he looked smaller and less confident. "The scholar's mate?"

"I believe that's the name for that particular opening, isn't it?" I was a half-decent actor when I wanted to be. "Or at least, that's the name that my father gave it when he taught me his favourite game for two hours a week throughout my childhood. He also taught me how to win, and if I ever have time to come back here, I'll be certain to prove what a poor player you are."

I had already left by the time he tossed the board over. "That's not fair. Letting me win is as bad as cheating."

I didn't turn back.

"You owe me for my time, Marius. I gave you that information in good faith." His brain was no doubt whirring as he considered what more he might extract from me. "You'll have to review one of my books for the newspaper. That seems like fair recompense."

I halted my retreat. "I'll happily tell everyone what a hack you are." I was about to say worse when a thought occurred to me, and I turned to look at him. "Why would you even want my recommendation? You sell ten times more books a year than I can."

He started to laugh, and it went on so long that I almost left before he could explain. "It's not your sideline as an author that interests me. Your career as a detective has brought you more attention than any novels could get you. If you were to recommend me in a major newspaper, it would be like getting Sherlock Holmes to review my book."

"Splendid!" For some reason that I truly can't fathom, I saluted him. "Then I feel even better about the fact that I will never, in a thousand years, write anything complimentary about you on so much as the back of a matchbox. Good day."

I walked off through the square with a spring in my step and a whistle on my lips. I should have known that it was a bad idea to indulge in such optimism and, when I returned to my car, it came as no surprise that the tonneau cover had been ripped open and the remaining files from Noel Carpenter had been stolen from the passenger seat.

ELEVEN

I felt as if I were investigating ten different cases at the same time. Several contrasting mysteries appeared to have been laid on top of one another only to be crushed down and amalgamated. And so, in addition to the near deafening refrain of *Why would anyone have murdered a dour but well-meaning banker?* I could now add this curious selection...

Why was Felicity Mortimer found guilty when there was so little evidence that she was to blame for her husband's death?

Was Richard Mortimer actually even murdered?

Why kill Carleton Hobbes years after he'd abandoned his mission to clear Felicity's name?

How had so many people done such a bad job of helping her when I'd found abundant evidence of her innocence after less than a week's investigation?

Where should I go from here?

Obviously it was this last question which now floored me. I felt that, even if the majority of Noel Carpenter's case notes had been stolen – and I was a dunce for leaving them in the car – I'd still accumulated a good deal of relevant information. It was certainly enough to write a contentious book on the topic, but that didn't mean it would right the wrongs of a faulty justice system. And now that I thought of it, how did a normal person go about doing any such thing?

I stopped at Bertie's house in Chelsea on the way home, and his wife cheerfully invited me to dinner, a bed for the night and – though less direct an offer – the chance to dine one evening with her eldest daughter, if I didn't mind waiting until she had returned from university.

"Come along, Bertie," I pleaded with him in his study. "You must know someone who can help me. Forget any of the prejudices you previously had. Forget the image the press propagated of Felicity Mortimer as a man-killing viper; she is innocent. I still have some work to do to make the case watertight, but there's no doubt in my mind. If she had been provided with a competent legal defence, she would have sailed straight out of court. Instead, she had a hostile judge and a well-meaning barrister in the twilight of his career who simply couldn't handle the wealth of evidence with which he was presented." I sat in an armchair on the other side of the fire from him as I laid out the case. "The fact that she still doesn't know that her husband consumed barely enough poison to kill a small rodent shows that this key fact was ignored during the trial."

I'd been chattering for some time when he finally offered a response. "Then what actually killed him if it wasn't the arsenic?"

I was happy that he was listening to what I had to say, as my chances of effecting any change were severely limited if I couldn't even get my close friend to accept my argument.

"I suppose it is possible that he died of one of the many illnesses that he insisted had kept him in bed for months. By all accounts he was hypochondriacal, but there may have been some underlying condition which had set him on that path in the first place. A more likely explanation, though, is that he had consumed so many toxic medicines over the years that they ended up killing him."

Bertie stared into the fire. I'd rarely seen him look so serious. I'd seen him jolly on countless occasions and lose his temper more often than I'd have liked, but this was different. "I do trust your opinion, Marius." There was a long pause as he made a meal of opening the bottle of whisky that was on the table at his side. "I should have believed you when you first came to me, but after the transformation I saw in Carleton when he was helping Felicity, it was hard to think anything but the worst of her."

"That's something else I don't understand," I cut in when he went back to looking at the blazing fire. "You told me that it became his obsession, but from what I've learnt, he didn't even talk to Noel Carpenter. He certainly didn't access the files that, just a few hours after they fell into my possession, both gave up an essential fact and were stolen from my car when it was parked in St John's Square."

"Stolen?" This only served to trouble him further. "Does that mean that someone followed you across London? I assume you drove from my office to Clerkenwell."

"I haven't taken the time to consider how they found me, but I suppose you're right."

He rubbed his eyes for a few seconds, apparently quite agitated. "That's not the first time this week that you've been followed, Marius. Have you 'taken the time' to question whether someone in London is pulling your strings?"

I opened my mouth to dismiss his fears, then realised I would be a fool to do so. "Do you mean that whoever followed me from my house to Charing Cross at the weekend was the same person who stole the files?"

"I couldn't possibly say. Although if it is the same person, he may also be responsible for murdering my friend this afternoon. He may have been watching us the whole time."

As if I hadn't been feeling dreadful enough about the world, this certainly knocked the wind from my sails.

"With regards to Carleton Hobbes," Bertie said to return us to my original question. "It was a strange situation. I'd never known him to be particularly interested in current affairs, but he threw himself into Mrs Mortimer's case apropos of very little. He volunteered to co-ordinate the response to her conviction and, whenever a public figure wished to be involved, he made sure that this interest was noted in the papers. When it was clear that, though she was spared the acquaintance of the hangman, there was no way to end her imprisonment, he fell into a terrible blue funk. I'd rarely seen such a change in a man. It was as if his very belief in humanity had been stripped away."

I thought back to my friend's earlier comments on the case. "That hardly proves that she misused him. If anything, it strengthens my conviction that she deserves our help."

He fell silent for a moment to consider this point. "You know, I remember the trial quite vividly. I read several accounts of the culmination and one image in particular has stayed with me. Most people at the time believed that the accused would be cleared of the crime. It was rare enough for a woman to be found guilty of murder if she hadn't been caught in the act, and even less common for someone of good standing like Felicity Mortimer to fall into that trap."

He raised his hand then, and I watched it tremble in the firelight as he continued with what he had to say. "I remember reading that a large group of women had gathered outside the court and that each of them held a single white rose which they intended to present to their long-suffering heroine. When the news filtered out of the court, all those respectable women dropped their flowers where they stood. Ever since then, I have held on to the belief that Felicity Mortimer was a killer. It was the only thing that helped me reconcile the disappointment of those women with the decision of the court. I still want to believe that the verdict was a fair one as, if not, I was witness to a great injustice and millions like me did nothing about it."

Instead of wallowing in my own mistakes, I concentrated once more on what we could do for Felicity. "And yet, I have no doubt that what happened to her was a great injustice. Once I find a medical professional to confirm Fortescue's interpretation of the post-mortem, and I secure witness statements concerning the dead man's temper and comportment, not to mention the length of time that he was kept away from his wife before death, I will have all I need to prove that Mrs Mortimer was wrongly imprisoned. What I don't have are the connections or resources to make sure that she is freed. You must know a judge or what have you who can help us."

He sat back in his chair and sighed. "It wouldn't be enough. Her case has already been reviewed by the Home Secretary. Only he can intervene at that level, and I've never met the man…" He paused for a moment, and I believe he was consulting the address book in his head where he stored the details of his numerous acquaintances. "Nor can I think of anyone who might be able to introduce us."

"I was afraid you would say that." I wrapped my right fist in the palm of the other hand. "However, there is someone who can help us. Bella worked in the Home Office before her father fell ill. The question is whether it would be more selfish to interrupt her at a time of mourning or leave Felicity Mortimer in gaol even a day longer than necessary."

We both fell to reflection then, and the only sound was the occasional click and pop of burning logs.

"It's not a question I can help you answer, I'm afraid." Bertie smiled for the first time since we'd sat down. "But I have every reason to believe that you will make the right decision."

"Thank you, Bertie. If only I had such faith in myself."

TWELVE

I stayed for dinner in their cosy mews house but declined lodging and any hint of matchmaking. When I got home, Mother was out doing one of the many activities with which she fills her time. She is forever attending painting, needlework, pottery and fencing classes, which I'm sure you'll agree are far healthier pastimes than poking into the affairs of dead people.

The flat felt cold and empty that night, largely because it was cold and empty. The absence of Percy's regular barks and yips was dispiriting, and the choice that faced me was turning in my brain like a ship circling a whirlpool. I hadn't stopped thinking of Bella for one moment since I'd last seen her, but interrupting her grief to secure an introduction to a family friend would have felt terribly cruel.

I stood in the doorway to the room where the poor man had been murdered, silently debating what to do. It came as something of a relief when Chief Inspector Darrington telephoned to tell me off.

"I told you to stay away from the Baines investigation. I did not wish to suggest that you should dip your toe into another murder investigation altogether." He was using his gruffest tone. It was quite effective.

"It really wasn't my fault this time. I was essentially minding my own business when we noticed a burning building in the centre of the city. I did what I could to help the man who lived there, but someone had already killed him before starting the fire."

Nothing but crackle came back to me for a few moments. "And I'm sure his death was in no way connected to a case you are currently investigating?" He knew more than I'd realised.

"Now, I didn't say that. But as my brief inquiry is more or less complete, you've no need to worry about me."

He grunted his disbelief and, as the opportunity was mine for the taking, I made the most of it.

"I don't suppose your officers have discovered anything pertinent about the man who was murdered in my flat?"

I could hear the impatience in his voice before he said a word. "I don't suppose I'm in a position to share such information with you."

"I'll take that as a no, then. I wish you well, Chief Inspector. Thank you for calling."

I thought he might tell me off again or warn me of the dangers of interfering in police business, but his tone softened a touch. "Try to stay safe, Marius. It is a wicked world we inhabit. Sometimes the only option is to avoid trouble of any kind."

The line went dead, and I was left with my thoughts. London in a rainy autumn can be depressing enough without meeting death at every turn, but at least the resolute policeman had put me in mind of a solution to my problem. I called Hurtwood House to make an appointment and went to bed with a slightly easier mind than I might otherwise have possessed.

. . .

I was out of London by eight the next morning. I can't imagine that I'm the only author in the world who wishes I had a more rigid timetable. If it weren't for my mother's presence, I might never change out of my pyjamas. It felt good to rise with the dawn, wolf down some food and leave the house before the postman had appeared on the square.

I drove faster than I ordinarily would. I believe that, unlike on my visit a few days earlier, I was looking forward to returning to the village where I grew up. It was the thought of hearing at least some report on Bella's well-being, and, yes, if I was lucky, spending a brief moment with my dear dog.

I made it to Surrey in record time. When I got to the village, rather than zipping up to the mansion on the hill, I took my time driving past the public house. Though closed at that hour, the Duke's Head had its usual selection of chirpy old men on the bench outside. I waved enthusiastically to Jeb Paignton, and, halfway up the hill, that irascible grump Sergeant Rossiter poked his head out of his police box to nod at me. I really must learn to stay glum for longer. All it had taken to cheer me up was the sight of a familiar face or two. So much for the tortured novelist, driven by his demons.

As I reached Bella's grand estate, I was animated by the thought of seeing her former maid Agnes, and Pullman, the Hurtwood House butler, who had always treated me as part of the family. My return to that stately manor in the countryside felt like a homecoming. The staff welcomed me with characteristic warmth and then, most discreetly, as I had instructed on the telephone, Pullman showed me up to the Duke's chamber.

The last time I'd mounted those old stairs, it had been a gloomy place, but things had changed. The invalid's quarters were no longer a tomb. The curtains were now kept wide open, and my host was not in bed this time but sitting in his wheelchair before an ornately carved desk. The room was just as

Gothic as when last I'd visited, but the Duke's renewed enthusiasm brightened the place.

"I'm so glad you called, Marius. I am always happy to have you here, but especially this week." He stopped to motion me towards an empty chair. "I'm sure you can imagine how disconsolate Bella has been."

"Do you think I should visit her, Your Grace?" The very idea sent a thrill through me, but I would not get my hopes up just yet. "Considering the past we share and what has happened to her fiancé in my very own home, I couldn't decide if calling on her would make things worse."

He smiled his typically sympathetic smile. "I don't see that it can do any harm. When she isn't locked away in her bedroom, she's calling poor Inspector Lovebrook to discover what news there is."

"Have there been any developments?" I asked, in case Darrington had kept them from me.

Even at this difficult time, the Duke had a level of positivity that I admired. "None on which I would waste the price of a stamp to inform you. It seems to me that the police are confounded by the whole affair." He came to a stop and peered awkwardly out of the window behind him. "I can't say I ever held Gilbert Baines in anything more than middling esteem, but it's a dreadful state of affairs when an ordinary man can be murdered in broad daylight without anyone noticing anything unusual."

It was hard to tell him that I hadn't come there to talk about Gilbert, but that was what I had to do. "I'm sorry to change the topic, but Darrington has made it clear that I'm not allowed anywhere near the case."

"Oh?"

"As a matter of fact, I've come here to discuss another matter entirely. I venture that you know the name Felicity Mortimer."

He looked understandably baffled. "The murderess?"

"In the eyes of many, yes. However, I have uncovered evidence which would suggest she was wrongly convicted. I know you are close friends with the Foreign Secretary, and I was rather hoping you might be acquainted with a colleague of his."

"Are you referring to Lord Verlaine?"

I suddenly felt presumptuous for barging into his house to ask him to use his connections to help a woman I hardly knew. I was about to explain my reasoning when he smiled and reassured me. "I've known Thomas since our school days. I'm sure he'll be happy to see you if you think the matter warrants his time."

It was one of the few moments that week at which I felt a little lighter than before. I would have told him how appreciative I was, but there was a knock on the door before I could. For some silly reason, I didn't imagine for one second that it would be Bella.

"Father," she said as she entered the room in her usual confident manner. Her chin was raised, her back straight, and the heels on her shoes clicked on the flagstones like the keys on a typewriter, but there was so much sadness in her tone of voice that I could tell she wasn't herself.

She would say no more just then. She came to a complete stop and stared at me as if to question whether her childhood boyfriend really was sitting comfortably in her father's bedroom. When she accepted what she was seeing, I doubt it was happy memories of our adolescence that my presence brought back to her: I imagine she pictured Gilbert dead in my writing room.

"I'm sorry, Bella," I muttered, though I wasn't certain why. I'd tried to spare her feelings by approaching her father for help instead of her. Perhaps I didn't want her to know I had found something to occupy my time besides hunting for her fiancé's killer. "I came to speak to the Duke because—"

"What are you doing here?" Her breathing was ragged, as if she kept forgetting to inhale and had to make up for the air that she'd missed.

I heard footsteps mounting the stairs and the sound of claws scratching against the tiles. Percy appeared in the doorway and, completely ignoring the mood of the room, came lolloping over to me with his tongue hanging out. I sometimes question whether he actually likes his unfeeling owner, but he couldn't hide just how happy he was to see me.

Inevitably this presented something of a dilemma. What is the etiquette when faced with a soppy basset hound in search of attention and a broken-hearted ex-sweetheart who has just demanded to know why you're haunting her house? In normal circumstances, I would have asked Percy who was a good boy, but I knew that wouldn't go down well, so I scratched him behind the ears and tried to sound contrite.

"I am very sorry that you found me here, Bella. I only hid my visit because I didn't want to upset you." I put my free hand to the back of my head and bothered the curls there as I considered what else I should say. "You see, I've been forbidden from having anything to do with the investigation into Gilbert's death, and so I happened upon a worthy cause of my own."

She turned to stare through the window as a tear descended from just one eye.

"I think you should leave." She didn't look at me as she said this. She glanced down at the floor and tried to stop her lips from trembling by pursing them together. "I can't see you now, Marius. I can't see anyone."

"You should at least listen to what he has to say, my sweet," her father told her with a note of pleading in his voice. "He came here for a noble purpose—"

"I don't care." The strength of her voice suddenly increased, and she clasped her hands together. "Get out, Marius. If you have nothing to tell me about Gilbert, then I don't want to speak to you."

I had no intention of arguing with her, so I stood, put my chair back in its place and walked towards the door. Once again failing to make sense of the emotion on display, Percy padded after me.

"I'm terribly sorry," I began, "but should I take my—?"

"Leave the dog," she snapped.

I considered reassuring her that I only had good intentions, but my words wouldn't come. I wished then that the last three days had never happened and that we could talk and laugh together as normal. There was nothing I wanted more than to pick over the Mortimer case with her. She always had such bright ideas on the crimes we investigated. I longed to see that spark that shines from within her whenever she tries to solve a taxing mystery. I longed to see her back to her usual happy self, but it wasn't to be.

I left the Duke's quarters, ran down the stone staircase to the long corridor that cuts through the centre of the house, and found myself back at my car. I sat in the driver's seat and counted to a hundred, hoping that she would appear. I started the engine and rolled out to the front of the property. I had never driven off the estate so slowly before, but it did no good. She wouldn't run after me, and I drove back to London feeling even more hopeless than I had before.

Of course, Bella always knows how to surprise me. Almost exactly twenty-four hours after I left Hurtwood House, her camel-brown Sunbeam 12/16 pulled to a stop in front of my flat, and there she was.

THIRTEEN

"There would seem to be a very obvious question that you've failed to ask yourself," she told me in my living room when I'd spent the best part of an hour trying to recount not just Felicity Mortimer's story but the most recent chapter of mine. Percy had come with her, too, and he was now wandering about sniffing everything, as though visiting the flat for the first time.

"I think that is very unlikely," I told her wryly. "I have had no one but myself for company all week. Mother has a more complete social life than me, and I doubt that there is a single original thought that hasn't passed through my head." I realised then that I was dismissing her suggestion and tried to make up for it. "But, please, tell me your idea."

"Unless I'm very much mistaken, someone is following you, and a man whom we both know to be a violent criminal killed Gilbert right here in your house." The briefest flash of panic was visible on her face. I'd seen it as she entered the flat and had to walk past the closed door to the writing room. Try as she might to focus on our discussion, she couldn't hide her pain entirely. "Despite that, you saw fit to set off on the trail of a woman, the knowledge of whom fell into your lap at an opportune moment."

I sipped from a glass of whisky that she had suggested we enjoy together. "That's more or less the size of it, but what have I failed to see?"

She breathed out loudly (and irritably), which made me feel that things were closer to normal than I had hoped. "That you have been manipulated from the start, quite possibly by Gilbert's killer."

I admit that I had not given this possibility a great deal of thought, but there was a reason for that. "Why would Lucien Pike want me to set Felicity Mortimer free?"

It was her turn for a pregnant pause as she sipped. "We can't possibly say, just as neither of us has struck upon an explanation for why Gilbert was murdered, or why that man keeps interfering in our lives. He's a monster, and we would be fools not to question whether he is responsible for everything else that has happened. You must surely have considered the possibility that the two bodies you discovered were killed by the same person?"

"I have indeed." I crossed my legs at the ankles and wondered for a few seconds why she would be so keen to believe this. "The one thing I will say is that, regardless of whether Lucien Pike is toying with us, if Felicity is innocent, then she deserves our help."

Percy had spent most of the last hour behaving like a puppy. He'd gone running up and down the corridor in search of Mother and then, when she'd spoilt him for long enough, he'd come scampering back to the living room and was now rolling about on his back in the middle of the carpet as though he'd missed his spot before the fire and wished to reclaim it for dogkind. It was somewhat distracting, as we were trying to conduct a serious conversation.

I moved to a chair beside the hearth and studied Bella for a moment. There was no sign of the pure, undiluted sorrow that had coloured her every move and breath the day before. She was dressed in an impossibly chic blue dress and grey overcoat, her silky black hair was artfully arranged on top of her head and her long, rounded nails drummed a rhythm on the table beside her as she considered her response.

When she took too long, I jumped in ahead of her. "I can't do it on my own, Bella. That's why I drove to Hurtwood yesterday. I believe your father would have come to see the Home Secretary with me, but you rather put paid to that idea, so there's only one route left available."

She tutted at the stupidity of my well-meant plan. "This feels wrong, Marius. This all feels wrong. What if the evidence you have is fabricated and Felicity Mortimer is as evil as the press described her? What if the mysterious man with whom she exchanged letters was Lucien Pike and we are about to set a killer free for her to reunite with her criminal associate?"

More than anything – more than the greenness of her eyes and the shape of her perfectly round cheeks – what I'd missed through our forced separation was the way in which she challenged me. It made me feel calm once more.

"Very well. Let's say she killed her husband. There's no question that he was a rotter. He once tried to strangle her. He had another family behind her back, and he allowed his sister to treat her like dirt. And let's not forget that I only had one brief, polite conversation with Felicity. I'm sure there is more to learn about Richard Mortimer that she didn't disclose."

"Your point being?"

"My point being that, if the very worst that could happen is for a woman who killed her cruel and callous husband to be released from prison after completing fifteen years of an inordinately long sentence, then I believe it is worth the risk."

She sipped her drink again and reacted to the sting of the

whisky. I rarely drink so early in the day, and the alcohol had certainly made its way north.

When she spoke again, there was a slight change in her, and I knew that she would do what was necessary. "Then how should we go about it? Do we march over to Whitehall and demand that the Home Secretary free the wronged woman, or do you have a more sophisticated plan to propose?"

"I propose that you call Lord Verlaine if you know him well enough and ask him to grant me an appointment so that I can present the evidence in support of Felicity Mortimer's innocence."

She looked so shocked I thought she would drop her glass. "Why on earth wouldn't you want me there with you?"

I realised that I could have explained myself better. "I wasn't saying that I don't want you to come. I imagined you would need time alone to—"

She slammed the glass down on the coffee table. "To sit at home feeling awful? To spend hour after hour crying, aware that there is nothing I can do to rescue the man I love from his fate? If you wish me to continue feeling guilty that our adventures brought about Gilbert's death, then that's what I will do, but there is no amount of punishment that can put right what has happened."

Finally conscious of the crack running through the room, Percy went to see his adopted mistress. He tried to put his head on her lap but was too short and could do little more than poke her legs with his nose.

"If you would like to come," I said slowly and clearly when the silence had settled around us, "then I would like you to be there. That is always true, and you need never doubt it."

She stroked my dog's velveteen ears for a few moments without saying anything. When she spoke again, her voice was brighter, as if she wished to pretend that the rest of the conversation hadn't occurred. "Daddy and Lord Verlaine were at school together. The pair of them were best friends with Lord Darnley."

I will pause here to mention that, while it might sound unlikely that the Duke of Hurtwood went to the same school as both the British Foreign Secretary and the Home Secretary – along with countless other lords and landed gentry – if you know anything about the British school system, this will not come as a surprise.

"Unlike my father, they grew bored looking after their grand estates and went into politics." This also explains a lot about the British political system. "I've known Lord Verlaine my whole life. He was there when I was presented at court, and he threw me my eighteenth birthday party at his house in Hampshire."

"So what you're saying is that he will listen to you if you come with me?"

She almost smiled then. "Something like that, yes." Her sea-green eyes locked onto me from across the room, then she rose with all the elegance of the debutante she had once been and walked out to the hall. I heard her pick up the telephone and, a few moments later, the faint sound of her voice as she spoke to the operator. I caught a mention of Whitehall but made out little else.

"It's done," she said very calmly as she reappeared in the doorway, and Percy continued rolling on his back. "We will visit his office after lunch."

FOURTEEN

It was hard to know how to treat Bella that day. She is my oldest friend, and yet I'd never felt quite so uncomfortable around her. Even the first time I saw her after failing to ask her to marry me hadn't filled me with such uncertainty. It was as if we no longer knew one another at all.

Mother was out... somewhere, and so I cooked a couple of chops and sautéed some vegetables as, despite the fact someone else often does it for me, I do know how to prepare a meal. Bella hardly made a sound as we ate in the kitchen together, and any topic of conversation I considered struck me as dreadfully insensitive, so we largely sat in silence. This was still preferable to sitting in silence in a public restaurant, worrying that the other diners were staring at us. At least Percy was there, and we could direct the odd comment towards him.

I can't say that I wasn't enormously relieved when the clock struck two and it was time to leave. Percy, on the other hand, was deeply disappointed that he would not be visiting the seat of government.

"Sometimes, you behave like quite the crackpot," I told him, and the fact that I was attempting to communicate such a complicated sentiment to a canine probably doesn't speak too highly of my own intelligence. "You know you can't come with us."

He stood his ground at the front door and wouldn't budge. It was not the first time he had mounted such a protest and, although I could have picked him up and put him inside, he would have been grumpy for days.

Bella was good at talking to all creatures – especially dim animals like Percy and me – and she crouched down to address him. "We won't be long, my lovely boy. I will come and visit you again very soon."

This promise was so promising to the dear hound that he could only whimper in excitement, and he finally plodded off to sit in the parlour and await our return. Bella's chauffeur Caxton, meanwhile, looked angrier with me than my dog had. He was a forever-snarling beast when I was around, and the only person in the Duke's employ whom I had failed to charm.

"It's so nice to see you, old stick," I told him when Bella had slipped into the vehicle, and he came to open my door. I like to be ever so polite to him in the hope he will one day bite my head off, and Bella will see him for the morose thug that he is. I swear that two small puffs of steam came out of his nostrils. He glared at me without a word being spoken. While I should probably learn not to unnerve him, where would the fun be in that?

"What is she like?" Bella asked as I took my place on the back seat. "Felicity Mortimer, I mean. Did you find yourself falling for her charms as so many men have before you?"

I almost told her how difficult that would be as my heart belonged to another, but I caught myself just in time. "I found her warm and considerate. There was a goodness to her that had not dimmed. Regardless of the clothes she wore or what she has suffered, it shone through."

It was lucky she turned to glance out of the window then, or she might have realised that I meant much of this for her just as much as Felicity.

I chattered on quickly in case she had noticed how I'd been looking at her. "But, no, she did not cast a spell upon me, and I don't think she is the devious charmer that the prosecution in her trial painted. She was just as interested in my own situation as what I could do for her."

For a few seconds, it seemed that Bella had forgotten her sorrow and was about to tease me as she often had throughout our friendship. "Oh, really? And what exactly is your—?" She cut herself short, and I saw what I took to be a momentary shot of guilt passing through her.

I kept talking for her sake. "I mentioned how inexperienced a detective I am and how unlikely it is that I can do anything to redress the injustice that had befallen her."

She didn't reply. She just stared out of the window and murmured a sound that I couldn't interpret. She remained in that state all the way to Whitehall, and I knew better than to disturb her. A sign of just how mercurial her mood was that day was evinced when, as we pulled up at the palatial Italianate building on King Charles Street, she snapped into an entirely new persona. She sat up straighter in her seat and I believe that, as she waited for Caxton to open the door, she became the smart young woman who had previously worked at that address.

By the time we had made it through the immense archway entrance and into the internal courtyard, she had fully regained her confidence. She spoke to the guards on duty as if she were the head of the whole complex and declined their advice on how to find Lord Verlaine's office, as she evidently knew the place better than they did.

The fact that she could put on this façade so easily made me reflect on what was whirling inside her. The mix of emotions must have been devilishly tricky to control, and it was hard to know whether our visit was the perfect way to take her mind off her troubles, or the prelude to a great implosion.

It was telling that I was more interested in the tumult beneath my companion's smooth exterior than the incredible surroundings through which we passed. We mounted a grand staircase with a polychromatic dome showing a selection of saints and angels. The walls were covered in marble, and there was glittering gold leaf wherever I looked. It made Bella's house in Surrey look rather drab, though that's not necessarily a compliment.

A secretary met us on the upper landing and greeted my companion as an old friend. Evidently the guards had telephoned ahead to communicate our arrival, and the two former colleagues conversed enthusiastically about everything and nothing in particular as we descended the corridor to the Home Secretary's office.

"Bella, my dear girl." Lord Verlaine's voice travelled through the open door as soon as we came into view. "It's been far too long. I blame your antisocial father."

"Uncle Thomas!"

He looked every part the politician, with his keen, birdlike eyes and slightly artificial attentiveness. He had hair on three sides of his head, but none on top, and wore the typical, nondescript black suit of most in his profession. I had the strangest sensation that I'd lived through a near identical scene with Verlaine's counterpart in the Foreign Office, who happened to be Bella's godfather.

In case you were wondering, the most powerful person that either of my parents have ever known was a man in Camberwell who enjoyed a brief burst of fame for his belly button trick at their local pub. I sincerely doubt that news of his talent reached the highest level of government, but then neither had talk of Gilbert's death.

Bella hugged her old family friend, and I waited my turn... for a handshake, I should add. I'm not known for embracing strangers.

"And this must be your young man." The tall, slim figure held one arm out to me, and having lived through a brief misadventure pretending to be Bella's sweetheart, I decided to nip that possibility firmly in the bud.

"I'm afraid not. Bella and I are just friends. We were at school together, much like you and His Grace, the Duke. My name is Marius Quin."

I thought that Bella might clarify further, but she ignored the issue and began to speak with her usual pep and gusto. "Marius is one of Britain's finest young novelists, but that's not why we are here." She really should have stayed in politics: she could have convinced her rivals to support any law she wished to introduce. "You see, together we have started our own detective agency. Marius does most of the—"

"Wait one moment." Verlaine retreated a step as though the very idea had knocked him backwards. "I heard something about this. Weren't you called to assist with a sensitive case at Mentmore Towers of which even I'm not supposed to know?" He signalled to two chairs on the other side of the room. We went to take our places, and he stood between us with his back to the sash window.

Bella's resilience was remarkable. She had forced down her sadness and looked just as sunny as a bright day in July. "We may have spent a weekend in Buckinghamshire this year, but I'm not at liberty to say anything more than that."

She had a certain lightness of touch that I knew to be false, and yet I found it entirely convincing. I could see how impressed one of the most powerful men in Britain was, and he didn't even know what my friend had recently lived through.

"It all sounds terribly *you*, Bella. You've always been the adventurous type." He closed his eyes as he said this, and I could tell that he was proud of his former assistant. I say assistant, though I don't actually know what sort of work Bella had done there. "Now, what has brought you here this morning?"

I sat back and waited to see whether she could maintain her ebullient attitude now that the time had come to ask a favour.

"Ah, you see, in the course of his work preparing a new book, Marius has uncovered what we believe might be a... well, a miscarriage of justice." It was a tough phrase to sweeten, but she did her best.

Verlaine gave a nervous laugh and smoothed down one lapel on his suit. "I can assure you, Bella, such things are far rarer than most people believe. The term is forever being bandied about by journalists and rabble-rousers, but in truth, in the twenty years I've been in government, both in this department and several others, I've come across very few cases in which the British court system has failed an innocent member of society."

I could practically feel a lecture starting.

He held the breast pocket of his jacket and gazed into a pastoral painting on the opposite wall as though admiring the landscape there. He had a thin moustache which moved jerkily as he spoke. "You know, countries all over the world have built their justice systems on the British model. It is something in which to take pride, not criticise." Even he must have realised that he sounded pompous, as his voice dropped, and he turned back to us. "Which isn't to say that it's impossible, and I will certainly listen to whatever you have to disclose."

Perhaps out of courtesy, Bella waited a few moments before saying two words that she evidently hoped would undermine his position. "Felicity Mortimer." It did the trick. As soon as the name had been spoken, the Home Secretary set off on a hurried tour of the room.

"Not her. Please, anyone but her. If there is one case that damaged my standing, it was the murder of Richard Mortimer." He wasn't just vexed that we had reminded him of what had happened. He seemed genuinely anxious. "I spent ten years in the wilderness after I spared her life. I was kicked around from one department to another before falling back into the good graces of the elite and being made Home Secretary once more." He stopped his pacing and addressed us directly. "There is nothing more I can do for that woman."

"But she's innocent," I replied before it occurred to me that such considerations were not a primary concern for men like Verlaine. "I have the evidence."

Bella stood up again, her long coat trailing behind her like a cape. "It's true, Thomas. Marius has worked ceaselessly to uncover the mistakes that were made. It turns out that there wasn't enough poison in her husband's system for it to have killed him. The case against her was built on a lie."

"There was more to it than just that." From the tone of his voice, I think that even he doubted this statement.

"There really wasn't. I secured a copy of her barrister's files." I produced the key report on the toxins in Richard Mortimer's body and placed it on the desk. "As I am sure you will remember from the appeal that was supported by a number of well-respected individuals, her conviction rested on the idea that she had poisoned her husband as she was seen handling arsenic before he died. This becomes quite irrelevant when we consider that the post-mortem found little trace of the stuff in his body."

I hoped this would be enough to convince him, but he returned to the chair behind his desk and once more stared into space. "This is like a terrible dream."

"Then you'll recall that, in order to cast her in a bad light, the prosecution promoted the idea that Felicity was adulterous because she had exchanged sentimental letters with another man. However, the judge forbade discussion of Richard Mortimer's unfaithfulness and violence and painted his poor, innocent wife as a scarlet woman. I spent yesterday contacting her friends and several can confirm her version of events. It seems to me that, from the beginning of the trial, the odds were against her."

"Yes, Lord Fenwick tried that case. He was never a nice man, but he took particular exception to Mrs Mortimer." He breathed out inordinately slowly. "However, that's not enough to reopen an old case or release a woman who has been in prison for the last fifteen years."

He was evidently thinking more of the impact that such a reversal would have on his reputation than the fate of the woman who was incarcerated.

"A man was murdered two days ago," Bella said out of the blue. "His name was..." she pointed at me without turning her head.

"Carleton Hobbes."

"Carleton Hobbes." Energised now, she clicked her fingers. "He campaigned for the release of Felicity Mortimer, and in the very same week that an accomplished detective examined her case with fresh eyes, Carleton Hobbes was murdered in his home."

This at least sparked a reaction from Lord Verlaine. "Are you suggesting that there is some sort of conspiracy at play?"

The way he said this deeply confused me. Far from questioning whether such a thing was impossible, it was almost as if he wanted us to come to this conclusion.

"I don't know whether I would use that word." I searched for a better one. "I think that there were certain... irregularities that combined to rob Mrs Mortimer of the verdict she deserved, and perhaps there are still people who would prefer her never to be free."

"I see." He leaned forward and displayed the large bald spot in the middle of his sandy hair. "Yes, I see what you're saying."

I looked at Bella in the hope that she would know what to say next. She presumably didn't, as she stared straight back at me, and we waited for the head of the British justice system to tell us what to do.

He adjusted a fountain pen on his desk, then ran his hands self-consciously through his tonsured hair. "I'm not denying that Mrs Mortimer deserves to be pardoned. If you possess the evidence to prove she is innocent, then I will accept it – regardless of any part I might have played in the original mistake. However, I need you to put the pieces together. It's not enough to show that Richard Mortimer wasn't murdered; I need you to prove that someone would gain from his wife's imprisonment."

I was still quite bamboozled by his reaction, but Bella managed to find her voice. "I'm sorry. I don't understand what you are suggesting."

One at a time, the Home Secretary put the tips of his fingers together and then pulled them apart again. "I doubt you were aware of the fact that I knew the Mortimers socially before Richard died." He didn't wait for a response, though in my head I was thinking, *Do all rich people in England know one another?* "His family live on the neighbouring estate to my own in Hampshire. Bella has been there many times, and I'm sure my wife would be only too happy if you were to pay a visit this weekend."

I imagine that it was clear from our expressions what we thought of this, as it spurred the oddest question I heard that day. Verlaine leaned forward to look at us intently. "You call yourselves detectives, don't you? Find out what really happened."

There was no charm left in him. He was tough and direct, and any fear that our revelation had inspired was now forgotten.

Bella presented a small problem with his plan. "It's one thing to go to your house, but that doesn't mean we'll be able to poke about in your neighbours' affairs."

"Yes, and poking about is rather an important part of a detective's work." I looked at Bella to see whether this had made her smile. "It is our forte."

Verlaine certainly wasn't amused. "If I know the dead man's sister as I think I do, she won't be able to resist calling to see the daughter of a duke. Deirdre Stradbrooke is the biggest snob I've ever met, and I'm the son of an earl."

"You won't be there with us?" Bella said, interpreting something that I had failed to notice.

"No. No, I won't." He looked at the stack of paper in front of him and seized a pen to scribble something down. I thought he might hand it over to us, but instead he rang a bell on the desk and his middle-aged secretary returned to seize it from him and scurry away. "I can't possibly be connected to this case any more than I already am. If you've any hope of my correcting the situation, the next time you come in here, you'll have to present me with the complete story without a single missing paragraph, page or chapter. I imagine that is something you're rather good at, Mr Quin."

Although it seemed he had the desire to set things right – even if he wouldn't sacrifice his career to do so – his manner had become a touch frostier. Did he feel guilty for what had happened to Felicity? Or was he merely upset about the damage that the case had done to his career? He had been the definition of warmth when we'd first arrived, then turned nervous, then hardened before our very eyes as he conceived of a scheme that, were it not coming from one of the holders of the Great Offices of State, I might have dismissed as hare-brained.

Bella was apparently just as mystified as I was. "We'll see you again soon." This was not the most obvious response. In fact, it sounded like the final throes of a social call.

Verlaine was now too busy to give anything more than an accepting wave of the hand, and we soon found ourselves outside his office, peering bemusedly at one another.

Bella blinked a few times and said exactly what I was thinking. "That wasn't what I was expecting at all."

FIFTEEN

Some murder investigations take place in a single location and are neatly tied up within the day. This wasn't that type of case. This was more of a week-to-ten-days-long affair with plenty of driving, stops for food, popping home to pack for the weekend and discussions about the logistics of what we had to do. We couldn't simply get into the car and make our way to Verlaine Towers (or whatever his house would turn out to be called). Bella's immense and immensely grumpy chauffeur drove her back to Hurtwood in order to prepare for the challenge ahead (sartorially, if nothing else). The plan was then made that she would pick me up the following morning and we would head to Hampshire together to make the acquaintance of a potentially murderous and conspiratorial family to whom neither of us had any connection.

This was the kind of challenge that I'd faced repeatedly since becoming a detective. I almost missed the days when my only worry was how I could afford to pay my mortgage and which character in my frivolous books I might bump off next.

As I had time to waste before Bella arrived, I sat in my writing room for the first time since I'd found Gilbert there. I can't say it was a pleasant sensation to picture a man being murdered literally in my place. Even if I hadn't felt some responsibility to find his killer and explain his senseless death, it would have turned my stomach. The thought of him struggling for breath as the garotte closed around his throat was almost enough for me to sell up my beloved flat and move to the country.

I also had to wonder how the events of that week might affect my future literary endeavours. There was no way that I could immortalise Gilbert in anything but an obituary for the paper, but the Mortimer case held all sorts of possibilities. I tend to have the most wonderful concepts for plots just before I go to bed at night. I foolishly believe that I'll remember them come the morning – only to find on waking that the spark of inspiration has been extinguished, and the hint of a story will never amount to anything more than that. To counteract this, I found a pad of paper and wrote down a description of the seed of a plot that I hoped would yet grow.

I loved the idea of including a fictionalised version of Felicity Mortimer in a novel. I knew she would make a perfectly soulful yet ambiguous central character whom my readers could mould in their minds over the course of the story. Was she the victim of a conspiracy or a woman wielding what little power she had to secure a life for herself? It would be up to the reader to decide – only for me to pull the wool from their eyes at the last moment. Or perhaps, in the course of writing the book, I would change my mind entirely about what should happen. Such was the uncertainty of my trade... well, both of my trades, as, waiting for Bella to collect me, like a student at the end of term standing at the school gates in expectation of his parents' arrival, I couldn't imagine what our imminent trip would involve.

When Bella eventually arrived, Percy was not in a co-operative mood.

"I believe we had this discussion yesterday, old boy," I told him, and I regretted even broaching the matter.

He stood in the front porch with his tongue hanging out and his oversized eyes ever so sad. He looked more like a drawing of a dog than a real one.

"Why don't you just let him come with us?" Bella asked. "He's been a great help on our previous cases. What's changed this time?"

I was tempted to ask her exactly how the lovable but largely tongue-tied creature had aided our investigations in the past, but I decided not to argue... this one point at least.

"We're staying with a person I've never met, in a house I've never visited, and we're looking into a complex case which involves any number of potential crimes. As such, I did decide to pack my smartest smart suit and a pair of comfortable shoes, but it did not enter my mind to invite Percy along."

I don't know why I thought this would convince her. Bella had already clapped her hands to encourage him to run to the car. It was only then that I realised it was for her sake that she wanted him to accompany us that weekend, not his. On the plus side, at least we didn't have to wait for him to pack.

Bella turned on the spot, so that the pale blue skirt she wore billowed around her and she skipped along the pavement with her new best friend. In the end, she had brought one of her family's Bentleys. It was a deep burgundy colour, and I was surprised to see that she would be driving it.

"Has Caxton gone in for repairs?" I quipped ever so wittily. "His neck was looking a little stiff yesterday. I hope the mechanic gives him a good oiling."

She didn't look at me as she helped Percy into the back of the car and rolled her eyes to show what she thought of my joke. "He is needed by my father, as it happens. And I thought you might like to travel in style."

She gave no further explanation but jumped into the

driver's seat and started the engine. "Don't look so nervous, Marius. I'm a very good driver." She looked up at my house fretfully as we drove past and inhaled a sharp breath, as was her way that week.

"I could have met you there, you know," I told her once we'd pulled out of the square. "You didn't have to come out of your way to collect me."

"I know." She almost sounded shy then, though it wasn't in her nature. "But I thought that we could talk on the way."

As soon as she said these words, it became quite impossible to follow this idea. How could we talk when there was something so great and oppressive between us that we were unable to address? It was not just Gilbert's death, but the fact we had been off gallivanting together when it happened. In contrast to the jolly atmosphere there had been when we'd taken the train to the coast the previous weekend, this would not be an easy trip.

We had two or three stabs at conversation on the near hundred-mile journey to the New Forest, but each one petered out before it got started. The ghost of her fiancé made light chit-chat seem insensitive, and the reality was that there was nothing to plan as we couldn't predict what would happen when we arrived. Lord Verlaine's wife might have known we were coming, but that didn't mean that her neighbours would make time for us. The whole affair left a bitter taste on the tongue, and I endured the drive to Hampshire with my teeth firmly gritted.

The countryside which bordered the A31 went some way to soothing my agitation. Even if the autumn had drained much of the colour from England's normally vibrant hills and fields, the leaves along the roadside were as varied as any kaleidoscope. The elevated road which crossed the Hog's Back of the North Downs offered such spectacular views that, for a little while, I didn't mind the silence. My first two novels had been so fixed within their stately settings that I'd had little time for bucolic description, but perhaps that would change in future publications.

When we reached Winchester, and I knew that our destination was relatively close, Bella began to chatter about everything and nothing. "Do you remember when we camped in my garden when we were children?" she asked quite out of the blue. "Father hung a tarpaulin between two trees, and we took thick blankets and as many pillows as we could carry. We thought we were being terribly adventurous, but in reality there was a footman assigned to watch over us, and Cook made us food every six hours."

It was hard to know why she would mention this now, and I could only think she was nervous about what we would find when we entered the New Forest.

"We were eleven years old," I said so that she wouldn't feel I lacked interest. "I was freezing cold for half the night and very relieved that you woke up early the next morning."

What I wouldn't mention was that I stared at her with something approaching love as she slept beside me. I doubt I knew myself how I felt, but Bella had always been a creature of wonder to me. She was the brightest and most beautiful person I'd ever met, even if it would be some years before I realised just what she meant to me.

"I tried it on my own once," she continued. "It wasn't the same."

She could sustain such light-hearted discussion for only so long before a look of melancholy came over her and she stopped again.

As we got closer to our destination, oaks, beech trees and alders grew right up to the edge of the road and gave me the sensation of being trapped within the boundary of the forest. Why couldn't it have been a sunny day with blue skies and a warm breeze as we attempted this foolish errand? That might have alleviated the unnerving sensation that was gnawing at my gut. But, no, we would be cursed with heavy grey clouds and a bitter wind until we drove back to the city two days later.

Even the entrance to Lord Verlaine's estate had an ominous look to it. There was an enormous stone gate with a glowering lion on one side and a rather disdainful unicorn on the other. The neighbouring foliage was overgrown, and strings of ivy spiralled up the wide stone gateposts, as though determined to strangle the unfortunate beasts. There was a crooked man on duty who didn't manage to communicate a great deal to us as he was coughing so much, but he opened the wrought-iron gate and waved us through.

Bella drove us along the apparently endless driveway, and Percy gave a yawn to remind us that he was still there in the back seat. The only sound we'd had out of him until then was an occasional snore, but he stood up now and put his head between the seats to see what was happening. He evidently didn't like what he saw of the dark path, as he immediately sat down again and hid behind me.

I offered what I hoped was a reassuring smile in Bella's direction, but her eyes were fixed straight ahead, and she didn't notice. I'm sure if we'd visited the place at the height of summer, I would have admired that very same tunnel of trees, but just then, the gloom made me shiver.

"Littleton Place," Bella muttered, when we finally emerged from the shade and caught sight of the early Tudor house on a rise in the middle of a large garden.

I couldn't have imagined such a welcoming view after the thoughts that had been running through my head. This was not the creepy Gothic mansion that I had pictured. It was a terribly homely and appealing sort of place. It was proudly asymmetrical, with an extra wing reaching towards us on one side and two small, crenellated towers attached to the main façade. Best of all, as Bella pulled the Bentley to a stop, there was a friendly looking butler waiting to greet us.

"Lady Bella, welcome," he practically cooed with delight. "I doubt you remember me, but—"

"Ainsworth!" Bella cut in before he could say any more. "Of course I do. I have so many happy memories of my visits here." She rushed closer to grip the tubby retainer's hands in hers.

"I and all the staff are simply over the moon to have you back."

This happy exchange continued for a minute longer before Bella remembered she wasn't alone. "Allow me to introduce you to Percy the basset hound and... Oh yes, I nearly forgot, his owner is here too. This is Marius Quin." She couldn't resist teasing me, and I couldn't resist showing how unimpressed I was.

"You will notice, Ainsworth, that Lady Bella's sense of humour has not improved since she was last here."

His ruby cheeks grew a little plumper. "I couldn't possibly comment, sir, but I must say that you are most welcome here at Littleton Place."

All this gaiety led Bella to suck in a breath and look understandably brittle once more. She clearly felt guilty for showing any kind of happiness so soon after Gilbert's death, and I wished I'd made certain that she really was ready for whatever lay ahead of us.

"Is Lady Letitia here this morning?" she asked in a more sombre tone.

"She is, miss," Ainsworth replied with a slight bow. "And although she sends her apologies, I'm afraid she is not receiving anyone at the moment. She has not been in the best of health recently, and it is difficult to know in what condition we will find her." Rather than dwell on this news, he swiftly changed the topic. "I will show you to your rooms rather than keeping you waiting out here in the cold."

He didn't give us time to ask any more questions but bustled off in that curious, mincing manner that butlers have come to adopt over the centuries. His white-spatted feet moved ever so quickly but took the tiniest steps. It was almost like a dance and contrasted with his heavy frame and deep, masculine voice.

We travelled so speedily, in fact, that I barely had time to take in my surroundings. I can tell you that the interior of the building looked just as old as the façade. There were no carpets, and the floor was hewn from stone. This lent the place a coldness, and the austere paintings on the walls – of long-dead members of Lord Verlaine's family – only enhanced the feeling that we were intruders there.

"Here we are." Ainsworth pointed to two doors at the top of a short staircase that led off the main landing. "I took the liberty of putting you in adjoining rooms so that you can keep one another company whilst you are here."

I couldn't imagine what he wished to imply with this statement. Was he suggesting that we required a different, more intimate form of company, or was he merely saying that we shouldn't expect to see too much of our hostess? Either way, his previously cheery demeanour had become subdued, and he bowed to show that it was time for him to go.

"Thank you, Ainsworth." Bella invested her words with more enthusiasm. "I am so grateful to you and your mistress for having us. If it isn't too much, however, I do have one favour to ask."

"Anything I can do, miss, I will try my utmost best."

"I imagine you know something of the reason for our visit, in which case it will come as no surprise that we are seeking the attention of Deirdre Stradbrooke from the neighbouring estate."

"You need say no more, Lady Bella." He opened his eyes and looked pleased with himself. "I have already made sure that certain key members of staff at Rhinefield House know of your presence here. Their mistress will already have been informed of your visit, and I'm sure she will appear forthwith." There was a knowing look in his eyes as he bowed once more and then ducked away.

"What do we do now?" I asked Bella, and we both opened the doors to look at our near-medieval bedchambers.

"I think you already know the answer to that question, Marius." There was no excitement left in her as she surveyed the dim room before her. "We wait."

SIXTEEN

A footman brought our bags up, and we took a short time to prepare ourselves for lunch. My room had all the accoutrements of luxury, including a bed the size of my spare room at home and a small bath set into an alcove, but the stone floor and walls were like blocks of ice and I couldn't feel truly comfortable there.

We took lunch in the great hall, of all places, and I had to move my place setting closer to Bella's so that we weren't sixteen yards apart down the table from one another.

"This is where I celebrated my eighteenth birthday," she reminded me as she gazed up at the vaulted ceiling. "I danced with my cousin because he was the only young man I knew who hadn't been sent off to war."

I didn't say anything to interrupt her daydream. I just followed her gaze as she examined the thick woollen tapestries which covered the lower half of each wall. She swayed a little, and I thought perhaps she was moving to the rhythm of the music in her head.

When she came back to herself, she straightened her shoulders rather primly. "Of course, that was a long time ago."

Something in her tone prompted a question. "Have you been back here since?"

She paused to consider the answer. "Not for many years. I don't know what happened really. Father still writes to Uncle Thomas on occasion, but we haven't come here as a family since shortly after the war finished."

This was clearly just as intriguing a situation to her as it was to me. I was about to ask her for more information on the Verlaine family, when she volunteered some of her own.

"Lady Letitia was always a fragile person. I didn't realise that she was ill, though."

"I wonder if we'll see her at all." I peered up at the ceiling as if to catch a glance of her through the wooden beams. There was something more important to discuss, though, and so I changed the topic once more. "What if no one from the neighbouring estate comes?"

"Then we'll walk back and forth in front of the driveway until they notice us."

A footman appeared with a carafe of red wine, and we waited for him to pour before I answered. "Mortimer's family may not be at home this week. They could be on holiday for all we know."

"Someone would have told us if that were the case." Her usual confidence rose to the surface and, before I could provide another pessimistic prediction to the contrary, we caught the sound of chatter from out in the corridor.

"Well, they won't mind me, now, will they, Anfield?" an artificially high-pitched voice declared.

"Yes, but madam—" the butler, whose name was not Anfield but Ainsworth, tried again.

"There's no need to stand on ceremony. I'm not that sort of person."

Ainsworth's fast feet could be heard pitter-pattering

towards us, though I imagine he must have taken bigger steps this time, as he reached us before the visitor.

"Lady Bella," the old faithful said between gulped-down breaths. "I am so very sorry to interrupt your lunch, however..." This was all he managed to utter before a storm of pink blew into the room.

"Now, now, Anscombe, I've told you there's no need for such formality with me. I'm just here to say hello, and then I will toddle off back to see my dear family at home."

She was dressed in a floor-length gown the like of which I had previously thought extinct. It was all ruffles and frills, and the skirt trailed along the floor a yard behind her. In her hand she gripped an ornate folding fan, though it was close to freezing inside and out, and her hair was a stack of tight curls approximately a foot high. I'd seen less complicated flower arrangements.

Ainsworth was doing his best to act as though the woman who had just invaded his employer's home was sane. "May I introduce Lady Letitia's neighbour, Deirdre Stradbrooke." He had to lean around her to deliver this information and then she launched herself over to us.

"That's right." She laughed a laugh that was as false as her squeaky and pretentious voice. "But you must call me Dreary, all my friends do, but I don't mind in the slightest. I love a good joke, do I, and it's funny because it's not true." She came to a stop a short distance away. Judging by the glum expression she now wore, she did not find this nickname funny after all.

Although I was not raised in any such refined surroundings, even I knew that it was poor form to interrupt someone while they were eating. I couldn't decide whether to rise to greet her or stay where I was, so I took my cue from Bella and didn't move a muscle.

"We're pleased to meet you..." Bella struggled over the next word, and I wondered whether, even for a modern woman like her, such informality was hard to stomach, "Dreary. This is my friend Mr Quin. What can we do for you?"

There was none of the usual warmth in what she said, but Deirdre Stradbrooke didn't appear to notice my friend's icy tone.

"It's what I can do for you that I've come to discuss." She wavered between sounding as polished as a silver kettle and as common as a pigeon. "I heard that you were visiting, and I felt quite beholden to extend the olive branch of friendship to you and yours." She nodded to each of us in turn and closed her eyes contentedly, as if she had done something truly altruistic.

It was hard to know how to respond to this force of gaudily decorated nature, and so we didn't.

"Oh, no!" she yelped with an amused colour to her voice. "I've done it again! My Arnold is forever telling me that I get ahead of myself, and I haven't even told you who I am." She put her hands together and held them against her sizeable bosom. I thought she was about to sing, but she merely went on to introduce herself better. "I'm Lord Verlaine and Lady Letitia's neighbour. We own the Rhinefield estate and its various properties. It's a lovely spot, nestled in the forest, of which my husband's family cleared large swathes to build a house that wouldn't look out of place in a fairy tale, if I do say so myself."

She discharged this information at such a clip that it was hard to make sense of it until she had finished. With this done, she stood looking proud and expectant and waited to see how we would react. Bella is better at hiding her feelings than I am, so I let her speak for the pair of us.

"It really is such a pleasure to make your acquaintance, and it was so very nice of you to come here and introduce yourself. I will be sure to tell Lady Letitia of your kindness."

Dreary looked suitably blank, but then, after a rush of realisation, she launched another barrage of words at us. "My goodness, I've done it again. I've forgotten the main reason I came here." She flounced closer and dropped her voice. I could only conclude she was worried that one of the servants might overhear. "I thought, seeing as you're new to the area, you might like to come to Rhinefield House for dinner and parlour games this evening from seven o'clock. We're expecting the whole family to be there, seeing as it's my birthday tomorrow. My sister and her husband are coming from Essex, and it would be my honour to have you there. I know Lord Verlaine is the son of an earl, but it would be a real fillip for me to entertain the daughter of a duke. And then tomorrow you are very much invited to the main celebrations."

I hadn't said a word until now, and so I decided that I should accept her invitation. "We would love to pay you a visit and have no particular plans for the coming days."

Even though we had travelled a hundred miles in the hope of securing an audience with the Stradbrookes, Bella clearly struggled to accept the fact that she would actually have to go to Rhinefield House. "We simply can't wait to join you there."

Our new friend practically purred with excitement, so she can't have realised just how hollow Bella's delivery of this normally cheerful statement was. Deirdre wobbled on the spot for a moment and then turned with a brief wave to leave us to our lunch.

Bella looked... well, she looked rather like she'd just walked through a hurricane, whereas I was very pleased with how the encounter had turned out.

"That was a lot easier than I had expected. Now perhaps we can have our lunch."

SEVENTEEN

We did not meet Lady Letitia Verlaine that day. I thought that I caught the sound of cries carrying downstairs to us from one of the towers, though that may just have been my overactive imagination and the feeling that I was inside one of my favourite children's books. I had come to picture Lord Verlaine's wife as being like the invalid boy in *The Secret Garden*, locked away from the world, seeing no one. Time would hopefully tell whether this impression was accurate.

As she was in no hurry to get to our neighbours' house, Bella retreated to her quarters, and I definitely heard her crying through the wall. The most remarkable thing about her that week was not her grief, but her ability to hide it. If I hadn't known her so well, I'm sure I would have missed those desperate sighs and far-off looks that came at least twice an hour. In between, she could be jolly and light, and she did a very good impersonation of a person having a lovely time, but our very civil lunch together had clearly exhausted her, and I didn't see her again for a few hours.

Being the hack that I am, I'd decided to treat the book I had pledged to write as nothing but a money-making exercise. And so, with Percy there for company, I managed to scribble down a couple of chapters of *Murder at Pemblewick Manor*. I found this new, more commercial approach to writing oddly liberating. I was no longer worried whether every word was perfect, as I didn't actually want the book to be any good. If Bertie saw just how dull and generic the tale I'd created was, he'd surely give me more freedom to write what I wanted in future. I made the characters excessively eccentric and frankly quite stupid. My detective, Inspector Rupert L'Estrange, was a mean and sniping bully, and I greatly enjoyed this little episode of self-sabotage.

I often find the main challenge to my writing to be the fight to cudgel the ideas from my brain. Now that I didn't have to worry how good my work was, the ideas flowed like a rushing river. I must say it was tremendous fun, and I was almost sorry when Bella knocked softly on my door and came inside.

"It's pitch black," she was quick to point out as I sat chuckling to myself about a witty depiction of a horrible suspect. "Have you not realised?"

Percy released a low, abbreviated howl, presumably to agree with his favourite person.

"No, I have not."

I was still quite tickled by the horrendousness of the scene I had just created but turned to Bella, who had changed her clothes and now looked— I struggle to think of a less effusive term than *radiant*. Her black hair caught the light, even where there was none to catch, and unlike the woman we would be visiting, her style of dress was simple but undeniably elegant. The sea-foam velvet hung loosely about her shoulders but cinched close at the waist to give her a silhouette from a modern tailor's sketchbook.

I tried to speak normally but surely stuttered out my words. "I'm ready to clear out if you are."

"No, you're not, Marius." She sounded just like any number of people in my life (from my mother to my editor, my aunt to my childhood schoolteacher) who feel it is their duty to tell me what to do. "Get changed and I will meet you downstairs. I'll ask the staff to bring the car around."

With this, she turned on the ball of her foot and marched out with Percy waddling after her. I huffed and puffed for a few minutes and then did exactly as she'd demanded. I am no materialist, but I do love my best suit. The colour is so pure and the material so thick that just feeling it between my fingers reminds me of last New Year's Eve and the glamorous yet disastrous party Bella and I attended together.

I broke from this brief daydream and got washed and changed as quickly as I could, then scampered down to the entrance hall. It was hard not to stare at Bella when I caught sight of her in a pool of light by the front door. She was standing just under a chandelier, and it poured down rays upon her like a starburst from the heavens. I'd got rather good at pretending not to be madly in love with her, and now that she was in mourning, it was doubly important that she didn't find out, but it was a challenge at that moment not to bow down at her feet and confess my feelings.

"Off we go, Marius," she whispered as she took my arm. "We have a conspiracy to uncover."

As she pulled me in closely at her side, and the cold air from outside hit us, I shivered for more reasons than one.

When we got to the car, I was both surprised and completely resigned to the fact Percy was waiting for us in the back seat. I was about to tell Bella that it is not the done thing to take pets to a stranger's house unless they have specifically been invited, but she predicted my complaint and cut me off.

"I know what you're going to say, Marius, and I disagree. If nothing else, he will help ease us into the conversation and disguise the fact that we are secretly investigating."

I considered informing her that the only other hobbyist

detective I knew was usually accompanied by a golden retriever, when she spoke once more.

"As it happens, I've come to rely on Percy. After all the affection and support he has given me over the last week, I would hate to leave him in this cold old building whilst we go off to enjoy ourselves."

I opened my mouth to speak for a third time and, for a third time, I was prevented from doing so.

"There's no sense in arguing. I've made up my mind."

She folded her arms, and we sat there for a few moments before she remembered that she was the one who was supposed to be driving. She started the engine, and we moved off along the path.

"Hello there, Percy," I turned around to say, now that she'd finished interrupting me. "It's lovely to have you with us."

I had more thoughts on the matter, but I could see there was no sense in sharing them. Within a minute or two, we had left Littleton Place and were rolling calmly along the road to the Rhinefield estate. I promise this is the last time I will have to describe a grand house or fancy location – on this case at least – but our entrance to the property was almost the opposite to the experience we'd had earlier in the day. The wooded drive that took us to the house was far more open and welcoming, and the ground around it so well kept that it looked as though a team of gardeners had filed down each blade of grass by hand.

And yet, when we came out in the open, the house was far more Gothic and imposing than the neighbouring property. I could tell that it wasn't much more than fifty years old, but the brick was dark and weathered in places and it was built in a Victorian Gothic style which, just as Deirdre Stradbrooke had attested, put one in mind of a fairy tale. On one side of the elongated building there was an impressive clocktower with an ornate stone trellis balcony leading off. There were barley-twist chimney pots cropping up at irregular points across the roof and, had the house been built a few hundred years earlier, the main arched entrance would surely have had a portcullis suspended from it.

It was both inviting and intimidating and I must say that it was nothing like the fussy modern palace I had imagined Deirdre calling home. Perhaps to make up for this elegance, she had provided another form of fussiness. Standing in front of the main façade was a guard of honour to welcome us. Our hosts had ordered every servant they had to stand in two lines facing one another to form a corridor through which the great Lady Bella and her insignificant companion would walk into the house. I'd never seen such nonsense and could only imagine that the Stradbrookes had mistaken my friend for a member of the royal family.

"Lady Bella," Deirdre sang from the end of the human tunnel. "If I may be so bold as to call you that!"

"Of course you may." Bella was usually capable of speaking to people from all walks of life but didn't appear to know how to react around this strange woman. "It is my name after all."

"You are too kind, Lady Bella. Too kind!" Deirdre stretched out the vowels in these two words so that they became a song.

She curtseyed and I noticed that her dress was even flouncier than the one she'd worn to interrupt our lunch. It had countless red flowers sewn on to it and small silver balls all over like a confectioner's embellishment on a wedding cake. It was hideous.

"And Mr Quin! Thank you, thank you, thank you for coming." I was awarded a bow and a shake of the hand, but that was already too much. "My nephew has just gone with our chauffeur to the railway station to collect my sister and her husband, so we'll soon be a larger party."

More importantly, there was no sign of Mr Stradbrooke, and I had to wonder whether missing spouses were a common phenomenon among the gentry of Hampshire.

"This way, please." A plummy butler peeled off from the end of one line to direct us. I believe he was putting on this accent, as I'm fairly certain that even Bella's lordly father sounded a lot more common than he did. He walked with his legs as straight as possible and reminded me of a wind-up tin soldier.

"Arnold is so very looking forward to your visit," Dreary informed us as we passed through the vaulted stone porch to reach a surprisingly modest and tastefully decorated entrance hall that was lined with a series of modern paintings by the French impressionists. "He's done nothing but talk about you all afternoon. It is a real thrill for all of us to have you here."

I wondered who "all of us" would turn out to be. I also had to consider the description that the woman's former sister-in-law Felicity Mortimer had offered of the unkind, controlling person who had treated her children so coldly. It was perfectly possible that the faffing and fanciful woman who had invited us there was the mastermind behind Felicity's unjust imprisonment, but it was frankly difficult to imagine her conspiring to conduct much more than a tea party.

"Here we are," she said as the butler hurried ahead to open a pair of rounded mahogany doors. "My husband is just in here."

We sailed through the arched doorway into a wood-panelled great hall – most of them tend to be, don't you know? There were all the usual accoutrements of such rooms: a grand alabaster fireplace with a frieze depicting armed men on horseback chasing after a child – I soon realised that the boy was himself in pursuit of a pack of dogs and a leaping deer, so perhaps it was a hunting scene rather than something more sinister. Above it on the chimney breast was one of the largest carved wooden family coats of arms I'd ever seen. And the man to whom all this belonged was standing beside a window at the far end of the room, looking out at the darkness over the grounds behind the house.

He did not turn to look at us even when his wife cleared her throat to get his attention. We were spared the embarrassment of this snub, however, as two young men arrived at this moment to distract us, and their mother hurried over to them.

"First allow me to introduce my sons, Peter and Paul."

"I beg your pardon?" I asked without meaning to say anything. It was a quite involuntary reaction. The words seemed to jump out of me. "Did you say Peter and Paul?"

"That's right." Dreary beamed at her two tall sons, apparently unaware of the children's rhyme about the little birds.

"It's an honour to meet you," the wider of the boys said as he kissed Bella's hand. He couldn't have been more than twenty, but I was fairly certain he was trying to seduce her! "Mother has told us lots about you."

Deirdre's laughter shot about the room like a firework. "Oh, you terrible boy. Be away with you."

Bella was amused by the young man's patter, but I was not.

"Yes, Peter, do fly away," I said with a smile so that no one noticed I actually meant it.

"He's a terrible tease, this one." His mother clung to him affectionately and I could tell she had never been much of a disciplinarian. "His brother has the brains, and Peter has the charm. That's what I always say."

Neither of the round-faced adolescents seemed aware of the fact that she had both complimented and insulted them simultaneously. Perhaps the two things served to balance one another.

"I'm Paul," the thin, supposedly brainy one said as if we didn't already know this. He had blue eyes that were as large and clear as his brother's brown ones. There was something terribly innocent about him, and I could tell that he was not the type to make sudden overtures to a woman he didn't know, as his brother just had. Whether or not he turned out to be as smart as his mother believed, I have to say I instantly liked him.

"Arnold!" Dreary yelped when her husband still hadn't come to speak to us. "Arnold, did you not hear me? Our guests have arrived!"

There was a definite count of five ticks on the clock above the door before the man finally turned to look at us. He nodded to suggest that his moment had come and then walked slowly across the long room.

"Welcome, both." He had a deep, earthy sort of voice which immediately made me think he belonged to one of those old English families from which his wife definitely did not hail. He bowed respectfully to Bella and then crushed my hand in his. "My game is international trade. I buy cotton from Egypt, sell it to traders in France, then buy it back from them for a profit before selling it again here for an even bigger profit. What about you?"

I was taken aback by the directness of the question and the pain shooting up my arm. I tried to hide both of these things and squeezed back far harder than I ever normally would. "I dabble in a number of fields, but writing is my main focus."

"Fiction?" His tone had become sharp and abrupt, and Percy cowered behind me as he spoke.

"That's right."

"Battles and shooting and that sort of thing?" He was apparently the kind of man who assumed that novels could only be about war, so I corrected him.

"No. I'm more about stabbing and poisoning and that sort of thing."

"You mean mysteries?" He had to swallow then, as it seemed that he found the idea quite appalling. "How interesting."

"How interesting, indeed," his wife interrupted as though

afraid what old Arnold might say next. "I had no idea that we were in the presence of a knight of the quill."

"I had no idea you were bringing a doggy." Paul bent down to spoil Percy, and I just had to hope that no Patricks or Peregrines would be at the party, as we had more than enough P names already.

Peter was trying to make Bella laugh, while his father gave due care to his truly masterful horseshoe moustache. It was thick and white and well groomed, but he couldn't resist smoothing it with two fingers as he continued to stare at me as though I'd offended him. Deirdre, meanwhile, looked nervous that the conversation wasn't developing as she would have liked.

"Games, that's my game!" she said a little opaquely, before explaining, "Parlour games, I mean to say. We should all have a glass of something with bubbles in it, and then we'll enjoy a round of Hot Cockles, or perhaps the Bull's Foot."

"I'm partial to the Simpleton myself," Paul added, still patting Percy.

Before any more oddly named suggestions could be made, a stripling of a footman appeared with a tray and six champagne glasses. Each held a fizzing pink concoction that I took to be some kind of Kir. Once we had each received one, Dreary led the toast.

"To new friends, and fun and games."

"And birthdays," Paul added in his usual wide-eyed, innocent manner. "And presents and cake."

"I'd best not start on the cake just yet, my boy, or I'll have no appetite for dinner." Deirdre's oversized laugh erupted once again, and we all drank while she calmed down.

I felt a touch awkward then as we all waited for something to happen, but the staff at Rhinefield House were well prepared and the butler stepped forward to direct us across the room. There were some chairs and a table with various paraphernalia already in place for the games. The fact that Bella and I would have to lark about like children in the hope of uncovering some damning information on our hosts showed me just how unlikely our mission was to succeed. I couldn't think how I might subtly change the topic to Felicity Mortimer and the mysterious case of Deirdre's dead brother.

I couldn't... but Bella could, and I was so relieved that we were back together.

"What a beautiful photograph that is of your family on the escritoire," she said quite incidentally to her admirer. "I bet I can guess which one you are, Peter."

I turned to see an image of not just the immediate family, but the whole Mortimer-Stradbrooke clan. It had clearly been taken years before, as Peter and Paul were little more than babies and there were no other children on the scene at the time. At the very edge of the picture, half hidden by the silver frame, was Auntie Felicity herself, heavily pregnant with her first child. From what I knew, this would mean that the photograph was taken a few short years before her imprisonment.

Bella walked closer to point at the first of the babies. "I think that's you, and that's your brother."

Dreary was the first to respond. She generally was. "You're absolutely right, Lady Bella. Peter has always had a rather *photogenique* quality."

"Mother says that my forehead is too big for that," Paul said with a gentle laugh.

"You're both beautiful to me, my darling."

I took in the other photographs that were on display. There was one of Deirdre and her boys, aged ten or so, and another of an austere, scowling lady in her thirties, her unsmiling husband and their four young children. I could only imagine that this was our hostess's sister and her kin. Perhaps unsurprisingly, there were no more images of Felicity, though I did spot one of Richard Mortimer with his sisters.

Before I could take a closer look, Arnold spoke up. "I

thought we were going to play Hot Cockles." This frivolous conversation had apparently vexed him further. "I'm fond of Hot Cockles – the game and the food."

Bella pretended not to have heard him. "Isn't that lady on the left an actress? I'm sure I've seen her face somewhere. Was she in a film with Alma Cavendish?"

Dreary couldn't resist this proposition and went running over to see who was in the picture. "No, my dear. That's not an actress, it's—"

"Come, come now, Mother." Peter's eyes narrowed as he interrupted her, but then he softened his tone. "Let's play the game, shall we?"

"How do you play Hot Cockles anyway?" Paul was quick to ask as Percy moaned in the hope of more attention.

"Oh, it's quite simple," his brother replied and then set out to confuse us. "A Penitent, chosen by chance, or by his own choice, hides his face upon a lady's lap, which lady serves as Confessor, and places herself in an armchair in the midst of the company..."

This explanation went on for approximately three minutes and I was no wiser as to the rules of the game at the end of Peter's winding speech than I had been before I was born.

"It's a little trickier to play than I remembered." This was the first time I heard any hint of sadness in Dreary Deirdre's voice. I should probably mention that, though it did rhyme, Dreary was a terrible nickname for her. She was full of colour and energy, and I still couldn't connect her with Felicity's description.

"Let's just play the Simpleton," Paul begged, showing his impatience.

With this impasse reached, Bella saw another opportunity and took it. "You know, the more I look at that photograph, the more certain I am that I know the woman on the left."

Deirdre was too fast for her family to stop this time. "You

may well recognise her, indeed, Lady Bella. The woman in that photograph is the murderess, Felicity Mortimer. That monster killed my brother. I keep that photograph there to ensure that I never forget her wickedness."

This was a perfectly dramatic moment at which, were I writing the scene myself, I would have chosen to end a chapter, but there was an even more significant development that I didn't notice until everyone turned to face the door.

A footman had arrived to announce the arrival of more guests, but as he opened his mouth, a trio of people pushed right past him. Each of them looked thoroughly miserable.

"Oh, Dreary," a woman I'd just seen in the photographs declared. She looked rather like the grim reaper. "What are you blathering about now?"

EIGHTEEN

Dressed in a long black robe, Ursula Tanner reminded me of a vulture I'd once seen when I was travelling in the Pyrenees. Though only around forty years of age, and decked out in feminine frippery, she had a sunken, masculine face. In a more egalitarian world, she could have turned a good trade as an undertaker.

She picked her way across the floor to us, as though she disapproved of the thick carpet beneath her feet. She certainly disapproved of her sister, towards whom she peered down her beak-like nose. "You've never been the most fascinating conversationalist, have you, dear Dreary?"

Poor Deirdre, for whom I suddenly felt an upswell of sympathy, could do little but laugh. "That's right, Ursula. I've a head full of sawdust and a malfunctioning tongue. Isn't that what you always say about me?" She turned to us to continue her self-critique. "In fact, it was my darling sister here who first started calling me Dreary. Oh, how we laughed!"

Ursula showed no amusement at her own joke. It was hard to imagine her smiling at anything. "Only because the name suits you perfectly, dear."

Arnold was still watching me, but he did nothing to defend his wife. I finally took notice of the other two new arrivals. There was a boy of perhaps fourteen who was carrying a clutch of presents and a few bags. He had the fuzzy beginnings of a moustache on his lip and was apparently unable to raise his bespectacled eyes more than a few inches above the floor. Standing next to him was a big burly chap who didn't appear to have noticed what anyone had just said.

"Am Jim," he muttered in the thickest Yorkshire accent I'd ever heard. For a moment, I thought he'd spoken some indecipherable phrase, the meaning of which I couldn't tell you, but then the words fell into their right places in my brain. "Am in cooal." A few seconds later, I realised that he'd made his fortune in coal, not cooal – whatever that might be. "'Ooh are you?"

As I was a man, he'd directed these remarks to me and barely glanced at Bella.

"My name's Quin," I replied, glad to have the chance to exercise my vocal cords for the first time in minutes. "Marius Quin. I'm a—"

"I know thee, Quin." He said this so sombrely that I thought he objected to the fact. "I've read both o' tha books."

Arnold made a noise that was somewhere between a gasp and gulp. "Of course! Quin, the novelist," he said as his wife looked at him with some concern. "I've definitely come across your name somewhere."

Jim once more continued as though he weren't aware of what had just been said. "I don't mind telling thee that they are a darn sight better than most o' the rubbish people write these days."

I must admit that I was happy he felt this way, but before I could enjoy his acclaim, he came over to squash my hand just as his brother-in-law had. It would take some time to recover.

"Don't be such a Deirdre, James," his wife berated him. "You'll bore us all to tears." Surprisingly, Ursula didn't land on a post from which to peer down at us or circle the room looking for carrion. She turned her attention to the boy, who was buckling under the weight of his load. I had to assume he was her son, as she soon took the opportunity to belittle him. "As for you, Neville, stop standing there so limply. You're like a piece of lettuce that has been hung up to attract rabbits to a trap. You've always had abysmal posture."

This was the sort of person I'd had in mind when Felicity had talked of her evil sister-in-law. It made me wonder whether I'd somehow got the names muddled.

Deirdre did her best to keep the proceedings light and friendly, but it wouldn't work. "We were about to play a parlour game, my dear sister. If you would like to—"

"How many times have I told you, Dreary?" Ursula interrupted. "Games are for children." She sat down in the comfiest armchair and closed her eyes so that she now resembled a disgruntled owl.

I looked from face to face in the hope that someone would think of a solution to melt the ice that had frozen the air around us. It seemed we had reached a stalemate as, if we weren't to play games, what could we do?

To resolve this dilemma, Deirdre dashed to a handsome baby grand in the corner of the room and began to play.

> "Of all the girls that are so smart
> There's none like pretty Sally;
> She is the darling of my heart,
> And she lives in our alley."

Her two boys and their cousin were evidently enjoying the performance as they went to accompany her.

Before they could open their mouths to join in, Ursula interrupted. "Your singing is not nearly as terrible as it once was, Dreary, and your playing has improved, too, but could you please keep the noise down? I've been suffering from the most dreadful headache this week. I don't know what has caused it."

After an awkward hush that lasted the best part of a minute, the unofficial head of the family declared, "Perhaps we should move ahead to dinner already."

Deirdre was still staring mournfully at the piano keys, and the three cousins (and Percy) were there to support her, but she could summon no enthusiasm for the idea. "I told Cook that we would eat at eight."

"And I appreciate that, but if you give your staff a talking-to, I'm sure we can sit down to eat within the hour."

Our hostess, more than anyone, looked unsure how to respond, and I had to wonder what the odious interloper held over the men there that they wouldn't come to Deirdre's defence.

"Come along, Dreary, get an iggri on! After dinner is over, we shall open your presents and have an early night. Won't that be pleasant?"

"But Ursula, my birthday isn't until tomorrow." She sounded truly lost then and looked at her imperial, though apparently rather cowardly, husband.

"Ah, now, I meant to explain. We'll have to leave immediately after breakfast. It's not that we don't want to stay, but..." Her talons curled together in her lap, and she leaned forwards a fraction, ready to swoop. We all waited for an excuse that would never come.

Deirdre brushed the frills of her dress with the back of one hand and looked at Bella and me quite desperately. "I suppose I'll talk to the staff about dinner then." As she left the room, something told me she wished to confide in us, but I couldn't imagine why.

"And the rest of you," Ursula continued as though she were

about to level some terrible accusation at her family, "don't you wish to feel a little cleaner before we sit down to eat? God gave us wash-hand basins for a reason."

The men began to drift from the room but, as Bella and I had nowhere to go, we stayed behind. She watched us for a few moments through suspicious eyes, then hurried after her husband, berating her still-laden son as they went.

"Really, Neville, you leave every room just as you find it, don't you? I wish you were more like your big brothers."

"Yes, Mother. Of course, Mother." The poor boy sent us a glance that reminded me of his aunt's pleading look.

"What a family!" Bella said under her breath when they had gone. Percy complained with a low whine, but I think that was mainly because everyone had stopped paying him attention rather than a comment on the company that evening. "How are we ever to unearth their secrets with that harpy calling the tune?"

"It's an interesting turn of events that sees Deirdre as the most sympathetic person here." I was about to say more (and worse) when there was a stirring in the corner of the room, and I suddenly realised that we weren't alone.

"I wasn't sleeping," a rather whimsical voice declared, and we turned to see an elderly lady dressed as an old-fashioned nursemaid.

Her black clothes and cap were almost the same colour as the chair in which she sat, so I can't say she stood out, but I was still surprised that we had missed her there. If she was who I thought she was, then she'd evidently become part of the furniture.

"I wasn't sleeping, and nothing you say will change the matter." She closed her eyes and, judging by her high, fluted breathing, went straight back to sleep. Taking his cue, Percy decided that her lap was the perfect place for a nap, so he bumbled over to see her.

I signalled to Bella to retreat to the hallway before saying anything more.

"That must be Felicity's old nanny. The one who got her in trouble," Bella explained before I could. "Why would they keep her around if there are no children in the house anymore?"

"Why indeed?" I said with an air of bemusement.

I was about to suggest we retreat to the gardens to talk when I heard footsteps from further along the dark corridor.

"Pssst!" Deirdre sent across the room to us. "If you want to know the whole story, you should come with me."

I didn't know to which story she was referring, but I was fairly confident I wished to know it. Rather than continuing towards us, she turned off the hall and evidently expected us to follow her. A few moments later, we reached a room on a narrow and nondescript passageway. I would surely have missed it if she hadn't opened the door for us, and I was really very glad that she had.

Within was a sight I couldn't have predicted. The room was resplendent with bright colours and the most exquisite decoration. I don't know enough of that part of the world to say whether it was Moorish or Arabic or whether those two terms are interchangeable when it comes to architecture, but it certainly wasn't a typical Hampshire sitting room. It reminded me of a secret cavern that Ali Baba might have come across in the *Arabian Nights*. A golden dome topped the octagonal space and, above head height, tiny windows with fragments of blue, red and yellow glass shone with light from outside. Skinny stone columns held up the roof, and the place was aglow with bronze and gold.

"We call it the Alhambra Room," not-so-Dreary told us. "Arnold took me to Spain on our travels one year, and we fell in love with the old Moorish temples we saw in the south of the country. I decided to build something similar, and this is what I gave him as a tenth wedding anniversary present, just after the boys were born."

"It's remarkable," I told her, struck once more by the tasteful adornment of Rhinefield House and its contrast with her tasteless dress. "I've truly never seen anything like it on these shores."

Even Bella looked impressed, but she is always more focused than me and returned us to what we needed to hear. "You said you had a story to tell us."

Deirdre appeared uncertain whether she should say anything and how much was acceptable to reveal. "I do indeed. And a terrible, wonderful story it is, but you see, my family don't like me to talk about it. That woman caused so much pain. I'd always had my suspicions of her, but then I found out—"

"I'm sorry, Deirdre," Bella interrupted, feigning ignorance. "But I don't know who you mean."

Having taken a seat on the cushion-strewn bench that circled the room, she adjusted her feet on the tiled mosaic floor. "The woman in the photograph is Felicity Mortimer – or Chandler, as she was when my poor brother Richard had the misfortune of meeting her. He thought she was so pure and innocent, but I saw from the beginning that she was trouble. He was two decades older than her, and people wondered whether he was wrong to ask her to marry him. The opposite was true. All those wags and gossips should have asked why a young girl like her would marry a portly clockmaker who was the laughing stock of London."

"Do you really believe that she murdered him?" I asked, and I required no theatrics to convey my wonder. It really did surprise me that she still thought this true.

"Oh, without a doubt." She shook her head as she spoke. "That woman is a poisoner. She must have married my brother knowing what she intended to do. I sometimes reflect on what would have happened if I hadn't caught wind of the game she was playing."

Bella paused before asking her next question and, when she did, her voice was more hesitant than I might have expected. "But what was her motive in any of it?"

"She was after his money, of course. We Mortimers may not come from high breeding, but we've all done extremely well for ourselves. For all his eccentricities, Richard was a very successful man. He was the head of his guild and held several other important roles. But our dear Nanny Yapp saw that creature Felicity harvesting arsenic from flypapers, and then we discovered that she was carrying on a romantic correspondence with a man who was not her husband. If it hadn't been for us, she would have got away with murder."

There was a tear in Deirdre's eye at that moment, and I realised that she really was still upset at the thought of what had happened. From somewhere under her ruffles, she produced an embroidered pink handkerchief, which she used to dab her eyes.

"The only miscarriage of justice in the case was when Lord Verlaine commuted the killer's sentence and spared her life. That was the real—"

She came to a sudden stop and looked at the door.

"What is it?" I asked, already walking over to see what she'd noticed.

"There were footsteps. I'm certain there were. I heard someone outside."

I pulled the door open with one sharp tug, then sped out to the hallway, hoping that I'd be quick enough to catch whoever was out there. The corridor was empty.

"I'm telling the truth," she insisted. "I definitely heard someone. I know I did."

"We don't doubt you, Deirdre." Bella moved closer to put a hand on our anxious hostess's shoulder. "I thought I heard something too, but it was most likely just a servant."

"There's certainly no one out there now," I told her in as reassuring a voice as I could muster.

In an instant, the red and white cloud became stormier. Deirdre rose to her feet and pushed past me, muttering as she went. "You know the story now. I hope that if you're ever confronted by such wickedness, you'll see it for what it is." She was out of the room in a moment, and I couldn't decide what I made of the whole affair.

NINETEEN

"What complicated people." This was the best word I could think of to define the residents and visitors to Rhinefield House. "I can't put my finger on any of them with much certainty."

When it came, Bella's response was more measured than normal. "She seemed so sure of her facts. It was almost enough to make me question whether Felicity really did kill her husband."

"Oh, please, Bella. Nothing she said disproved any of the information we've obtained." My response was a little keener than I'd been intending. "The facts remain the same: there wasn't enough arsenic in Richard Mortimer's body to kill him."

"I'm aware of that, thank you, though we wouldn't be good detectives if we didn't at least keep the question at the back of our minds."

I smiled then and felt a touch guilty for being so short with her. "You know full well I've never considered myself a good detective."

Bella was unsettled by Deirdre's self-assuredness whereas, as we left the Alhambra Room, I tried to make sense of how our hostess could be so wrong. While I believed in the evidence that had brought us there, it was curious to remark just how differently two people can see things. Of course, Felicity had told me what Deirdre was like and, even if she wasn't cold and monstrous like her sister, nor as empty-headed as she'd first appeared, I had no reason to take her side in the matter.

Outside the great hall, a young maid directed us to the room where we would have dinner. I don't think I've ever come across a building with so much wood panelling. Unlike the other parts of the house we'd seen, where it finished at head height to give way to the plaster underneath, it covered all four walls and even the ceiling of the dining room.

"You've arrived," Arnold Stradbrooke called, and I got the sense that we had entered at the wrong moment. There was certainly no enthusiasm in his greeting, and the way his eyes lingered on me made me nervous.

With his frock coat and monocle, he was every bit the traditional old boy, and I had to wonder how he fitted in with this diverse group. The Mortimer sisters, though haughty and proud in different ways, were a million miles apart from their husbands.

"Aye." So far at least, his brother in-law Jim Tanner was a man of few words, and many of them seemed to be aye and thee.

He was another interesting cog in this machine. He'd evidently made enough money in coal to keep Ursula content, but his working-class accent and rough manner were so distinct from Arnold's that I couldn't help imagining the two of them appearing in a music hall sketch. Toffs and working men failing to understand one another always inspires plenty of laughter on a Friday night at the Holborn Embassy, but these two seemed perfectly at ease together.

As we awaited the other ladies before sitting down, the three cousins arrived, and I tried to remember who was who. Were Peter and Paul twins? They were certainly close in age –

that odd in-between stage that bridges childhood and adult life. Their younger cousin Neville was slight, hunched and less confident than them, but without his mother there to criticise him, he was at least capable of meeting my gaze. In fact, he seemed quite at ease, and I had to wonder whether this dual personality was a sign of duplicity.

The one thing I could say for certain was that, as he was not born when his aunt was sent to prison, we could rule him out of the conspiracy that put her there. Peter and Paul, on the other hand, were very much alive, though they would have only been around three at the time. Still, let's say that the youngsters were to blame. Solving the case so swiftly would enable us to get away from Rhinefield House and the uncomfortable meal we were about to endure.

I warmed myself by the fire, but the wind that blew down the chimney almost undid the flames' good work. Like everything else in the room, the chimney breast was made from polished oak. It depicted an armada of ships battling a stormy sea, and I thought it summed up the mood in the house rather well. Arnold clearly concurred with this assessment, as he kept pouring drinks down his neck – one after the other like a man preparing for the gallows.

As I stood there, I tried to ignore Peter's continuing flirtation with Bella – and Percy's attempts to charm everyone else in the room. Instead, I listened to Arnold and Jim discussing the latter's wife.

"She's a terribly good woman," Arnold assured his brother-in-law. There was already a slight slur in his voice, and was that a hint of sarcasm? "Selfless is another word for her. I've always said that I don't mind Ursula taking the reins of the family because she has a sensible head on her shoulders and knows what's best for those around her."

Jim seemed less confident on the matter, but he agreed in principle. "Aye, Ah married a good woman, and Ah won't hear a word against her, tha knows. She's raised our bairns as they ought to be raised. There's no doubt about tha'."

"And she's steered you well yourself, eh, Jim?" Arnold laughed a deep, inappropriate laugh as the alcohol worked its way around his body.

Poor Jim winced, and I had to wonder how he really felt about the woman who, as she now entered the room, brought a chill to the place that could not be put down to the draughty chimney.

"Come along, everyone," she exclaimed as she surveyed the party. "It's time for dinner." Her browbeaten son immediately sped across the room to pull her chair back before she could even reach the table.

Whatever suggestion there was that this was Deirdre's soirée had long since been forgotten. Although she gave the orders to begin the meal, the butler appeared at Ursula's side whenever she wanted something that was *hors menu*. She glared at me for much of the meal, and I wondered whether she knew more about me than she'd revealed. I had the sense that she was watching me because she knew I was there to watch her.

The one saving grace of this experience was the food itself. There were seared scallops from the nearest port at Southampton, followed by a rack of well-trimmed New Forest lamb. A second seafood course offered crab, turbot and some tiny cockles, which went to prove Arnold's previous claim that he liked them, hot or otherwise. The only thing that wasn't notably local was the dessert, which went a good way to proving the pastry chef's credentials. The flaky praline Paris–Brest that I ate that night was as good as any I had tried in Paris (or Brest, for that matter). It left me in something of a happy stupor, as the first mouthful had sent me shooting back to my days living in France after the war. There was a particular bakery I used to visit on the Boulevard Saint-Michel which... really isn't important just now.

The point I'm trying to make is... well, I'm no longer quite sure, but the food was delicious and once more spoke of the good taste of our hosts. The only small hiccup was an exceptionally pretty maid, who, having spent much of the night lingering in the shadows and occasionally huffing her disapproval at something, accidentally tipped a glass of red wine all over the tablecloth in front of Bella.

With stern and single-minded Ursula there, the bonhomie which the meal inspired didn't last long. She clapped her hands, and we fell silent. "If you are all now adequately refreshed, I think it would be best if we forego the cheese course and take drinks in the library. The sooner I get to bed, the sooner I will rise." This marked the end of her lukewarm address to the group. She tapped her husband's hand and said without any attempt at tact, "If we're lucky, we'll be home in Essex by midday tomorrow."

I really did feel for Deirdre. Not only was her sister coldhearted and critical, with all the warmth of a wet rock, her birthday celebration had been hijacked and now curtailed.

"We will definitely still be here for your big day," I found myself telling her, though my eyes immediately strayed to see Ursula's reaction. "I am greatly looking forward to discovering what you have planned to entertain all your friends who will be here to enjoy the celebration."

"Friends?" Ursula parroted. "I was not aware that anyone else was invited." Her eyelids opened very wide and then narrowed again.

My comment apparently gave Deirdre the strength to answer back. "That's right. It will be quite the occasion. If you're too busy to stay, you will be missed." Her smile was the most authentic thing I saw from her that day. She was one of those people who spend their lives trying (and failing) to be someone whom everyone will like. As she delivered this retort, however, she thought only of herself, and I approved.

"Never mind all that." Ursula pushed her chair back, and its feet shuddered noisily across the floor. "Let's open your presents. You'll like that, won't you, Dreary?" Even when she tried to sound cheerful, there was an undertone of disdain. "Why you still celebrate anything so childish as a birthday is beyond me, but this is your house." She bustled across the room with her skirts noisily following her and, as the staff were all busy with other duties, she snapped at her adolescent son for assistance. "Neville! Door!"

How many dead bodies have Bella and I come across this year? Five maybe? Or is it six? Whatever the number, I was confident that there would be few tears shed if Ursula turned out to be the next victim. It was hard for me to imagine why Arnold and Jim would describe her in such charitable terms when even her son presumably couldn't bear her. He looked so downtrodden the whole time and was prone to long, slow sighs. My heart went out to him. It really did.

There was one thing on which sallow-faced Ursula and I could agree, and that was our desire for the evening to conclude as soon as possible. I thought I might catch Bella's eye to communicate this very thing, but she was still immersed in her role. She tittered away at every word Peter said. Well, it was either that or she really had forgotten all about her dead fiancé and planned to take up with an immature replacement.

As we once more trailed through the passages of the house, I fell in step with Jim Tanner, who was almost as interesting as his wife was kind.

"The thing with cooal," he told me quite sincerely, "is that it may look dull and ordinary, but it conceals a great secret. It's as civilising an influence as anything else tha can name – from t' written word to Christianity. Without it, we'd be livin' in t' *dark ages*."

He evidently considered this a fine pun. Sadly, he would continue to talk about coal for a while longer, and I soon lost the ability to feign interest. His son Neville, meanwhile, was happily chatting with his friendly cousin, Paul. It was nice to discover that the younger boy knew how to smile, as I'd seen little evidence of it until then.

When we reached what Ursula had referred to as the library – which was more like a smoking room and lacked the key ingredient of any books whatsoever – Deirdre's presents had been arranged on a table by some unseen servant. There was a big stack of the things, piled up in a pyramid, and our hostess's chestnut brown eyes shone when she saw them.

"Really!" she said, as though surprised by the number of presents. "You're all far too kind."

"It was nothing." Ursula could summon no glee at the prospect of watching her sister unwrap them. I was curious to discover what a woman like her would give someone as a birthday present. From what I'd seen so far, she was not the generous type.

We took our seats around the piled-high boxes, bags and packages. There was a suitably roaring fire in the grate, and I'm sure I don't have to tell you that every surface in the room that was not upholstered was made of dark wood. I could only assume at this point that the builders of the house had chopped down so many trees to clear the land, that they'd had to find creative uses for all that they'd felled.

"Open mine first, Mother!" sweet-voiced Paul sang like a child as he ran to pull out his gift from the tower. He was certainly no less than eighteen, but there was something ever so juvenile about him, and I finally accepted that he was not the simpleton he wished everyone to believe. His innocence was an affectation, just as his lothario brother's lustiness didn't quite ring true.

"A painting!" Deirdre looked proudly at her dear little boy's artistic effort. "It's just lovely, Paul. I'll put it with the others in my sitting room."

She displayed the framed picture of a boat at sea. It was colourful, imprecise and quite ugly, but we all made sounds as if we were impressed by the young man's skill with a brush.

"I'm next, Mother," Peter said in that ever so smooth voice of his. He crumpled his brow and wore a confident smile as he took his turn to remove a present without making the whole lot tumble down.

I should probably mention that Ursula was already tutting impatiently. Arnold was clutching a glass of wine as if he hoped to strangle it. Jim showed little interest in the proceedings as he puffed on a pipe, and Bella observed the scene with a keen eye. We'd lost Percy at some point, so I could only assume that a member of staff had taken him off to the kitchen to spoil him.

Peter's present turned out to be inordinately well-wrapped, and it took his mother a whole minute to extract it from layers of tissue paper, wrappings and ribbon.

"Oh how nice," Deirdre inevitably cooed as she revealed a framed photo of her son, who was gazing away from the camera, as if admiring a pretty landscape or perhaps a sunset. "I know the perfect place for it."

With little conversation and no great fuss even from the birthday girl, this scene continued for what felt like hours. I should probably have felt out of place there, seeing as I was a complete stranger invited along to a private event. They were such an unusual bunch, though – on a scale between hostile and effusive, friendly and reserved – it was hard to feel that I was intruding. It didn't hurt that, except for Arnold who kept nodding off anyway, barely anyone noticed my presence. I was a fly on the wall, and that served me well.

One by one, and sometimes repeating if they'd been generous, the various members of the family handed over their presents to our hostess. She clucked like a happy hen at each of them. Her husband bought her a necklace, and her nephew gave her a pile of recently published books from Dorothy L. Sayers, Virginia Woolf and G. K. Chesterton – this made me like him a good deal more, though, admittedly, if he'd bought her a Carmine Fortescue book, I would have been forced to blame him for his aunt's imprisonment, and Carleton Hobbes's death while I was at it.

It came as no surprise that Ursula's presents would be the main event of the evening. She turned to face her sister – having sent Neville to collect the three small boxes – and showed interest in the process for the first time.

"I do hope you'll find them useful. It is difficult to know what to buy someone like you." These last three words almost suggested that the two of them hadn't known one another their whole lives.

With some trepidation, Deirdre slid off a ribbon and opened the first paper box. Her face, as she peered inside, told me that the contents would do nothing to bolster her mood. "You shouldn't have," she managed to whisper as she showed everyone there the wooden coat hanger that her sister had chosen for her.

"It is engraved with your name to ensure you never lose it." Ursula closed her eyes, and I wondered if she expected praise for her choice of gift.

Trying her best to remain positive, Deirdre moved on to the next present. It was a plain white porcelain soap dish, and now even she couldn't pretend to be anything but numbed by her sister's selection. There was worse still to come.

"Aren't they wonderful?" Ursula asked, and it was the first time that night she'd sounded the slightest bit animated.

Deirdre looked confused as she took out a bundle of feature-less rectangular cards and held them out to us.

"They're notelets. You can send them to people to say thank you for your presents." The grim sister looked quite proud of herself, though I believe it was the chance to impart a moral lesson that she particularly enjoyed. "I've always said that gratitude is the most important element of any gift."

"Well... thank you, Ursula." For a moment, I saw a flash of true discontent on Deirdre's face. She tidied these last few presents away under her chair as if she couldn't bear to see them anymore. Her stare was free of any humour or light, and I really thought she might tell her sister what she deserved to hear.

The anger or pain or whatever it was that flowed through her then didn't last. She smiled, looked around the room at us and said, "Well, I truly appreciate all of your generosity. This weekend wouldn't be the same without your presence. Especially yours, Lady Bella." She nodded across to my friend, who replied with a polite smile. "We are all so honoured that you would participate in this family event. And I am particularly—"

"Wait a moment, Mother," Peter interrupted her. "There's one last present."

We turned to look at the table that was now empty, and when no one could make sense of what he meant, he got up to show us. Leaning against the neighbouring sofa, somewhat hidden in the shadows, there was a long packet covered in white tissue paper. It wasn't as well wrapped as the others had been, and it was tied together with packing string.

"Here you go." Peter's smile shone once more.

There was an awkward lumpiness to the package and, had I been wrapping it, I'm certain I would have put it in a box first. Deirdre must have noticed just how odd the presentation was, as she gazed about at us curiously.

"Whose present is this? I really didn't expect so many."

In return, all she received was a sleepy nod from Arnold. Perhaps aware of the silence that had fallen, she clumsily tried to untie the knotted string, before giving up and ripping the paper to extract the contents. It took me a moment or two to realise what she now held. Deirdre raised the strange object to the light, and it was her brother-in-law who first identified it.

"Tha's a noose." Jim started to laugh but then cut himself off sharply. The abruptness of the change made the hush that followed all the more jarring.

It wasn't the heavy kind of noose that you'd find on a gallows. The rope was a lot skinnier, but it had been tied in a way so as to look like that very thing. There was no doubt in my mind of the message the giver had intended to convey.

"Who is responsible for this?" Deirdre demanded in a surprisingly confident tone, and her eyes swept the room like a torchlight.

Ursula's face was suddenly quite flushed. She looked back at her sister in something approaching defiance, and it made me wonder why she took this question so personally.

"It was evidently someone's idea of a joke." She turned to the three youngest members of our party, but for their part, the cousins looked just as nonplussed as the rest of us. When no one would say anything more, Deirdre spoke for the lot of us.

"Thank you all for being here this evening. I'm afraid the party is over."

TWENTY

"I take back everything I said," I told Bella as we reached her car. "It might have been easy to get inside that house, but it's impossible to know what any one of them is thinking. I encountered more transparent characters in a Danish-language play I once accidentally bought a ticket to see at the theatre."

She sat in the driver's seat saying nothing for some time, and so I continued to ramble.

"Deirdre was perhaps the biggest surprise. She may well be the best of a bad bunch," I told her, but still nothing came back to me. "I doubt I need to say anything about her sister, but if she doesn't turn out to be involved in the conspiracy against Felicity, then I am the head of the Catholic Church."

I know little of Bella's feelings about the Vatican, or my role within its hierarchy, so this made no impression whatsoever.

"Are you quite all right, dear friend?"

My question brought her back to the present and in a flat, nervous voice, she said, "Someone wanted to scare Deirdre. It must all connect to the events that brought us here."

Before I could ask more, she'd started the Bentley's engine, and we moved off around the property and back to the long, dark driveway.

"How can you be so certain?"

She would need a few moments to answer, but when she did, she spoke more urgently than before. "What do you think I was doing all evening with that rude boy? He may have thought he was subtly seducing me, but he was not."

"You went fishing for information?" I betrayed a note of surprise. "You clever thing."

"I was trying to find out what I could about his family."

"So...?" I prodded her. "What did you discover?"

"Well, we couldn't really talk when his parents or aunt were there to overhear, but whenever I got the chance, I changed to more relevant topics." We had reached the road that led to Littleton Place, and she stopped to make sure that no cars were coming before pulling onto it. "All I could get Peter to admit was that his family had a lot of dark secrets. He says that even he doesn't know the full story, but there was all sorts of chicanery going on when he was tiny. If he ever knew what was behind it, he says he has forgotten."

I reflected on what cunning techniques she might have for extracting such information and decided not to think about it too carefully. It was good to see her so engaged with the case. It at least suggested that, however briefly, it had taken her mind off Gilbert.

"What about you?" she asked. "Did you discover anything useful through your reconnaissance?"

I was about to defend my frankly sparse findings when I remembered a story my father had once recounted. When he was a newly qualified solicitor, he'd defended a man whom he knew in his heart was innocent. He didn't have enough evidence to rule out his guilt but, desperate to see justice win out, Father found a way of speaking at great length on the case whilst saying very little of any substance. The jury were so bowled over by his vague but impressive speech that they came to trust him and ended up clearing his client of all charges. It was not a strategy he would employ again, but I hoped it might work for me now.

"I think, all in all, when you consider the various points and the key evidence we have accumulated over the course of the last week, what we must strive to define is what we are really trying to—"

"You haven't discovered anything of use then?" she interrupted with a look of satisfaction.

"That's going a bit far. I certainly have plenty of opinions on what's happened. The noose is very telling, wouldn't you say?"

"It might be." She looked a little mischievous in the moonlight before we once more plunged into the ominous darkness of that long tunnel of trees.

"I think it comes back to the discussion we had in the Alhambra Room. Whoever left the noose amongst the presents did so at short notice. Let's say he (or she, as Ursula may well be the culprit) heard Deirdre telling us about Felicity Mortimer and conceived of a way to make her shut her mouth. All the blighter had to do was find a rope and tie it into a noose, then steal a piece of tissue paper from another of the presents to wrap the thing up. It would only have taken a few minutes if you knew where to look... and how to tie the thing."

The car's headlights reflecting off the trees offered just enough light to show Bella nodding to herself. "That's quite possible, but there is another explanation." I waited for her to tell me what it was. "Deirdre came across as truly angelic at times this evening, especially when compared to her sister. We would be naïve to rule out the possibility that she knows just who we are and what we're doing here. It would explain why she was so eager to tell us about Felicity."

"So you're saying that she put the noose there in the library to suggest that she's not the person we're after?" I didn't wait for her to answer, as I'd already spotted a flaw in the theory. "It wouldn't have made a great deal of sense to invite us to her house in the first place if she knew we were investigating a crime she'd perpetrated."

She kept her eyes straight ahead as she navigated a bend. "Perhaps the whole thing was for our benefit. Perhaps she wants to send us off on the wrong path. She may even have invited her unbearable sister here so that we would think that Ursula was the mastermind."

"Surely it would have been a better defence simply to ignore us. If she really knows who we are and wishes to stop us finding out anything negative about her or her family, all she had to do was bar us from the property and there would have been nothing we could do."

The sound of the tyres crunching over gravel filled my ears for a moment before Percy yawned on the back seat. Knowing him, he would fall asleep fifteen seconds before we pulled up at the house, and I'd have to carry him to bed like a very heavy baby.

"I think a more likely scenario," I continued, "is that Deirdre was desperate to have you there tonight in order to show you off to her nasty sister. While it is our job to suspect anyone we meet, that does not make every last person in the world a criminal."

"I suppose you're right," Bella eventually conceded. "But something has clearly frightened the killer if he decided to hide a murder weapon in among Deirdre's birthday presents."

I don't like having to be the sensible one, but that role does sometimes fall to me. "The killer? Aren't you getting ahead of yourself? We don't know that Carleton Hobbes's death has anything to do with these people. Bertie told me that Hobbes had done countless jobs over the years. Perhaps his death is quite unconnected to Felicity Mortimer and it was just bad timing."

The car jerked forward and then back again as Bella pressed on the brakes. There were lights on in almost every room at the front of Littleton Place, and I could see her clearly as she fashioned her response. "Of course this is all connected, Marius." She pulled at the fingers of her driving gloves one at a time to loosen them. "Hobbes must have discovered something about the Stradbrookes or the Tanners. He was surely about to prove Felicity's innocence when the killer came for him. The house was set on fire to destroy the evidence he had of their moral turpitude."

Something about her choice of words, and the glimmer of obsession in her eyes, told me that she was using our case as a surrogate for the one we were unable to investigate. I could hardly blame her, so, rather than taking her to task, I reflected on something that had disturbed me all week.

"I can't help imagining what it was like for Felicity to move here when her husband's family were so very set against her. He was already in poor health. Deirdre disliked her from the start, and the best thing you can say about Ursula and her family is that they don't live close and wouldn't have been here too often."

For some reason, though the car's engine had been silenced, neither of us moved to leave. Bella looked up as though trying to search for the stars beyond the roof of the car. "If all that weren't bad enough, just think of their attitude when he became really ill and they suspected her of poisoning him."

Perhaps this was too horrible to spark any more discussion. We waited until Percy's snoring had become so loud that we couldn't ignore it any longer and then, silently, and with a head full of thoughts, I lugged him inside.

"I'm afraid my mistress is not at all well and is unlikely to see you tomorrow either, miss," Ainsworth appeared from below stairs to inform us as we crossed the wide entrance hall.

Though this was the least of her concerns, it seemed for a moment that the news would be too much for Bella. She looked truly distraught, and the stack of worries that had been growing day after day might have toppled over altogether if I hadn't answered for her.

"That is a great shame. We can only hope that she feels better on Sunday." I stepped in front of her – not to be rude, but simply to hide from the butler how downtrodden she looked.

It did the trick. Ainsworth didn't appear to notice anything. In fact, he smiled curiously and posed a question of his own. "I hope it's not impolite to ask, sir. Was your visit to Rhinefield House a success?"

I put Percy down and then led the man away by the shoulder, as though to confide in him. "No, no. It's not at all impolite." I ran one finger across the stubble on my jaw as I considered how to answer him without giving too much away. "We have certainly made some progress, and I believe that no one knows anything of our motives for coming."

He wobbled a little on the spot, as the very idea of our covert investigation was enough to excite him. "How fascinating. So what happens next?"

I looked about the entrance hall, but there was no one there to overhear us. "Let's just say that we will be going back to visit your neighbours at the first opportunity we get."

"Wonderful. That's wonderful." With a definite spring in his step, he turned to leave before remembering his duties. "If there is anything you should need during the night, there are bells in your rooms to call for assistance."

I nodded my gratitude, and he hurried away, perhaps to share the nugget of gossip I'd provided with his colleagues.

On any normal case, this would have been an obvious moment for Bella and me to exchange quips or an innocent barb. Instead, I kept quiet but offered her my arm for the short journey up to our bedrooms. She wasn't just distant: she was a hundred miles away. I could see that she was willing herself back to London to find that her fiancé hadn't been murdered after all and was waiting for her at home in his slippers and dressing gown – waiting to bid her goodnight before he retired. For her part, she did not bid me any such thing. She made the faintest sound as she slipped through the door into her room, and I didn't see her again until morning.

I went to sleep with ghosts that night: ghosts of the living and the dead. As I drifted off, I pictured Felicity in her cold and cramped prison cell, Gilbert in the final moments of his life as he trustingly followed his killer into my flat, and Bella as she'd glided into her bedchamber and forgotten all about me.

I woke before her and took breakfast in a comfortable nook downstairs. I sat looking over the extensive grounds of Littleton Place, eating buttered muffins and feeling thoroughly spoilt. I didn't like to consider what lay ahead of us – or how Bella would cope with an investigation that was forever on the precipice of failure – though, as it happens, I needn't have worried.

"I've come to a conclusion," she said when she found me enjoying a mug of tea and the warmth of the fire. She was terribly focused on the task before us, though not in the excited way she had been at times the night before. "I think that, whatever the reason that noose was given to Deirdre, we can use it to our advantage."

"Oh really?" I said without sharing my feelings on the matter.

She spoke fast and with great determination. "Yes, really. It's come to the point at which, if we wish to find the culprit, we can no longer hide why we're here. We must go to Rhinefield

House and tell the owners that we believe Deirdre is in danger. We'll tell them all about our endeavours over the last year, explain that we are well placed to protect them, and hopefully they won't throw us out on our ears."

"That," I said before dabbing at my lips with a napkin, "is a plan."

Bella was so het up that I thought she might want to sprint across to the neighbouring estate, so I was happy when I discovered that the Bentley was ready for us to drive. The Littleton Place chauffeur had washed and prepared the car for our really not very long trip next door. It sparkled in a brief burst of morning sunlight, and Percy was somehow already in place on the back seat. For a moment, I was worried that I had left him in there overnight, but I distinctly remembered placing him on a bench beside the fire in the entrance hall. He didn't beg for food, so I knew he'd been looked after by the staff.

He released a short, eager bark, and from the look on Bella's face, I half expected her to do the same. We accelerated away from the house, with the wheels of the car spinning on the gravel beneath us, and followed the path to the gloomy trees that pointed us sullenly off the estate.

Percy didn't lie down for once, or try to sneak a quick nap. He stood watching the road through the windscreen, with his head sticking through the gap in our seats. It only took a few minutes to reach Rhinefield House, and when Bella brought the car to a stop, my unusually motivated canine pushed forward so that he could leave through my door as soon as I'd disembarked.

The two of them marched purposefully towards the house, and I followed behind with the feeling that I was being swept along by an unexpectedly strong tide. I thought Bella might roll up her velvet sleeves and Percy would growl at whoever opened the door to show that they'd come there with a purpose and would not be dissuaded from their task.

Oddly though, no one had noticed our arrival. There was a

black metal bellpull in the porch, which Bella pulled accordingly, and then we listened to the sounds of the house. She was quite impatient, and kept her eyes fixed on the door, willing it to open.

"Are you perfectly all right?" I felt I should ask her, not for the first time that weekend, but then we heard footsteps, and she chose not to reply.

"Good morning, Lady Bella, Mr Quin," the same toffee-voiced butler from yesterday greeted us with something approaching fluster. "Do you have an appointment to see..." His words faded away, and it was clear that he was not himself. "Perhaps you should come in."

I was about to ask what had happened when there was a scream from somewhere deep within the house. It was not just a single note that you might hear when someone has a brief fright: it repeated over and over.

There were two young footmen in the hall and the attractive maid from last night's dinner beside them, but none of them appeared to know what to do as the lady's screams continued. The butler did nothing to direct us, so I ran along the corridor and up the right-angled staircase to the first floor, from where, I could only conclude, the distress emanated.

One featureless wooden corridor led to another, as Bella and Percy stayed close at heel. I caught the sound of men talking in loud, panicked voices, and then the screaming started once more. I'm not sure I've ever heard someone make such a noise for so long, and I had a feeling that it had to be Deirdre even before I reached her. I turned the corner to find an open doorway and half the household assembled just inside.

Dressed in a flowing pink negligée and satin dressing gown, Deirdre was kneeling at the foot of a large four-poster bed. Her husband was laid out on the floor in front of her, and I didn't need anyone to say it aloud to know that he was quite dead.

TWENTY-ONE

Arnold's brother-in-law Jim decided to pull the new widow away from the body.

"Come along, Dreary. There's nowt thee can do for him. Tha had best move back." He was not the sort of man who excelled at choosing reassuring words in a crisis.

Even as the poor woman's sons looked on, it fell to Bella to put an arm around Deirdre and usher her over to an armchair at a safe distance. To be perfectly honest, I think this served my friend just as well. From the way she looked at the corpse, I could tell that Bella was equally tormented by the scene.

I should probably mention that it wasn't the tone of his skin or a certain look about his wide-open eyes that told me Arnold was dead. There was a knife handle sticking clean from the left-hand side of his chest. Well, clean isn't the word for it, actually, as his checked shirt had turned as red as a postbox, and the blood had started to seep down onto the carpet beneath him.

Considering how well-kempt Arnold had been when we'd met him the day before, it was more than just his internal organs that were a mess. His previously neat hair and moustache looked as though they'd been slept on overnight, and he had creases on his face and forehead to suggest that he'd only recently woken.

"Who found him?" I asked when no one offered an explanation.

No one said anything. No one moved. It was almost as if they wished to preserve the scene exactly as it was until the relevant authorities arrived. Of course, that prompted another pertinent question.

"Has anyone telephoned the police?"

"The police?" Peter asked, as if I'd suggested we dance the Dashing White Sergeant or strip to our underwear and go for a swim in the nearest lake.

I took a few steps closer to gaze down at the body. "Yes, Peter, the police. It seems very unlikely that your father accidentally stabbed himself whilst cleaning his knife. And even if that was the case, it would be down to an inspector to rule out any more nefarious possibilities."

"You think he was murdered?" clever old Paul asked, then had to sit down opposite his mother as the reality of this sank in.

"Of course 'e were murdered, ya gawby!" His uncle had lost his cool and went striding across the room without purpose.

"Does anyone recognise the knife?" I thought I should ask before we went any further.

The only person who hadn't spoken yet – aside from Bella and the screaming widow – was the dead man's nephew. Neville was standing in the corner of the room with his hand over his mouth and a look of fear plain on his face. There was no sign of his mother, though I suppose she wasn't the sort of person to worry about other people's suffering. A scream down a hallway was unlikely to rouse Ursula from her morning tasks.

"Ah found the body," Jim finally answered, and I had to wonder whether all my questions would receive delayed responses. If I waited long enough, perhaps I'd learn that someone recognised the knife. "Ah were on m' way down t' breakfast when Ah noticed the door were open and saw a pair o' feet pointing up at t' ceiling. Ah wou'n't a looked inside if not."

My brain had switched to full detective mode, and practically everything everyone said for the rest of the day would sound suspicious to me. If I'd walked past a bedroom and seen someone lying on his back on the floor, I doubt that my first thought would have been to stick my head inside. But there was something even more urgent I had to address.

"Where were you at the time, Deirdre?" I turned to our hostess, but she wasn't really with us. She was still in her chair with Bella kneeling beside her, but in terms of her awareness of what was happening in that room, she was far from present.

"She weren't in here when Ah came," Jim explained. "Ah went to find a servant to tell 'em what 'ad 'appened, and she must have found poor Arnold while Ah were at it."

Deirdre did nothing to confirm or deny this story, though it did fit with what I'd seen. The servants had evidently known about the murder when we arrived, and it sounded as if Deirdre only just found out after the door was opened to us and the screaming began.

"What about you, Peter and Paul?" I really should have switched their names around. It sounded as though I was about to read them a bedtime story. "When did you arrive here and where had you been before?"

It was inevitably headstrong Peter who answered, and he really wasn't happy. "Are you suggesting what I think you are? Who are you to come here and accuse us of murdering our father?"

I'm sure he would have continued in this vein had Bella not interrupted him. "Marius happens to be a very capable detective." Her quiet response did little to soothe his temper, and so she told him something more pertinent. "By ruling out the possibility that you were involved, it will make it much easier to find the real killer."

He took a step back and ran his hand through his hair so that his long blond fringe was returned to its place behind his left ear. "It's obvious who killed him, isn't it?" He glanced about at his relatives, but when Jim and his son said nothing, he explained his thinking. "One of the servants must have done it. That's the only thing that makes sense."

"Why?" I could probably have fashioned a more complete response, but this summed up my thoughts rather neatly.

"Because they're poor. We know that none of us would have hurt Daddy. One of them obviously tried to steal his watch or what have you and was caught in the act."

"What absolute tripe!" Uncle Jim didn't take kindly to this conclusion, and it made me wonder about his path to riches.

Unexpectedly, to me at least, it was young Neville who would correct his furious cousin. "That's a terrible thing to say. You can't assume someone is a murderer just because he's poor. Most of your staff have worked at the house for years. Nanny Yapp has been here for decades! Are you saying that she could have murdered your father?"

"Not Nanny, obviously. I meant..."

I think that the truth of the matter became clearer for Peter just then. He calmed down a fraction and stepped back from the centre of the conversation. His brother, meanwhile, had begun to sob, and his sorrow woke their mother from her trance. She reached her hand out to him and suddenly she was the one doing the reassuring.

"There, there, my darling. There's no need to cry. This will all be a distant memory one day."

They truly were a fascinating family, and I felt that one of those famous brain doctors over in Switzerland or Austria or wherever such people reside could have done an intriguing study on the psychological identities of the various players. Deirdre had switched from shell-shocked mourning to doting mother in a second. The sudden change was striking, and

Bella wasn't going to miss the opportunity to put a question to her.

"I'm sorry to ask this, Deirdre, but where were you when Jim found your husband's body?"

There was another transformation as the sadness of her loss and the fact of her potential involvement in the murder came home to her.

Her lip trembled as she replied. "I was... I was in the bath." This word seemed to cause her even more pain and a great cry broke from her. "He was here getting dressed when I left him. When I returned half an hour later..." She couldn't finish the sentence, but we didn't need her to.

I looked at Arnold and considered whether I could work out when he'd been killed. I even crouched down to put my hand to his head and, though far from hot, there was still some warmth in him. He was dead but, to put it clumsily, I'd definitely seen deader men before. There was every chance he'd been murdered in the last half an hour. Not that this proved Deirdre was telling the truth.

"What are you people doing here?" Peter asked, finding his anger again. "I don't just mean this morning. Why did you come to this part of the world in the first place?" I watched as new doubts occurred to him. "And for that matter, how do we know that you aren't the ones who did this?"

I was about to answer his questions – a courtesy which had not been extended to me – when, to my genuine surprise, Paul came to my defence.

"Let them ask what they want, brother. It'll do the innocent no harm whatsoever." There was no arguing with this, and so he continued to explain what he knew. "I was in my bedroom when I heard a noise. That's why I came when I did." He paused to recall the scene. "Jim must have let out a cry when he found our father. As I arrived here, he came hurrying out looking quite distressed. He warned me not to go inside while he found someone to assist us, but I couldn't resist." His voice wavered then, and I thought he might cry. "I think I knew it would be Daddy even before I opened the door. Though he might not have seemed it on the surface, he was always the more vulnerable of our parents."

His mother shot up from her seat and pulled his head against her almost as if she were cradling a baby.

"I can confirm Paul's story," Neville muttered in a tiny voice from his spot in the corner. "I don't know where he was ten minutes before that, but I was sitting with him upstairs reading a book when we heard the commotion."

This sparked another significant question, but I was determined to hide my suspicions for the time being.

"I was with them," Peter suddenly decided. I didn't trust him for a second but, even when spontaneously making up this alibi, he spoke with that unwarranted confidence that so perfectly summed up his personality. "Tell them, brother."

Paul hesitated, and I could tell just what he was thinking. Was it worse to betray a sibling or lie in the middle of a murder investigation?

"That's right," he eventually replied in a half-hearted mumble. "I was with Peter and Neville up in my room. I was the only one to go downstairs. Neville continued reading his book. Peter... had his own concerns to consider, but they both came running when Mother screamed."

Even as he protected his wayward brother, he showed his disapproval. I wondered what Peter's concerns were that he had found so troubling. There was no time to ask, as someone had just rung at the front door.

TWENTY-TWO

"Would you believe it?" the inspector said as he went around the room shaking hands with everyone there. He was apparently unworried by what his stomping might do to any evidence. "I was visiting an old friend of mine in Brockenhurst village. I called up Scotland Yard on the off-chance something required my attention and here I am. I doubt five minutes passed between your butler calling the police and my arriving at your front door."

Inspector Falk was perhaps fifty years old but, in his soft rural accent, he spoke as if everything came as a great surprise. I was already curious how he would react when he found out what we were doing there.

"M' brother-in-law 'as been murdered, Inspector." Jim found his voice, having fallen noticeably quiet around the time Bella had mentioned I was a detective. "I'd like to know, what do tha plan to do about it?"

Falk fished into the inside pocket of his rather tatty suit. Finding nothing there, he moved on to the outer pockets and so on and so forth until he discovered what he needed. He was one of the most remarkably unremarkable men I'd ever met. His height, build and features were all very average and, were it not for his shiny head, with its few remaining strands of hair spread out like a fan atop the dome, I might not have been able to remember a thing about him.

"Here we are!" he exclaimed as he finally located a pencil in his trouser pocket. He then went on another adventure to find the small pad that was close to his heart (literally). "I plan, sir, to make careful notes on everything I learn here. A pencil and paper are a modern police officer's most important tools." He nodded a few times as if pleased with the sentiment and then turned to inspect the body.

There was already a rumbling of discontent from the dead man's family, but I was beginning to think that Peter was born discontented.

The confident inspector just ignored him. "A tricky case. I think I might struggle with this one," he muttered far too honestly and then, looking around the room, perhaps in the hope that he would stumble across a signed confession or someone with blood all over them, his eyes fell on me. "My goodness, you're him, aren't you!?"

I wasn't quite sure that I was, and so I shrugged and waited for him to explain.

"You're Quin! The detective I read about in the paper. Why, you've solved more crimes in the last year than I have in my whole career."

"I told you he was a good detective," Bella said to reinforce her previous claim, and I realised that she still hadn't mentioned her own part in our enterprise.

"And, oh my golly goodness! Lady Bella Montague, I cannot believe it!" The inspector was duly bowled over at meeting his apparent heroes, and this reaction led the others to take an interest in us once more.

"Then perhaps Marius should be investigating Father's murder," Paul suggested, and Neville stepped forward to agree.

"That sounds like a fine idea." He stopped to consider whether this was true. "Well, someone should be having a go. Aren't we wasting time even discussing it?"

Somehow, I had been elevated to the most authoritative person there. Falk looked at me with a quizzical expression which said, *Where would you like to start?*

I cleared my throat and did what I could. "Very well. I say that we must confirm the time of death, and then—"

"Time of death!" the inspector said, waving his pencil at me excitedly. "That's exactly what I was going to suggest."

"And then we should interview everyone in the house to find out where people were for the last forty minutes or so."

Falk clapped his hands together as though I'd said something quite brilliant. Bella looked a touch amused by our change in circumstances, but she said nothing.

"Perhaps your constables could get the basic facts from each of our suspects?" I asked the inspector, and he turned a little furtive.

"That is most definitely an excellent idea, Mr Quin." He walked over to shake my hand before admitting, "Though I will have to ring the local police station, as I haven't requested any constables yet. But leave it to me."

And with that, he turned and walked from the room.

"What a very strange man." Bella's eyes were as big as magnifying glasses, and she was evidently as confused as I was by what we'd just seen. To be frank, this was better than the panic I'd seen in her when we'd first entered the room. I'd been afraid the sight of the body might overwhelm her as it had our hostess.

I was about to issue orders to the suspects when Deirdre rose from her armchair, tossed the long skirt of her dressing gown behind her and declared in a beseeching voice, "You must find him, Marius Quin. You must please find my husband's killer."

Like a queen with her entourage, she glided from the room, and her two sons followed after her at a respectful distance.

Only Neville and his father remained, and I would have taken this opportunity to put some questions to them, but Jim started rattling off the answers I needed.

"Ah didn't kill him, tha knows. Arnold and Ah were from two worlds that rarely come together, but the truth is that, o'er the years, 'e's come to be m' friend."

He spoke very fast and, the more nervous he became, the more his Yorkshire accent emerged.

"No one is accusing you of murder just because you found the body," Bella reassured him, and then our first suspect pointed straight at me.

"Ma'bee not, but 'e were thinking it." I might have attempted to deny his claim, but he had proof. "I saw his face when Paul said what 'e and me lad 'eard from upstairs." He looked at me accusingly, as if I were cruel to think so poorly of him. "I'm no idiot. Thee reckons that the commotion weren't me finding the body but Arnold breathing his last. Thee reckons that Ah'm to blame. Don't ya, Quin?"

I don't know why I felt guilty about this, but I scrambled for an explanation. "I wouldn't take it personally, Mr Tanner. I think everyone is guilty until we can prove otherwise. It's the nature of any investigation."

His son stepped forward with one tentative hand stretched out. "What do you mean, Dad? Why would it matter what we heard?"

Jim took a deep breath before explaining. "It's nowt to worry yourself for, lad. Mr Quin over there had the mistaken idea that thi uncle weren't dead when Ah came in 'ere, but 'e were when Ah left. He thought that the sound that disturbed you were Arnold yelling out, not me."

A ripple of indignation travelled through the adolescent. "He wouldn't do that. Not my dad. He's a good man."

I would have loved to pounce on this comment, but Bella stepped forward to place herself between us. "People say that your mother is a good woman, too, but I can't say that she's struck me as particularly saintly."

It was interesting to watch the impact that this comment had on the two men. I swear they were more frightened by the mention of that grim figure Ursula than the threat that now hung over them as suspects in a murder.

"You may not have seen the best of her," Neville began, picking his words with great care, "but Mother always means well."

This was faint praise indeed, and so his father tried harder. "My wife 'as 'ad a tough life. Don't forget that she lost her brother. And it took us many years t' 'ave bairns of our own. All the failures and lost babies we 'ad 'urt her more than Ah can tell thee." He stopped himself then and, perhaps realising that his defence didn't go far enough, added one more point. "Nay but she's a canny wife and mother."

His son spun away from us and went to stand by the door. I don't believe it was just his desire to leave his dead uncle that sent him there; it was clear to me that his mother's misfortune had hung over him for years. Was this what drove Ursula to needle and criticise him all the time? Was he a disappointment after their first miracle children who came along? This seemed an unlikely explanation, but I had definitely heard her comparing poor Neville unfavourably to his older siblings.

"Well there's an obvious question that no one has yet asked." Bella's hair moved like liquid metal as she stepped into a rare ray of light that cut into the room. "Where was Ursula when her brother-in-law was murdered?"

TWENTY-THREE

Neville turned back to us with an apprehensive mien. I felt certain that he was about to reveal something significant, but his words died even before they reached his lips.

His father answered the question instead. "My wife were doin' what ladies do at this time o' day. She's not one for fuss nor gossip, which is probably the reason she ha'n't come to find out what t' noise were." Whatever fear Jim had previously shown, it had been replaced by the stirrings of his anger. "Now, if you've finished accusing m' family of terrible crimes, I think it's time we left."

"Thank you for your help," Bella said in the most polite yet perfunctory voice she could muster.

Unable or perhaps unwilling to tell us anything more, Jim grabbed his son by the arm and pulled him from the room.

"Well, this is a mess," I told Bella.

She didn't answer but went to look at poor Arnold. Her expression was filled with such sorrow and sympathy as she peered down at him that I was tempted to ask yet again whether she was all right.

"Just like every case we've investigated." Her voice was oddly steady and emotionless.

"Perhaps, but it feels as if we need to tie three crimes together over a fifteen-year period when we can't prove that any one has a bearing on the others."

We could have continued chattering for some time, but Bella decided to do something more useful. She put on the pair of gloves that she now apparently took wherever she went and, with a quick glance over her shoulder, went looking in the dead man's pockets for clues.

I would have worried that this could be seen as tampering with evidence, but I knew who Scotland Yard had put in charge of the case and decided she'd done the right thing. As is often the way at such moments, it was the last place she looked that held something worth finding. From his right trouser pocket, she fished out a small, bloodstained piece of paper and held it up between two fingers.

I had to walk closer to read the tightly scrolling handwriting. "*Holborn 1263*. We'll take it as read that this is a telephone number rather than a place in time."

"I think it's fair to assume." She looked rather happy at her discovery. "I had a friend who lived on Russell Square, and she had a Holborn number. I don't suppose this could belong to Carleton Hobbes?"

I was just as encouraged as she was. "I couldn't tell you, but I know several men who can."

She moved towards the door. "Ye of little faith, Marius. Just two minutes ago you were terribly glum and said we would struggle to connect the killings. You should have known that things would turn out well before long."

"I agree with you entirely, however there is something you've forgotten." I lingered in the middle of the room and pointed at the cooling corpse.

"Oh, yes?"

"No matter how permissive Inspector Falk is of our presence here, I think it would be better for us not to remove evidence from the scene of the crime."

"Oh, you're probably right." She glanced at the paper again then hurried back to hide it once more.

We left Arnold and Deirdre's bedroom, and my head was full of possibilities for what lay ahead of us on this increasingly curious case.

"Is the story already writing itself in your head?" Bella asked halfway along the corridor.

I couldn't help smiling. "Sadly, it's not one single tale. There are fifty of the things, and for the moment, the characterisation in each of them needs some work. The endings are hazy, too, and I haven't a clue how to link the mid-sections to anything else."

"Well, I've got a new thread for you, and I think you might like it." We'd come to the top of the closed wooden staircase, and she put one hand on my arm to keep me there. "It feels significant that, after the noose was given to Deirdre last night, her husband was the one to die today. Perhaps the pair of them knew about the murder in London and were threatened by the killer to keep quiet."

"I was working on the principle that Arnold killed Carleton Hobbes. Why else would he have the man's phone number in his pocket? He certainly behaved oddly when he learnt my name last night."

A maid appeared from behind us at this moment. It was the same fair-faced girl who'd attended us at dinner the night before. Far from bowing her head and hurrying discreetly past us as most servants would, she cocked her chin back confidently and continued along the corridor. The look seemed to say, *I know what the pair of you are up to.* I was tempted to tell her otherwise, but she disappeared too soon.

Bella was not distracted and answered without hesitation.

"That would suggest the family is full of killers when surely one single culprit is more likely. And besides, if Arnold were to blame for Hobbes's death, why would anyone have killed him?"

"There are all sorts of reasons," I said, then took a moment to consider whether this was true. "Perhaps someone here knew the victim and sought revenge. Or perhaps Arnold and Deirdre know the same incriminating information that got Hobbes killed. The killer threatened one of them, and when that wasn't enough, he murdered the other. Or perhaps this whole affair is simpler than we first considered." I'd moved away from her hypothesis by this point, but she looked eager to hear what I would say. "Maybe Deirdre killed her husband, then jumped in the bath to wash away the blood. She could have been the one to leave the noose with her presents before she came to distract us with talk of Felicity in the Alhambra Room."

"Isn't that what I suggested last night, and you said was impossible?" For a moment, she looked like Bertie when I'd forced him to read an early draft of one of my books. "And where does Carleton Hobbes fit into any of that?"

I was fairly confident that I was about to amaze her with my interpretation of the evidence, but whatever clever idea had entered my mind flew clean out again. "I really don't know. As I've already told you, the story I'm piecing together needs a lot of work. There is one thing of which I'm certain, though."

"Amaze me," she said as if she could hear my very thoughts.

"The person who is most likely to know what's been happening to this family is Ursula Tanner, and she's the only one of them who hasn't made an appearance since Arnold was killed."

"Brilliant. So how do we find her?"

If I were a real detective, I'd have a wise yet ever-so-discreet retainer who could provide vital information like this in a flash. As it was, Bella and I hadn't decided which of us was the main sleuth and which the assistant, so, the only option we had was to descend the stairs and look for a member of staff. Before this could happen, there were some less useful people to meet.

"Excuse me, Nanny," I asked the doddery old lady who had nursed various children in the family and now haunted the halls of Rhinefield House. "I don't suppose you could tell us where Mrs Tanner has her quarters when she stays here?"

She was sitting on a polished wooden bench in a shadowy spot beside the front door. She couldn't have been less than eighty, but she reminded me of a little girl nervously waiting to discover her punishment for putting a frog down her teacher's back.

"I don't suppose I could," she said matter-of-factly. "I have strict instructions not to tell anyone anything, and I must say that I'm doing a very good job of it. I've rarely been so suited to a task."

"Who told you not to tell anyone anything?" Bella asked, perhaps optimistically.

"I couldn't possibly say, but the first rule of working in a family like this one is never to share secrets."

"You shared Felicity Mortimer's secrets," I reminded her.

She closed her mouth tightly, and I didn't think she would say another word. Eventually, a mumbled, "I don't know who that is," escaped her lips.

I considered asking her a further question, but I doubted it would help.

"Thank you so much, Nanny." I gave her a respectful (though slightly sarcastic) bow just as the inspector appeared with four perfectly smart constables in tow.

They marched into the house in a line and tipped their helmets to me in perfect synchronism. As we were in a part of the English countryside which isn't known for its high levels of crime, I could only assume that they had a lot of time to practise such flourishes.

"Right you are, men," Falk told them once they'd fallen into a neat row at the bottom of the stairs. "The coroner is on his way to examine the body and establish the time of death. You're to talk to everyone in this house about where they were and whether anyone else can confirm it."

All eyes turned to us, and so the inspector added a caveat. "Except for them. They're on our side." He gave us a cheery wink. He was a very odd man indeed.

"Perhaps you could also confirm the whereabouts of each suspect at the time of the murder on Tuesday this week of a man named Carleton Hobbes," Bella suggested, and the inspector looked grateful for her contribution.

"How interesting, miss. Do you believe there could be a connection between the crimes?"

"There might well be."

I decided to offer a few relevant details. "Hobbes was murdered at one in the afternoon on Tuesday in Queen Square, London. It would help if you could establish and confirm any alibis not just for the staff but also the guests and people who live here."

"You heard the gent, get to it." The officers filed away, and their superior rubbed his hands together as he walked closer. "Have you discovered anything that might lead us to the killer?"

Bella glanced at me, and I told him of our first real clue. "We found something on the body."

"You went looking through the pockets of a man who had just been murdered?" He sounded alarmed by this, and I thought perhaps we'd underestimated him. The feeling didn't last long. "I should really have done that myself!" He removed his pad from his pocket and began to scribble down a note. I know that was what he was writing as he read it aloud as he did so. "Must remember... not to get distracted by ... my swift arrival at... scene of crime... and forget basic tasks." Putting it away again, he added. "You'll have to forgive my excitability. This is my first murder in rather a long time."

"We found a telephone number," Bella told him as soon as he'd put the pad back in its place with a satisfied nod. "We believe it could belong to a man called Carleton Hobbes who was murdered near Russell Square. That's why we asked your men to confirm the suspects' alibis. But we'll need you to check the telephone number."

"Wonderful!" He clapped his hands this time. "I will be certain to do that very thing."

Without waiting another second, he sprinted across the hall and up the staircase in search of the number that we knew off by heart. He obviously wished to support us in any way he could, and I already realised that I should only give him instructions once I was ready for him to carry them out.

Bella and I were getting used to Falk's eccentricity and continued with our task as if nothing had happened. We soon found the butler, who helpfully directed us to the western wing of the building and up a different flight of stairs. It was simplicity itself to stroll along a corridor, knock three times on the door to Ursula Tanner's bedroom and answer the shouted question that came back to us.

"Who's there?"

"It's Lady Bella Montague," my companion replied in a terribly formal and correct voice even for her. "We'd like to talk to you about the events of this morning."

There was some huffing and complaining from inside and I thought, perhaps, that Ursula had stubbed her toe. Despite this, I still expected the door to swing open and for the grumpiest person at Rhinefield House to grant us admission. That is not what would happen.

She muttered to herself for a little longer, then called, "I have no wish to speak to you. Goodbye."

TWENTY-FOUR

Mrs Tanner was evidently smarter than any of the killers we'd met before. She had realised that the best way to avoid incriminating oneself in a murder investigation is to refuse to talk to the upstart detectives who have stuck their noses into it. In order to go about killing another human being in the first place requires a certain amount of arrogance. Each of the culprits we'd encountered before that day must have thought that they could dupe and manipulate us into believing that someone else was to blame. They were wrong, and Ursula was wise not to try.

As I stood outside that firmly shut door, I couldn't decide whether this made her the most likely candidate to have killed her brother-in-law, but I did know that there was nothing we could do to make her talk to us.

That didn't stop Bella from trying to persuade her otherwise. "There is a very serious situation, Mrs Tanner, and we believe you can help."

"I am not interested," Ursula responded rather dismissively. "Now if you would please leave me alone, I..." She paused to think of an excuse and failed. "Well, as I've already stated, I do not wish to talk to you."

"But..." Bella began, and I stepped in to prevent her from knocking again.

"Give up, Bella. She's not going to say anything unless she has to. We'll come back later with the inspector. In the meantime, we're better off speaking to another of the suspects."

I'm sure she would have argued with me next, but I heard a sound from further down the corridor and followed it before she could disagree. It was an unusually happy and out of place noise, not least for occurring so shortly after a man had been killed.

I came to a stop in front of a door that was illuminated by a small window at the end of the hall. Before disturbing whoever was inside, I decided to put my ear against the thick oak to listen.

"... always been that sort of person, don't you think? I remember when we were children, and he made us take a holiday in Brighton as he felt the sea air would be good for us. It rained the whole time we were there, and he refused to leave the hotel." There was more laughter, and I could already tell that this was not the sinister sound of conspirators plotting; it was too light and nostalgic for that. "I'll never forget the sight of him with his trousers and sleeves rolled up, sitting in the hotel sun lounge trying to enjoy the gloom of an English summer's day."

"Or the time he took us all out to show off his ability at map reading." This was almost definitely Peter talking... or his brother. The door was quite thick. "He got us lost in the space of an hour and we needed Neville's skills as a boy scout to direct us back to the car."

This really sent them into hysterics, and I decided that it would be safe to knock on the door.

"Come in?" a softer voice replied, and I think I recognised Paul's slightly cheerier tones.

Bella arrived alongside me, and I opened the door. The

looks on the faces of Peter, Paul and their cousin Neville suddenly changed, and I was certain that they felt guilty to have been found in such a jovial mood so soon after Arnold had been killed.

"It's not what you think," Peter was quick to assure me.

"How do you know what I think?"

His brother came to his defence. "He means that we were only reminiscing about our father. The fact we were laughing shouldn't suggest that we are unaffected by his death."

I decided not to say anything. I could tell that this would unsettle them more than any retort I could make.

"They're telling the truth." Neville had a pleading tone of voice at the best of times but now sounded desperate for us to believe them. "We were telling stories about poor Uncle Arnold to cheer ourselves up. He was a wonderful uncle to me."

"You can say what you like." Bella sounded so confident then that it was hard to imagine she had gone through a similar experience to the Stradbrookes just days earlier. "But your behaviour is far from normal less than an hour after a brutal murder."

Peter's anger flared, much as I had expected it to. "Just because we're not weeping like old maids at a funeral, that doesn't mean we're not mourning him." He really wasn't the nicest young man.

Paul was once more called upon to make his brother seem more reasonable. "What my brother is trying to say is that we loved Father. We really did."

Neville seemed to be forever on the outside of any situation and sat apart from his cousins, who were lounging on the floor beside a messy pile of books.

I still didn't answer but walked further into the small sitting room and sat down in an armchair. It was a leather Chesterfield, in laurel green that matched the floor-length curtains over the windows. There was a bureau plat in one corner, and the place smelt of books and old wood. It was a rather sedate, old-fashioned sort of room and, at a push, I would have guessed that this was Paul's domain rather than his brother's.

Bella leaned with one elbow on the bookshelf beside the door, as though uncertain whether to stay or go. "That may be, but Marius has investigated several different murders this year, and laughter is not the usual accompaniment."

"Then it's a good thing we all have alibis for the time at which Father was murdered." Peter fixed his eyes on the (obviously) wooden floor. "We are not the types to fuss and cry."

"Neither was Father," Paul added in a melancholic tone that rather contradicted what his brother had just said.

"He certainly seemed like a restrained sort of person," Bella conceded, having switched to her usual, friendly persona. "It must have been odd growing up with two such very different parents."

Peter sneered, Paul attempted a smile, and Neville was clearly wondering whether he should be present for such a private conversation.

When her sympathy sparked no further response, Bella tried to be more direct. "Your mother is obviously a blunter instrument than your father was. Do you think that left a mark on you?"

"I'm sorry, Bella." There was nothing apologetic in Peter's manner. "But you clearly think that by leading us around in circles, we'll end up saying something that shows who the killer really is. I've already told you; we were together at the time that Dad was murdered. None of us could be to blame, so you had better go and investigate the third footman, who's only been here for a few months, or the gardener with a squint, as we are not—"

"You don't all have alibis," I interrupted him.

"I beg your pardon?" The look on his face could have turned a man to ice.

"I said that you don't have an alibi for the time at which your father was stabbed to death." If anything, my response made the room even colder. "You got carried away when we spoke to you earlier. Instead of forcing your brother to say that the two of you were together at the time of the killing, you secured an alibi for the time at which the body was discovered. You really should have been more careful."

Peter looked terrified. He certainly hadn't been so distressed when standing beside his father's body. "It doesn't change anything, I—"

Before he could talk his way out of the situation, I turned to Paul. "Where were you at nine o'clock? Based on what I saw of your father's corpse, that was the approximate time of death – some twenty minutes before Jim found the body."

Paul didn't dare look at his deceitful brother. He knew that he had a reprieve from his earlier dilemma and could now tell the truth without going against Peter's will. "I left Neville reading in my bedroom and went for a walk in the grounds. My brother and I had... Well, the truth is that we had argued. I was in a stinking mood and went to get some fresh air."

I could hear the steam building in Peter's head, but I wouldn't address him yet. "What about you, Neville? Was Peter still in Paul's bedroom at that time?"

Now it was the cousin's turn to hesitate. His eyes flicked to the most sympathetic person there, and Bella silently urged him to tell the truth.

"No, he wasn't with me. I get lost in my reading very easily and barely noticed, even when Paul returned to his room after Uncle Arnold was killed."

This was interesting, but there was no time to chart the course of Paul around the Rhinefield grounds, or interrogate Neville further, as Peter was about to explode.

"You swine, Quin. You come to our house on the darkest of days to accuse me of this barbarity." He was up on his feet and swinging his arms around like a bad actor. "You really are the lowest of the low, and I won't—"

"Calm down, please, Peter," Bella intervened. "No one is accusing you of murder. We simply wish to find the killer." She was a genius at making our probing sound innocent. "It's in your own interests to tell us exactly what happened."

Her words had done the trick. Though, at first, he gripped the back of Neville's chair so tightly that I thought it might break, Peter soon sighed and appeared to relent.

"Very well, I was all alone when Father was murdered, which means I will now suffer everyone's suspicion. Had he died when I was downstairs having breakfast, then my life would be a lot simpler."

I considered telling him that, had he been upstairs at the right time to stop the killer's knife, his father's life might have been spared, but he wasn't the type to worry about other people, and I wasn't the type to interrupt Bella when she was working her magic.

"Thank you for your honesty, Peter." She paused for a moment, and I noticed that Paul shook his head just the tiniest bit. "Could you tell us where you actually were at the time?"

"I was..." He swallowed then, and it was hard to say whether this gave him the time he needed to think up another lie or he was struggling to come to terms with the truth. "I went to my room."

This really piqued his brother, who had to bite his lip to silence himself.

His reaction provided me with my next question. "What did you and Paul argue about that sent you off in different directions?"

Brother looked at brother, and I could see the struggle between them. It spoke of an imbalance that had lasted for years. Paul was sensible and studious, if a little naïve, whereas Peter was showy and smug. One was the type to fall constantly into scraps and scrapes but get out unscathed. The other had his every move appraised by their proud mother.

"This is ridiculous," Neville finally intervened when neither would answer. "Are you really willing to incriminate yourselves in a murder to hide some petty secret?"

Peter's gaze switched to focus on his cousin. "You know it's not that simple."

"Can't you take our word for it that it's not important where Peter was?" The sadness in Paul's voice suggested that he already knew the answer. "He's not a violent person. I promise."

Bella looked a mite flabbergasted by the idea. "I'm afraid that's not how murder investigations work. You can't tell a police officer that, while you admit to keeping potentially damaging secrets, you promise that they are unrelated to any criminal activity." She let out a long, harried breath before softening her approach. "Listen to Neville and tell us what you were really doing this morning – and why you argued with your brother, for that matter."

The brothers stared at one another again before Paul turned away. I took this to mean that whatever Peter was about to tell us would be a lie.

"The truth is that my brother is angry with me because I got drunk and drove his car into a hedge."

"And why would you lie about that, you dimwit?" Can you tell that I was beginning to lose my patience?

Peter still wouldn't yield to common sense. "If you don't believe me, go down to the garage and ask Father's chauffeur to show you the Napier T75 that was in an accident on the way home from London this week."

"You're more of a fool than I imagined if you expect us to believe that."

As his ruse had failed, he tried to look hard done by. "But it really is there. I'm not making it up. I drove Paul's car, but I'd had two drinks too many, and he was furious with me. Isn't that right, brother?"

I felt too sorry for Paul by this point to let him answer – not just because he now found himself in the awkward position of having to confirm these half-baked stories, but for having a brother like Peter in the first place.

"Good liars weave their falsehoods into the truth," I said to rescue him. "I imagine you did crash the car, but your explanation doesn't make any sense because there is no reason for you to hide such a petty fact from us. I'll ask you one last time, Peter, why did you and Paul argue this morning?"

A stillness took hold of the room. I, for one, didn't move a muscle as Peter attempted to work out how to get out of the hole he'd dug. In the end, someone did it for him.

"This is too much," pale-faced Neville rose from his chair to exclaim. "He doesn't want to answer because he's more frightened of his mother disowning him than he is of being suspected of murder."

The at least guilty-seeming, if not outright guilty, Peter was only a foot away but yelled his response. "Don't say it!"

It was enough to make Neville doubt himself. It was too late to hide the secret now, though. I knew what it was.

"You were with a woman, weren't you?" I dared guess, but Bella could already go one step further.

"You don't wish your mother to know that you were with a young lady who is below your social standing." She pushed her silky black hair behind one ear as she considered the inevitable extension of this theory. "It must be the maid who served our dinner last night."

Paul and Neville looked suitably impressed by her reasoning, while Peter was knocked backwards. When he managed to free his tongue to speak again, he could only murmur rather pathetically, "Who are you people, and how can you read minds?"

Bella tried not to show how pleased she was with her own deduction. "The poor girl stared at you every time you and I spoke, and there was nothing accidental about the wine she spilt at the end of the evening. Was she warning me not to get too close to you?"

"No, it's just... You could never understand."

"Oh, I think we do," I couldn't resist telling him as I sat back in my comfortable armchair.

"I don't mean you can't understand what has happened between Emily and me. I'm talking about my parents. If Mother knew what we were doing, she would..." His voice trailed off before an unexpected declaration burst out of him. "I love Emily! Is that what you want to hear? I love her, and we were together when my father was killed, but neither of us can say anything because..."

He fell silent, apparently stunned, and I turned to his brother instead. "So this is what you were suggesting when we spoke to you earlier. These are the concerns that you said were occupying your brother."

The sweeter of the two siblings hung his head in shame. "I wasn't trying to get him in trouble, if that's what you imagine." This was not what I'd been thinking... until now, at least. "I was just angry that he'd made me lie for him when I would never normally do such a thing – and angry he'd started this ridiculous liaison in the first place."

"I love her!" Peter shouted over him, and I believe we were all clear on this point by now.

I don't know about most people, but when reading a mystery novel, I tend to fix on one culprit early on. The same thing can happen during our investigations, but this time the obvious culprit kept shifting. When I'd met Felicity, she'd made it seem as if her sister-in-law Deirdre was behind the conspiracy against her. On arriving at Rhinefield House, it was Ursula who seemed to hold the power. Her nephew Peter was devious enough to have killed Carleton Hobbes and his own father, but now I was forced to wonder whether his brother was the one pulling the strings. And just for good measure, I decided not to overlook their bookish cousin.

Right you are! Let's say that Neville did it. All we needed now was any proof whatsoever.

Paul hadn't finished unburdening himself. "The fact is that I argued with Peter because I can't stand such lying and subterfuge. He went to see Emily, and I stormed off to feel a little less gloomy about the world."

"And I continued reading my book," Neville added, then jabbed the cover of the weighty volume he held.

Peter must have seen his chance to deflect attention away from himself as he pounced on this comment. "That's hardly an alibi, Nev."

"Perhaps not, but I imagine you've never been forced to read dry philosophical texts like *Leviathan*." He looked rather sad about his task. "The one good thing I can say about it is that it is marginally shorter than the volume by Jeremy Bentham I have to read after this. Mother gave me a big pile of books and says I have to finish them before the end of the month, but they're all so abstract that I have to read each sentence seven times to make any sense of it."

Bella bit her lip, and I knew she'd realised something important. "This is your sitting room, isn't it, Neville?"

It took me a moment to realise how she would have guessed this, but we knew that the three boys had previously convened in Paul's room, and I suppose she couldn't have imagined Peter choosing to spend time in such a worthy (yet dusty) place.

Neville gulped before answering and evidently didn't like the light that was now shining on him. "That's right. My aunt kindly allowed me a space of my own here."

"And when we arrived," she continued, "you had just left to

collect your parents from the railway station. Do you live here at Rhinefield House?"

That tome fell from his hand onto the floor in front of him. For a moment, he was a caricature of an excessively nervous adolescent, of the kind you might find in *Punch* or another of the more satirical magazines. "I... I don't exactly live here. My school isn't too far away, and so I come to visit from time to time. I don't get on well with my supposedly perfect older siblings – my mother never stops comparing me to them – but when I'm here no one bothers me."

This was a sensible enough reason, but we were getting far from the heart of the case, and so I decided to take control. "That's all very interesting, but there's something far more important that we are yet to discuss." I paused to make them nervous. "What can you tell us about Felicity Mortimer?"

TWENTY-FIVE

For a moment, the three young men fell silent. It was hard to say whether the very name had shocked them, they'd never heard of this person, or they were unwilling to share what they knew.

It would require another prompt from Bella to get them to speak. "We have discovered evidence which could link Arnold's death to that of your uncle fifteen years ago."

Paul looked quite awestruck. "You mean that whoever killed Father killed Uncle Richard?"

"It's possible," I said before taking the time to consider his point. "But there's also a strong chance that your uncle wasn't murdered. I believe that your aunt should never have been sent to prison."

Neville pushed his thick, black-framed glasses further up his nose, but he said nothing.

"I've had enough now," I finally told them. "We've been in here for far too long without any of you telling us the slightest thing that relates to the case. The way I see it, if the staff can be ruled out as suspects, the only people who could have killed Arnold this morning were the three of you and your parents.

One of you must know something. So you had better talk, or I'll send for the inspector."

This sounded like quite the ultimatum, and I wasn't about to tell them that the man charged with investigating Arnold Stradbrooke's death was only a little more useful than a paper jacket in a rainstorm.

The cousins exchanged glances as if to say, *Perhaps the time has come.*

Peter was the first to speak. "Our parents rarely talk about her."

"My mother won't let them," Neville added. "I hadn't been born when Uncle Richard died, so I've never really understood the story, but I know that Aunt Felicity isn't popular here."

"We all know that." Bella's tone was stern now. "But the man who tried to overturn your aunt's conviction died in a fire in London this week. We believe that his phone number was in Arnold's pocket when he was killed."

"Carleton Hobbes was—" I started to speak but Paul interrupted.

"I read that name in Father's paper. Wasn't he murdered?"

Still lingering by the door, as if she wished to escape, Bella looked at me to confirm that we should disclose even this simple fact.

"That's right. I found the body," I answered. "His throat had been slit before the killer set the house alight."

"What has any of this got to do with our father?" Paul demanded in a guileless manner as he poured himself a glass of water from a carafe on the table beside him.

"That's what I need you to explain. Have any of your parents revealed what happened all those years ago?"

Peter was a touch less evasive than before. "I've spent my whole life wondering about it. A murder in a family leaves a mark, you know."

His brother was next. "The thing is, Mother is the only one

who ever talks about Uncle Richard. He was living here at the time he died, and the whole sorry affair affected her a great deal."

"Because she was involved in framing her sister-in-law for the crime or because she misses her brother?" I could probably have chosen my words more carefully, but this was no time for discretion.

The three of them kept their eyes on me then. Even Neville, without his mother there to barrack him, looked more confident and he soon gave his view on the matter. "I've rarely heard my parents mutter that woman's name. Aunt Deirdre is more vocal on the topic, of course, but she mainly talks about what a monster Felicity was... or *is*, maybe. Is she even still alive?"

"She is. Prison may change people, but it takes a long time to kill them outright these days. I went to see her myself this week."

Paul was most impressed by this. "You met our mysterious aunt?"

His brother, meanwhile, was unnerved by the admission. "So then that's what brought you here. You're not friends of our neighbours. You're just poking about in other people's business, like journalists or spies."

"You're wrong," Bella began, before clarifying her response. "I've known your neighbours since I was a child. My father is a close friend of Lord Verlaine's, and we came here because an injustice has been done. There is little evidence that your aunt murdered her husband. Everything we have discovered suggests that there was a conspiracy to find her guilty. What we don't know is who was behind it."

They looked between themselves once more, and I wondered whether they were all terribly good actors, or they knew just as little of the affair as they claimed.

"We can't help you." Paul spoke when the others couldn't. He had a low, plaintive voice, and I almost felt sorry for him for coming from such a family. "Peter and I were toddlers at the time and have no memory of her. Neville wasn't yet born. And if anyone here plotted against the woman, they've never told us about it."

This was easy enough to say, but I wanted to know more. "That doesn't mean you don't have an opinion on why two people who were connected to the case have been slain. Why would anyone kill both Carleton Hobbes and your father?"

There were more blank faces, but Paul had clearly been raised to oblige his guests and didn't like to leave my questions unanswered. "What do you want us to tell you? Father was a kind man; he had no enemies, and I can't imagine that anyone in the family wanted to hurt him. Even if he were somehow responsible for an innocent woman going to gaol – which I still very much doubt – that doesn't explain why one of his closest relatives would have killed him."

This was the dilemma we were facing. A murder in the family is always... well, usually hard to imagine, though we couldn't rule out any of the most likely suspects.

Bella maintained her gentle manner to conclude the discussion. "We're not looking to hurt you or your family. But there is a killer on the premises, and he must not go unpunished." She could be so authoritative when necessary, and I felt that her words had more impact on them than anything I had said.

She nodded to show that she'd finished, then motioned for me to follow her from the room. For approximately half a second, I was relieved to escape, but the hallway was oppressively dark, and the case was starting to overwhelm me.

"It feels as if we are moving back and forth between suspects without ever finding out anything for certain."

"Don't be so grim, Marius. We've barely started."

I took a step closer to her, if only to make out the lines of her cheeks in the darkness. "That doesn't change the fact that, beyond a near-senile former nanny, the only suspects are from the same family. They could all be telling lies to protect one another."

Rather than indulge my pessimism, Bella walked further along the corridor and began trying different doors.

"What are you doing?" I stayed behind to ask.

The first opened and she peered inside. "That's just the airing cupboard."

She moved off to try the next one, so I strode after her. I arrived just in time to see a messily organised chamber with a pile of clothes on a chair by the bed and a large pile of books on the floor.

"I would imagine that this is where Neville sleeps. It smells of boy."

"What are you hoping to find?" I asked but, seeing as she hadn't answered my previous question, I wouldn't hold out hope this time.

She moved to the next door and did the same. She found a silver room, complete with a perplexed-looking footman who was hard at work with cloth and polish, a bathroom, which was thankfully unoccupied, and a small study with paintings of long-dead family members covering practically every inch of the wall.

When we reached the far end of the house, she shed some light on her task. "We know that Richard, Felicity and their children were living here when he died, so it stands to reason that..." The door handle upon which she had just placed her hand wouldn't turn. "...this must be it."

I tried the next one with the same result. In fact, there were five rooms arranged around the end of the corridor that would not open. "You think that this is where they lived all that time ago?"

"We'll need the keys to find out." She was energised once more, and I realised that it had been at least an hour since she'd looked despondent over Gilbert. Who would have thought she would require a new pair of murders to take her mind off the previous one?

On cue, our ever-eager public servant arrived. "Mr Quin, Lady Bella, I have some important information to share with you," Inspector Falk revealed.

"You've found out to whom the telephone number belongs?" Bella asked a little too optimistically.

"Not quite, but the operator called it and there was no answer." He stood for a moment, silently awaiting the praise that wouldn't arrive. "The operator was not able to tell me who owns the line."

I bit my tongue, and so Bella composed herself to reply. "And you didn't think of speaking to her bosses to find out?"

The inspector played with his shirt buttons as he replied. "I did indeed, and I am expecting a call with the answer. That wasn't what I came to tell you, though. The news I wish to share is that, except for a maid by the name of Emily Smith—"

"With whom Peter claims to have been at the time," I felt I had to interrupt to explain.

"In which case, all staff were accounted for in the half an hour prior to James Tanner finding the body. Furthermore, they were also here at home on Tuesday when Carleton Hobbes was murdered. Further furthermore, the coroner has confirmed Arnold Stradbrooke's time of death as being very close to nine o'clock. To me, this suggests that the killer must be a member of the family... or that mad old nanny."

"Well done, Inspector," Bella humoured him. "You've done an excellent job."

He looked expectant once more, and much as if I were addressing my dog, I felt that he needed me to gee him on, too. Before I could give him a pat and tell him what a good job he'd done, something popped into my head.

"My goodness, I haven't seen Percy for hours. I hope he's all right." Admittedly, I was also wondering whether Peter's girlfriend Emily had been involved in the murder of Carleton Hobbes. She might well have wanted to kill him to get on the family's good side, but if that was the case, why murder the father?

Falk moved closer and spoke confidentially. "Never fear there, sir. Your hound was in the Great Hall the last time I saw him. I have set a footman to watch him. I thought it wise given the circumstances."

"Oh, yes, of course..." I muttered, unsure which circumstances these were. Did he imagine that the killer would target Percy next?

The well-meaning fellow was genuinely eager to help, and there was one small task he could do for us.

"We need a key to these doors," Bella told him. "We believe that these rooms belonged to the—" Presumably realising that it would take too long to explain, she changed her mind. "We believe that it will be useful to look inside. But please go about your task without alerting anyone in the family. We don't want to catch the killer's attention."

"I will get right to it!" he responded, then ran away again before I could ask him to keep us up to date on Carleton Hobbes's telephone number.

"Blast! I'll have to do it myself."

I walked back along the corridor to the study where I'd noticed a telephone on the wall. A minute later, I was connected to Bertie back in London.

"Is Carleton Hobbes's telephone number Holborn 1263?" I asked, then heard my editor bumbling about his office in search of the information we needed.

"1263? Yes, you've hit the bullseye."

"Well, that was easy," Bella muttered beside me, and I put one finger to my lips to shush her.

"I've been wondering about something else, too, Bertie." A thought had only just occurred to me, and I would need a moment to know how to phrase the question. "Am I right in thinking that you told him that we were coming to visit that day?"

There was a brief pop on the line and then his crackly voice came back to me. "I certainly did. I telephoned in advance to ask whether he would be free. He was happy to know what you'd been up to after all he did to help that woman." Even now, he couldn't hide a note of disapproval when he mentioned Felicity.

"Thank you, old friend. You've been very helpful."

"Marius, is everything all right with the two of you? Is your investigation going as you hoped?" He always turned on the concern when it mattered.

"In the sense that there's only been one dead body discovered today, which is fairly low by our standards."

He soon perked up again. "Wonderful. Then I hope to see you back at my office within the week with new chapters of *Murder at Pemblewick Manor*."

Sadly, I hung up before we could discuss this further.

Bella was quick to draw her conclusions. "So it *was* Hobbes's phone number in Arnold's pocket? The two killings are definitely linked."

"Did you ever doubt that was the case?"

I opened the door to the study and Bella walked through ahead of me as she made a suggestion. "Our conversation with the three young gentlemen didn't get us far, so we must talk to their parents before they make it even more difficult for us to solve the case."

A smile spread across my face then. "I was about to say the same thing. Perhaps we should find Inspector Falk. He might have to convince Ursula Tanner to speak to us."

Even as I said this, I heard raised voices, and we made our way to the room of the woman who had been absent all morning.

"We must admit what 'appened," I heard her husband exclaim in his usual direct manner. "It's the only option now that Arnold's dead."

"The only option?" Ursula replied, the incredulity apparent in her voice. "Yes, I suppose it is if we wish to *destroy our family*!"

Bella and I both held our breath so as to hear what they were saying. I caught the sound of footsteps and concluded that Jim had crossed the room to speak to his wife.

"But our family is already fractured, Ursula. Three of our bairns 'ave 'ad nowt to do with us for months. As for Neville, the poor lad—"

"That's enough!" These two words were delivered at such a volume and with such authority that they made me take a step back from the door. They gave way to silence before Jim made one more attempt to convince his wife.

"What we did were wrong and it has consequences. If you're not willing to admit it, then perhaps Ah will. Ah've lived with our mistake for years. Ah may not entirely regret it, but Ah will do what it takes to—"

"You'll do nothing of the sort." Ursula's high and haughty voice killed the conversation, and we would hear no more. Instead, the sound of movement travelled out to us, and we both turned to run away.

TWENTY-SIX

"They're guilty," Bella told me when we found our way to a secluded spot in the gardens.

"Yes, but of what exactly?"

There was a long narrow pool of water which cut across the patio from the house. It was covered with lily pads and brightly coloured fish swam lengths to and fro. Alongside it, elegantly arranged flowerbeds displayed autumnal plants and, in the distance, I could see a team of gardeners tidying a plot beside an ornamental stone temple. If we'd had time to spare, I would have liked to explore the gardens better, but there were more important things to see to just then.

"If they didn't kill Arnold and Carleton Hobbes, they must surely know something about it."

I paused to consider her point. "I'm not convinced that anything we overheard proves that. Perhaps they are afraid that, now Arnold is dead, they could be next."

Bella strode across to a bench that faced the rectangular pond. This was an obvious moment for Percy to come and make a fuss of her, but we still hadn't seen him. In his absence, my companion could only focus on the case.

"So you're willing to rule them out as the killers then? I had the feeling, after our conversation with her son and nephews, that Ursula was your primary suspect."

She'd helped me to realise something pertinent. "I certainly want that to be true. She's a cold-hearted person with no blood in her veins of any description. The thought of putting one of those comparatively genial young men or even her silly sister-in-law behind bars is hard to bear. However, that doesn't change the fact that we haven't discovered anything sufficiently damning to convince the police she's a killer."

"You didn't think that Peter was so genial when we spoke to him. Were you really convinced of his innocence just because he confessed to falling in love with a maid? If anything, that makes it more likely he's to blame. Perhaps they weren't canoodling in a cupboard at nine o'clock this morning but killing Arnold. Or it may well be that she was put in charge of doing the deed, so that he could be spotted elsewhere at the same time."

"But he wasn't spotted anywhere!" I felt I should remind her. "He claims to have been with his secret love at the time of the killing, which is hardly an impartial alibi."

Bella didn't reply. She just stared into the water and presumably turned over the various pieces of evidence we'd discovered. I must have looked quite pensive then myself. Each new comment she made unlocked different possibilities, and for a moment, I was transported back to the imaginary room in my head where I like to plan my books and do any important thinking. I stood in a hallway with a hundred doors leading off it and was about to open one, when she spoke again.

"I don't know if you've noticed, but I've been playing down my role in our detective work and playing the fool as much as possible."

"You could never be a convincing fool, my dear Bella," I said a little too sweetly, and she waved away the compliment.

"You know what I mean. I didn't want any of our suspects to think that I was considering their guilt, but it has done me little good. I really hoped that I'd won Peter's confidence last night and he would seek me out to reveal what he knows."

I perched on the arm of the bench next to hers. "I will admit that he is an interesting fellow. I took him for something of a bounder at first – and there's no doubt that he lied to us – but his forbidden love affair does explain his desire to hide the truth."

"So that's the three boys, Jim and Ursula you're willing to declare innocent. Why not go the whole way and rule out Deirdre and the nanny while we're at it?" Her smile was playful just then. It reminded me of the way she used to talk to me when we were children, and it sent a tingle down the back of my neck.

"I'm not ruling anyone out." I glanced at the reflection of the exquisite house in the water. "All I'm saying is that the evidence we have is inconclusive. Ursula and Jim were discussing their guilt, so the obvious conclusion is that they were involved in the plot to get Felicity Mortimer sent to prison. But that doesn't explain why either of our victims were murdered or who was behind it."

She stretched her arm out along the back of the bench. "I hadn't thought of it that way. And you're right, of course."

"Oh, of course." I looked back at her with a teasing grin of my own.

"Don't be flippant, Marius. Let me concentrate."

She looked up at the changeable sky just as a ray of light burst through the clouds in the distance. It was rather majestic, and I think it spurred her on to consider the case before us.

"Let's say that it was Ursula who engineered Felicity's conviction for murder. It would explain why Deirdre seems to know so little about what happened back then. After all, her sister clearly views her as a dolt and wouldn't involve her as a co-conspirator. But what would Ursula and Jim have gained from such a plan?"

"We should never underestimate the attraction of a substantial inheritance. Richard Mortimer was presumably quite wealthy when he died, but Felicity would have received his estate. The surviving children could make no claim upon it if they were given up for adoption and never told who their real parents were. Which meant that the vultures were free to divide the carcass as they saw fit."

We were playing with theories and, as attractive as this simple solution sounded, it didn't go far enough to explain the events of the past week.

"That still doesn't provide a clear motive for the murders." Bella bothered her top lip with her pretty white teeth for a moment, then picked apart my hypothesis. "Even if Arnold knew of their plan, he wasn't about to confide in us. The killer had no reason to fear that he would reveal any secrets, so why was he murdered first thing this morning in a house full of people?"

I had no answer for her, so she sighed and changed tack. "Whoever is responsible, he must be desperate to have got rid of Hobbes and Arnold in quick succession."

A rush of ideas suddenly came crashing into my head. "What if we're wrong about all of this? What if the killer isn't covering up the conspiracy that occurred fifteen years ago but punishing those he hates?"

Bella's imagination fired once more, and she rose to consider the facts. "That would make sense in the case of the dead man you found in London."

"Precisely. If the killer were responsible for having Felicity imprisoned, then he would loathe the man who tried to save her. Isn't it possible that he believed enough time had passed and that no one would connect Hobbes to what happened back then? If I hadn't been at the scene with Bertie, it's unlikely that the police would have considered the two cases alongside one another." I nodded somewhat vigorously, then immediately lost my confidence. "But that still brings us back to the question of why Arnold had to die."

"That's just it." Even Bella's enthusiasm had drained away. "Whatever conclusion we come to only fits one of the murders. It's hard to say why someone would have targeted both of the victims."

"You know, it is possible that Arnold's death wasn't planned. Perhaps he stumbled across the killer's identity and paid the price."

I picked up a stone from the paved ground and threw it a little testily into the pool. It caused a small splash of water to erupt into the air, and a frog disappeared under the surface as the ripples reached him. It was appealing to do much the same thing and hide from my failures, but I decided to go back to the beginning instead.

"It's tempting to believe that Richard Mortimer really was poisoned, and that's what Ursula and Jim were discussing. Of course, if there had been enough poison in his system, that would surely have been the first point of evidence against his widow."

"I suppose that anything is possible," Bella replied with a barely perceptible huff. "There are still so few certainties. Inspector Falk couldn't find a flower in a florist's without our guidance and, to be perfectly honest, we're not doing a great deal better."

We sighed in unhappy unison, and I was tempted to throw another stone to scare another frog, but I heard a noise behind us and turned to see Deirdre Stradbrooke standing in a gap between two hedges.

"There is one suspect you've barely considered," she said in a mournful tone, befitting of the day. "Me."

TWENTY-SEVEN

"I never expected you to give me much thought, of course. What use have I ever been to anyone?"

Our hostess was already crying by the time this sentence was out. Bella and I did not have to discuss who would be the one to comfort her. I felt quite confident that I would have only made things worse.

"Come, come, Deirdre." My friend steered her towards the closest stone bench. She'd done a lot of steering, ushering, leading and directing already; a little more wouldn't hurt. "We certainly don't think of you like that, and there's no reason why anyone else should."

Deirdre quietly scoffed. "They call me Dreary, and it's true. I'm a dull, petty person, and the one man in this world who could ever love me has been taken away."

Bella produced a clean handkerchief, and Deirdre blew her nose with great noise and animation. She sounded rather like an elephant I'd once seen at the Ménagerie du Jardin des Plantes in Paris. I was tempted to address the issue of why she'd been hiding behind some bushes, listening to our conversation, but I truly felt for the woman and wouldn't be so cruel... yet.

"That's all nonsense. We saw it from the beginning," Bella insisted. "If anything, it's your sister who is dull. She is so severe and unfeeling. I would rather spend time with you than her any day of the year."

This seemed to go some way to reassuring Deirdre, and she responded accordingly. "You're too kind, Lady Bella. Too kind. My Arnold used to tell me much the same thing, and my boys are ever so good to their old mother, but I've never been a great believer in myself. Try as I might, I just can't get beyond the thought that I suck the joy and life from whoever I meet."

"Why on earth would you think such a thing?"

Deirdre looked back at Bella as if the answer were obvious. "Because Ursula often tells me that I suck the joy and life from whoever I meet. I've always looked up to my sister. She's so capable and, no matter what you think of her, she is a selfless person in many ways. You can't overlook all she has done for those children of hers."

She shook her head then and looked quite amazed. As good a mother as Ursula Tanner might have been, I could only think that the constant veneration of her by the rest of the family was down to the mythology that she established for herself rather than any good deeds on her part. She struck me as a thoroughly unlikable person, but everyone spoke of her as if she were Joan of Arc.

"That doesn't mean she has the right to treat you so cruelly," Bella insisted. "My eldest brother, Kenton, has always been very fond of himself. He used to order me around and tell me that his views were more valid than mine because men are born with bigger brains or some such rot. Do you know what I did to him in return?"

I knew exactly what she'd done, as I'd been standing next to her at the time, but Deirdre just shook her head.

Perhaps inevitably, Bella smiled as she revealed the answer. "I pushed him into the lake and only fished him out when he promised never to utter such rot again. He cried all the way back to the house, and I'm happy to say he was true to his word. Of course, he still has a high opinion of himself, but I make sure to put him in his place whenever I hear him talking down to others. People like Kenton and Ursula need to be reminded that they aren't the perfect, charming geniuses they think themselves."

"You *are* wicked saying such things, Lady Bella." As she covered her mouth and gave a titter, Deirdre looked much younger than her forty or so years. "But it isn't just because of Ursula. Much as your brother has a high opinion of himself, I've never thought that I was worth the clothes I put on each morning. You know, my brother, sister and I came from practically nothing. We're not fancy and sophisticated like the pair of you."

I had never expected to have to console a grieving widow by discussing her home furnishings, but that was what was about to happen. "Whatever you think of yourself, I can assure you that your talents are far more evident to me than those of your sister. Your house is beautifully decorated and there are elements here that are unique. You've evidently left your mark on this building – some parts of which still look like the interior of a sixteenth-century galleon."

She held her hand to her chest and was apparently touched by my words. "Oh, Mr Quin, that really is one of the nicest things anyone has ever said to me. My Arnold always claimed that I would bankrupt him with my expensive tastes, but I wanted to leave my stamp on the place. I couldn't stand living here thinking that his family still owned it. I did my best to make it ours, though I must admit that I do like the finer things in life."

"Don't we all," I muttered, still feeling bad for spending my first year's income as a writer on a flat that I couldn't afford.

A look of grave worry came across her face then. "You don't think that was why someone hurt my husband? Perhaps the killer hated us for showing off our wealth like that. Maybe that's why I was sent the noose and Arnold was killed!"

I can only imagine that I failed to hide my incredulity at this comment. Had interior design ever been a motive for murder?

"I can't believe that anyone would kill for such a petty reason," Bella reassured her as I stood there looking blank. "But we do have some questions regarding your husband." She took a deep breath, and our witness looked up expectantly as she waited. "It seems that almost all the servants at Rhinefield House were occupied elsewhere when he was murdered, and it's unlikely that someone could have got onto the estate and up to your bedroom without being seen. That would suggest that the killer is one of your relations." She had chosen her words ever so carefully, but this still drew a short gasp from Deirdre.

"I can't bear the thought that someone so close to me would have hurt him." She held her hand to her prominent chest, which was encased in pink satin. "Please say it isn't true!"

Bella allowed a few seconds to pass before doing the opposite. "I'm afraid we have to consider the possibility. And so I'd like to ask whether he'd had a disagreement with anyone here recently?"

Deirdre's innocent expression turned to one of sadness. "No one disliked my Arnold. He had a very good heart."

"You didn't answer the question," Bella tried a little more forcefully. "Was there anyone in the family with whom he didn't see eye to eye?"

Deirdre's jaw hung open and her eyes became fixed to the ground. "I did hear him arguing with Ursula one day. I assumed it was over a shared venture, but he always told me that when it came to business, his was none of mine. He said it jokingly, but he was a private man in that respect and preferred to control anything to do with money himself. He wasn't always like that, but something changed around the time our children were born."

"He seemed to get on well with Jim," I reflected in a mumble that was mainly for myself.

"That's true," Deirdre confirmed. "They were quite different in many respects, but they were very good friends. Perhaps being married to two Mortimer sisters meant that they could console one another when times were bad!" There were the makings of a laugh in her voice as she put herself down once more, but it never quite materialised.

"And what of your boys and their cousin? Did Arnold ever butt heads with them?"

Bella and I awaited the answer expectantly, but Deirdre just shrugged. "At their age, young men are generally not the easiest people with whom to interact. But either way, Arnold left the child-rearing to me. Our boys can be boisterous and a little silly, and Neville is a serious young man, but we all get on famously."

Though most of what she said was comparatively obvious, there was an interesting thread buried in it that I had to pull. "Why did Neville start visiting so often? Did something happen in his family that drove him and his siblings away from their parents?"

Until this point, Deirdre had appeared either sad, grateful or alarmed, but a conflicted look passed over her features, and it was clear she would have preferred not to answer. "It really isn't for me to say, but I know that Neville's three siblings are angry with their parents for some reason. It's been a long time now since they came here as a family. Ursula plays down the argument they had, but I know that whatever was said drove a wedge between them."

"You honestly don't know what upset her children?" Bella sat down on the bench beside Deirdre to ask.

Deirdre thought about her response for a moment or two. "It's much as I told you: she dismisses me as a nuisance and won't tell me her business. Neville and I have become quite good friends over the last few months, and I try to lend him an ear whenever he needs it, but even he hasn't revealed much. All I know is that each of them feels they are in the right. In my family, we are one as stubborn as the other."

The words *a soup of nothingness* entered my mind then, and I came to accept that yet another suspect had offered us little of any value.

All of a sudden, Deirdre's expression became more strained, and she put her arm out to touch Bella's. "There was something I was too upset to tell you earlier. You see, the knife that killed my beloved husband was his own. Arnold was the only hunter in the household, and it makes my blood boil to think that some heartless individual would murder him with his own knife."

"Your boys never went with him?" I asked, knowing how fathers are when it comes to such matters.

Deirdre smiled sadly. "They did from time to time to keep him happy, and Jim would go out on occasion, but none of them had a passion for it like my Arnold did. He was a real marksman and often brought home our Sunday lunches. I'm not too keen on rabbit myself, however—"

Bella hummed softly, as if giving this careful thought. "That's very helpful, thank you, Deirdre. But if you overheard everything that Marius and I discussed before you appeared, then—"

It was our hostess's turn to interrupt in her usual flustered manner. "I did indeed. As I'm sure you must understand, I was sitting alone out here feeling miserable. I would have said something when the pair of you arrived, but you were so deep in discussion, and by the time I had the courage to come out, I knew you'd think the worst of me. I promise that I hadn't meant to eavesdrop. That's the last thing I'd want to do to a guest."

"If you overheard our conversation," Bella continued without hesitation, "then you'll know that we have been looking for a connection between the murders this week and what happened to Felicity Mortimer fifteen years ago."

There was something of a snarl on her lips just then. "I don't even like hearing that woman's name – which is a good thing, as Ursula swore me off mentioning it after the murderess was convicted. My sister took Richard's death very poorly. I think that's why she doesn't like to remember what happened."

"Did you all attend the trial together?"

"That's right." Deirdre seemed rather happy with this assertion. "Arnold and I were there every single day to ensure that justice was done, whereas Ursula only attended with her husband to give evidence."

"Which of you selected Felicity Mortimer's barrister?" I interrupted, as this had been hanging over me for some time. "We heard that it was Richard's sister who chose him, and I assumed that it was you because you were living here at the time, but perhaps Felicity got her wires crossed."

"Barrister?" The innocent look that often consumed her oversized brown eyes was back, and she reminded me of my hound. "I left that side of things to Arnold and Ursula. But why would they have anything to do with Felicity's defence?"

Bella and I glanced at one another for the briefest of moments before she asked the next question. "Then do you think that your sister could have intentionally hired a barrister who had fallen some way from the peak of his powers to prevent an innocent woman from having a fair trial?"

She rocked from one side to the other and back again, and I could tell that she didn't appreciate the phrase Bella had used. "Felicity wasn't innocent, as was proved in court. She killed my brother and got what she deserved. As for the man who represented her there, if Ursula had anything to do with his hiring, she certainly never told me."

Neither of us could summon a reply, and I felt like jumping

into the pond in frustration. When no one spoke, Deirdre rose to bluster away.

"If you've nothing more to say to me, I will be in my bedroom. But let me state one thing with absolute certainty: Felicity Mortimer is a killer. She was carrying on with another man behind her husband's back. She was seen tampering with poisons just a short time before Richard died, and I have never been shown the slightest fragment of evidence that could disprove her guilt."

"But you kept her from him for days before he died," I replied before she could get away. "Even if she had access to arsenic, she couldn't have administered it without a nurse seeing, and there wasn't enough poison in his system when he died for that to have been the—"

"That is all I have to say, Mr Quin." I was yet to see a fierce side to Deirdre's personality, but her eyes narrowed as she fixed them upon me. I don't mind telling you that she was quite intimidating. "You've heard my thoughts on the matter, and I will bid you adieu."

TWENTY-EIGHT

Bella and I slumped back onto the bench. We sat in silence for a whole minute before I tried and failed to throw a stone to the far side of the pond.

"Nine steps forward, nineteen steps back," I whispered.

I thought for a moment that Bella would join me in an enriching bout of glumness, but she wasn't the type. "Stop feeling so sorry for yourself." There was no humour in her words and the underlying message was, *Neither your husband nor fiancé has been taken away from you.* Had such a statement been made in anything other than our heads, I might have countered that I'd spent ten years mourning the life I could have had if the war hadn't broken us apart. It really wasn't the time for such honesty, but I replied quite calmly.

"We're back to where we started, and I know why."

She sat up straighter and pretended that she was taking me very seriously. "Please, enlighten me."

"Because we keep prodding at different members of the same family, trying to get one of them to talk. The fact is that even Deirdre, who is ill-treated, overlooked and outright ridiculed by her sister, won't say a bad word against her. It was too much to hope that they would eventually turn against one another."

She let out a despairing groan from somewhere deep inside her, and I instantly wished I could make her feel better again. Luckily for both of us, her negativity was inversely proportional to my own. Perhaps it was because we couldn't bear to see each other looking forlorn, but I pulled myself up to sitting and had a stab at being optimistic.

"I'm sorry if I've made you blue. The fact is that we should be proud to have solved ninety per cent of this case many times in countless different ways. All we need is for the last pieces of the puzzle to fall into place, and the culprit will be locked up before lunch."

Mentioning lunch prompted an awareness of my own hunger, and I looked up at the sky and wondered what time it was. It felt as though we'd been at work for days, but it surely wasn't noon yet. To confirm this fact more accurately, I glanced at my watch to discover that it had just gone half past eleven. When I turned back to Bella, I could see that her sadness hadn't passed. She was just as despondent as at any time that week. At least when I'd broken the news about Gilbert, it was so fresh that her pain hadn't truly arrived. But now she looked entirely without hope: *une belle dame sans espoir*.

"Bella..." I began, but nothing else came. I didn't want to patronise or upset her. I didn't want to remind her of the tragedy she had gone there to forget, but I wanted to make the situation better in some small way, so I searched for something – anything – to distract her.

"There's still hope," I said before swiftly explaining what I meant. "The killer is here in the house with us, and we will find him."

My half-hearted promise was not enough to make her move a muscle, let alone laugh or smile. The nearest frog was back on his lily pad, though, and something about that simple creature's resilience made me try again.

"I'm sorry if I've upset you, old friend."

"I'm quite all right," she finally replied in the voice of an upper-class liar. I'm not besmirching the aristocracy with this comment. I've merely learnt over the years that blue-blooded types like Bella (and her father, mother and Arnold Stradbrooke for that matter) are taught from an early age to pretend that everything is fine when it is not. "We'll just have to try again."

"Yes, of course." My voice had fallen quieter, but I was about to give it another go when she wearily pushed herself up off the bench. "Come along, Marius. Perhaps the police have discovered something useful in their interviews with the suspects. Or maybe Inspector Falk will have done the unthinkable and achieved the task we set him."

In the time we had been out in that gorgeous garden, a mist had swept across the woods to obscure the house. I sat watching Bella walk along the path beside the pond and, in a moment, that cloud of white seemed to swallow her whole. I had an inexplicable fear that I would never see her again. I can't begin to describe what caused it, but an urge shot through me, and I ran after her, determined to find something to remove the frown from her perfect face.

It can only have been ten seconds before I saw her again but, much as when I sit down to write without a thought in my head and the words flow from my mind to my pen just like magic, as soon as I caught up with her, I knew what to say.

"We won't be beaten," I told her and took her hand in mine. "We'll start by talking to Neville on his own. If anyone in the family can tell us what his parents have been up to, it's him."

She nodded tentatively, and I suddenly doubted whether, though I'd meant it as a friendly gesture, taking her hand was such a good idea after all.

I kept talking to stop myself from wondering either way.

"We heard Ursula and Jim discussing their past transgressions. If anything, they have the most to gain from the murders, so they're the ones we'll investigate until we are certain they're both innocent."

I'm not suggesting that this was exceptional detective work by anyone's standards, but at least it distracted Bella from whatever she was feeling.

"Yes," she said resolutely. "Ursula is a nasty sort, and I would enjoy nothing more than exposing her as a killer."

In the end, it was this thought that dispelled her grim mood and put a certain vigour back in her step. I opened the door to a small conservatory – thus providing myself with a subtle opportunity to drop her hand once more – and we entered the house. We followed those endlessly wood-panelled corridors back through the building and up to the guest wing on the other side of the property. By the time we arrived at Neville Tanner's sitting room, I was (perhaps unrealistically) hopeful that he would tell us what we needed to know to convict his parents of a litany of crimes.

"I've already told you everything I can about Arnold when you were here before," the fourteen-year-old insisted, having admitted us to the room in his normal polite manner.

We were seeing him alone for the first time that day, and I had to wonder what his cousins were doing now that they'd left his side. He sat down in his usual chair and placed that same philosophical text on his lap without opening it.

"Does your mother always tell you what books to read?" I asked, thinking back to the conversation we'd had in that room an hour or so earlier.

He brought his shoulders up to the level of his chin and then slowly down again. "Only since I was four years old. She believes that it is her job to improve me as a human being. Apparently, I have never lived up to her idea of what one of her children should be."

"Whereas your siblings have?" Bella asked, before adding a more contentious question. "Even though they've recently fallen out with her?"

He had to swallow then, and I could see he was surprised by how much we'd discovered in our short time apart. This was in stark contrast to my feeling that we were still several thousand miles away from identifying the killer. It reinforced my optimism a little.

"Nothing could dim their brilliance in her eyes. The only thing I can think is that she would have preferred to stop at three children. It goes without saying that I am her eternal disappointment and shame."

"You seem perfectly nice to me," Bella reassured him, and much as I would have if a beautiful, sophisticated young lady had paid me a compliment at his age, he blushed rotten. "And the fact that you've made it through even the first chapter of that dry-as-dust book suggests you're more persistent than I am."

I glanced down at the silver lettering on the front of the pale brown book: *Leviathan – Thomas Hobbes*. I doubted the coincidence of the writer's surname being the same as our first victim's would prove important, but anything is possible. "Try as I might, I can't consume philosophy as I do novels. It starts off fine, but I soon find myself craving intrigue and excitement. My mind starts to wander, and then I lose track of the point that's being made."

"It's funny you should say that," Neville replied, full of excitement, "I feel the same way myself and—" He stopped himself short and his eyebrows curved down cautiously. "I'm sorry. I can't imagine you came here to discuss my thoughts on old books, did you?"

"Not exactly," I told him as cheerfully as I could without coming across as a loon. "The truth is that we'd like to know more about your parents."

He sucked in a gulp of air in a manner that suggested it was in short supply. "Ah... my parents."

"You might not know why your Uncle Arnold was killed, but there's every possibility that you've heard something over the years that can shed some light on the case before us."

He put his hand on top of his book as though swearing on a Bible. "Are you saying that you think Mother and Father were involved in the killing? And even the one in London this week?"

I looked at Bella and was very grateful when she answered for me. "We honestly don't know who the culprit is, but in such a tightly knit family – when there are so few people who could be the killer – we have to explore every possibility."

"Have you asked them?" Neville's question was straightforward enough, but that didn't make it any easier to answer.

"Your mother won't speak to us, and you were there when we talked to your father. He seemed quite shaken by your uncle's death."

He looked off through the room's one small window. "I can't say that such secrecy is out of character for either of them, but what do you expect me to tell you? That I've witnessed some terrible cruelty that no one else will admit?"

"Have you?" I was a little too quick to ask.

"No, of course not. Mother is a true dragon, and Father goes along with whatever she demands, but that doesn't make them murderers. Her fiery breath is usually far worse than her bite."

I'm not sure that this metaphor worked, but I hadn't gone there to give him tips on literary devices, and Bella soon presented a more relevant topic.

"We'd like to ask you about your aunt who was sent to prison."

"You already have," he was quick to remind us. "And, as Paul told you, I was not quite born when she was locked away."

If I'd worked out little else that weekend, at least I'd been able to estimate his age with some accuracy. I'd never met a boy who looked more fourteen than Neville Tanner. Despite that, there was a purposefulness and fluency to his speech as we talked, and I was amazed to think of the contrast I'd seen in him whenever his mother was present.

"That doesn't mean she hasn't been discussed in your presence," I jumped in again. "You told us that your parents rarely mention her. Rarely is not the same as never. Your aunt keeps a photograph of her downstairs, too. So Felicity clearly hasn't been erased from everyone's memory."

His nervousness had returned, and his gaze drooped, much as if his mother had appeared in the doorway.

"I don't know what you want me to say." This is the kind of one-size-fits-all statement that witnesses often produce when they know something they don't want to reveal.

"You can start by telling us why your mother won't allow your aunt's name to be mentioned."

"I can't," he insisted. "It wouldn't be loyal."

It took all my strength not to shout aloud that Deirdre was threatened just minutes after she spoke of Felicity Mortimer in our presence, a scene that coincided with the arrival of Neville's family to Rhinefield House. While I knew this wasn't enough to mark his mother, father or indeed Neville himself as the killer, it at least gave me something to put to Ursula should she ever deign to speak to us.

Bella decided to slow the pace of the conversation. "Neville, the truth is that we wanted to talk to you alone. We thought you might be more comfortable explaining what you know without anyone else hearing."

I appreciated the soft tone she had used and tried to mimic it. I doubt I did a good job. "We've met people like your mother many times. We understand if you'd rather she didn't hear what you have to tell us, and I promise that we'll never tell her."

"My mother isn't a murderer!" he snapped at me without really raising his voice. It was impressive in a way, but then the fight went out of him, and he conceded a good part of what we needed to know. "Or at least, I've never seen any evidence that could prove she is."

I was quite happy leaning against the mantelpiece, but Bella moved to kneel down a few feet away from Neville. Once again, this is something that could greatly unsettle a fourteen-year-old.

"If your parents weren't involved in any of these crimes, then they won't be punished."

He was shaking now. His hands trembled as they rested on the arms of the chair, and he suddenly breathed more deeply. "But what if something I tell you leads to their arrest?"

I could feel the atmosphere change – the tension rise. I could feel just how much he was suffering to be in the centre of the spotlight we'd shone on him.

"There is a woman who has spent the last fifteen years in prison for a crime which there was no way she could have committed." My voice had risen steadily, and I had to reduce the theatricality, as I realised that I sounded like that famously stentorian actor, Henry Snow. "Her children were given up for adoption, and she may never see them again. Can't you think about her for a moment?"

It wasn't just his eyes that dropped. His head bowed and his chin touched his chest as he faced this dilemma. As soon as I'd walked into the room, I thought I knew which way up the coin would land, but as his laboured breathing continued, and he gave no other sign of having heard my question, I began to doubt myself.

"You're probably right," he finally whispered, though it would be ten seconds before he clarified in which way. "Aunt Deirdre has a collection of old newspapers on the case. I read through them recently and, from what I understood, I think that Aunt Felicity was wrongly imprisoned."

"There you go, Neville!" I said, clapping my hands together

even as he pushed his glasses back up his nose and added a caveat.

"But I'm sure that neither my mother nor father played a part in sending her to prison. For one thing, they don't have control over the courts. There is no way they could have forced the judge and jury to pass down the sentence that she received."

"Yes, but there were measures they could have taken to exert their influence. And frankly, the judge's behaviour was unprecedented." I could have said a lot more, but Bella raised one hand to make sure I let the boy speak.

"Father says that Mother took it very badly when my uncle died. She only went to court on the days she was required to speak, and I get the impression that she was terribly depressed by the whole thing. She'd already struggled to have children when she was first married. Perhaps the wait to have me ignited those feelings once again."

"Your father told us something similar." Bella was as cautious in her phrasing as she knew how to be. "How long is the gap between you and your next sibling?"

He tipped his head back quite suddenly, and I realised that, even if he was willing to help us, he still had no intention of criticising his parents. "I'm not sure the length of time was the problem. It was all those things coming one on top of the other." He fell quiet and blinked a few times as if to compose himself. "I'm sorry, but I doubt that any of this is relevant to my uncle's death... or rather, either of my uncles' deaths. All I wanted to say was that I don't believe she was in any state to involve herself in the trial. Personally, I don't see why anyone made such a fuss over Richard in the first place. From what Aunt Deirdre has told me, he was a conceited bore."

This reminded me of Bertie's run-in with Richard Mortimer at a London party. Of course, the fact that few people liked the man didn't rule out the possibility that someone hated his wife enough to conspire against her.

"If anything, it was Aunt Deirdre who involved herself in his life," Neville continued. "She invited her brother and his family to live here after he became ill. She kept Aunt Felicity away from him when his condition became worse, and I know she was there at the trial every day because it said so in the newspapers."

"So you're saying that she…" Bella began before abandoning her enquiry and waiting for Neville to reveal more.

"I don't think my aunt killed her husband or anything like that," he said, clearly imagining what she might have asked. "But if someone set out to incriminate Felicity, it would have to be Aunt Deirdre. She's the only person in my family who has admitted to hating her sister-in-law. That's why my mother won't let any of us talk about it; she knows how her sister becomes as soon as the name is mentioned."

This certainly wasn't what I'd thought when I'd heard him speak of his mother's ban on mentioning Felicity, and I was once more forced to question whether anything Deirdre Stradbrooke had told us was true.

Neville turned back to the window, as if searching for answers in the low clouds that hung around the building. "I began to wonder about her last night when she opened the final present. She's been so kind to me over the months I've been visiting. She's always eager to talk about what happened all that time ago. I think she liked the fact that I was interested when no one else in the family would talk about it."

"Did the noose make you question the part she'd played in the conspiracy?" Bella got her whole question out this time and, to begin with, he could only stare back blankly.

"Not exactly. I just wondered why someone had left such a threatening object among her birthday presents. If Uncle Arnold was involved, too, it might explain why someone here was so angry with them. I've spoken to my cousins at length about it, and it's the only solution we can muster."

There were so many possibilities turning over in my head that it took me some time to form a response. "So what you're suggesting is that one of your relatives cared so much about Felicity Mortimer that, when he discovered what Deirdre and Arnold had done, he sought revenge?"

His brows knitted together, and he looked a little queasy. "I'm not sure now. Perhaps that's what happened." His breathing became markedly louder. "Or perhaps I know just as little as my mother always tells me, and I've got it all wrong."

TWENTY-NINE

"We went looking for a solution to an impossible problem and found one that contradicts every feeling we've had on the case until now." Bella was decidedly pensive as we left young Neville's sitting room.

I wasn't much better myself. "But it makes more sense than anything else we've considered. It's the solution we keep coming back to, as well. Instead of forcing a square peg into a round hole, we've simply drilled an extra hole and now we need to find two round pegs to fit... Sorry, I don't actually know what I'm trying to say."

We came to a stop at the point where the guest corridor reached the narrow staircase down to the ground floor, and Bella took up my thread.

"If Deirdre and Arnold interfered in the trial to secure Felicity's imprisonment, then they have been manipulating us ever since we arrived. Just think how she pulled us into the Alhambra Room to tell us about Felicity last night. She must have found out who you were and decided to convince us of Felicity's guilt so that we didn't suspect her involvement."

My first reaction to this was that not mentioning Felicity Mortimer in the first place would have been an even better way of hiding the truth, but we were short of theories, so I kept such thoughts to myself. In fact, I ignored every reason that we'd encountered for why Deirdre couldn't be the killer and looked for something to support the idea.

"It does make sense in one way for Arnold to have been involved. He may have come from an aristocratic family, but this doesn't appear to be a working estate. It's surrounded by trees, not farmland, and he told us that he was an international trader."

I paused to see whether she wanted to draw her own conclusions from this, then continued when she remained silent. "Fifteen years ago, the war was on the horizon. Military alliances had been formed, and the arms race was in full swing. Selling goods from one nation to another across Europe and beyond was becoming increasingly difficult, and Arnold must have feared for the future of his business. If you consider the expensive tastes that his wife has, and her clear desire to refurbish this house to those standards, he might well have fancied his brother-in-law's inheritance to pay his bills."

She leaned back against the wall, and a narrow shard of light hit her face from a lamp on the landing beneath us. "So he and Deirdre made it look as though Felicity was a killer in order to steal the money that was due to her. If there is someone here who cared for the prisoner, it would explain why Arnold was killed and Deirdre threatened."

She came to a stop and, when she spoke again, Bella's voice was high and alarmed. "Marius, what about the letters that Felicity wrote? Don't you think it's possible that the man with whom she was in love was Jim Tanner?"

I barely heard what she was saying, because the question of how Carleton Hobbes fitted into any of this still hung over me.

A killer motivated to help Felicity would surely have approved of Hobbes's attempts to overturn her conviction, unless... A new hypothesis presented itself, and I was about to tell Bella when we heard someone coming up the stairs.

The shabby inspector soon arrived, and I tapped my head a few times to remind my friend not to forget anything we'd just discussed.

"Lady Bella, Mr Quin," he said rather formally, "it has taken some time, but the constables and I have been able to ascertain the professed whereabouts of every last person in the house at the time of the two murders."

Bella and I were both a little taken aback by his sudden proficiency.

"Well done, Inspector Falk," I told him quite sincerely, and, as he stood to attention, he even looked a little more professional than normal. I had to wonder whether his previous behaviour was just an act. "And has a clear suspect emerged based on the information you've obtained?"

He hummed in a hesitant manner. "I'm afraid not, sir. Except for the old nanny, who rarely sets foot outside, most of the inmates of this house were at large on Tuesday when Carleton Hobbes was murdered. Any one of them could have been in London. I've sent one of the men to telephone the staff at the Tanner family home in Essex in order to confirm Ursula Tanner's story that she and her husband were there at the time."

"Remarkable." Bella's reply was presumably a comment on the good work he'd done rather than what he'd discovered.

Buoyed by our praise, he continued outlining his discoveries. "I am also happy to inform you that the butler believes he has located the keys to the doors at the end of this corridor. He says they were locked up before he came to work here fourteen years ago. It turns out that he's the longest-serving member of staff... except for Nanny Yapp, of course."

He raised aloft a long rusty key, as though it held great importance. I put my hand out to accept it and he presented it with a bow. I got the impression that he had seen a state function like a coronation or some such thing and wished to add a little ceremonial flourish to proceedings. As I've already mentioned, he was a truly odd man.

We walked back along the corridor, past Neville's sitting room, and up to the first locked door. We looked at one another expectantly as I put the key in the lock, and Bella smiled. We were finally getting somewhere.

"Here we go," I said quite breathlessly before disappointment hit. "Oh, it's the wrong key."

The inspector began muttering to himself and shaking his head as he checked the pockets of his suit jacket. "I should have known it wouldn't be the first we tried. Things like this are never straightforward. Have a go with this one."

I exchanged the key I had for a similar one and this time it unlocked with a click. "Here we go," I said again, and the first thing I saw when the door swung open was a tall pile of ladies' blouses.

"It's a cupboard." Bella made no attempt to hide her disappointment.

"Not to worry," the inspector reassured us, "there are four more to try."

I'm happy to say that this wasn't one of those situations when you try all the options and the last yields results. We moved on to the neighbouring door and, when we used the next key from the selection that was, for some reason, distributed around different pockets on Falk's person, we all three walked inside.

"The nursery," Bella muttered, in case we hadn't noticed the crib, the toys, the rocking horse or the pastel colours in which the room was decorated.

"It's creepy that this place has been left like this for so long," the inspector commented with the shiver of a man who has read too many ghost stories.

There were thick blankets draped over two of the beds, but for the most part, the room had been left as it was when Felicity Mortimer's children last slept there. There was a shroud of dust over everything, and at least this meant we could rule out the possibility that the killer had been poking around in there.

I had seen the two photos on the walls above the cot in the newspaper. The first showed Felicity at her most elegant in a white beaded dress with her hair in tight ringlets, and the other, facing hers, was the head and shoulders of her husband. He looked glum and disdainful, as though not quite approving of the carefree expression on his young bride's face. With little else to interest us there, I moved to the adjoining door.

"This must lead to another of their rooms," I hazarded and was relieved that the handle turned, and we would not need to go through such a palaver with the keys for a third time. As it happened, the four rooms that interested us turned out to be a u-shaped suite with the nursery at one end.

I don't know if it was my imagination which lent this second space a more pungent, musty air, but I instantly knew that this was where Richard Mortimer had died. It contained no furniture except for a bed, a chest of drawers and a washstand, but the bottles arranged in lines on the window sill, and several ceramic bowls that were placed haphazardly on the floor, indicated that this had been a sickroom.

Much like the nursery, it was frozen in time. The sheets had been thrown back on the bed, never to be replaced, and there was a book lying open, face down on the rug. I could quite understand the staff locking the door and never wishing to set foot inside. Not that anyone who had been employed at the time was still working at Rhinefield House.

It reminded me of a museum I visited on Doughty Street in London. Some benevolent fund recently purchased and restored Charles Dickens's house, and it is much as it would have been when he and his family lived there. If you care to visit, you can marvel at his library, manuscripts of his books and even take a look at his wife's jewellery collection and sitting room.

No one would go to such trouble for Richard Mortimer. He was a wealthy but unloved merchant who would already have been forgotten if it hadn't been for the trial that followed his death. His final week on earth had been preserved, but it was more through happenstance than intent, and if the house were ever sold, or – dare I say it – the family ended up behind bars, the rooms would be gutted and all traces of him removed.

Bella continued to the next bedroom before the inspector and I had finished our solemn observation. I already had a sense that the room would belong to Felicity, and I was right. The feel of the place changed once more, and I was reminded of the effortless kindness that I'd seen in her when we met. The room was just so, and I was sure that she had arranged it to her specifications when the family moved there. There was a chair beside the uncurtained window with light blue cushions arranged on it and an unfinished piece of knitting that could perhaps have become a scarf or a jumper. On the nightstand stood three silver-framed photographs of her infant children in their christening robes. They were tiny, fragile creatures, and I felt her pain at losing them once more.

I was aware as I walked through that we were not the first to do so. The police would have examined every item in there after Richard Mortimer died, and I had no reason to think that we would find a simple explanation for the chain of events that had led to the various injustices we were investigating. Luckily, Bella was more hopeful than I, and she moved on impatiently to the final room.

There was a white silk shawl draped over the back of Felicity's dressing table, and I couldn't help but tease its dangling tassels with my fingers and reflect on the rags I'd seen her wearing in gaol. In fact, everything I saw took me back to Holloway Prison, and I might have stayed there daydreaming had it not been for my more composed associate.

"Marius," Bella called to me and, when I didn't respond, she appeared at the door once more. "Can you tell me who you think previously lived here?"

The room into which she now beckoned me was smaller than the others we'd seen. It was simpler too, with little decoration but the cream wallpaper, which had a vertical grey line descending every foot or so.

"I suppose it must have been the nanny's," I eventually answered. "The door is directly opposite the nursery, so she would have passed through the corridor to see her wards and was on hand to help with the invalid when necessary."

Bella moved to a corner cabinet, which displayed a small collection of photographs. "Everyone says that Nanny Yapp was very close to the family. She's been with them for decades."

I accepted her explanation for why a member of staff would have pictures of the family who employed her, but it wasn't the thing that most interested me just then.

The inspector had finished in the room next door and, with a scratch of the head, appeared alongside us. "What have you found here, then?"

There were pictures of Ursula and Jim on their wedding day, looking resplendently young and oddly cheerful. I saw another of Deirdre and Arnold's elaborate celebration – there were more flowers at their nuptials than you'd find in a meadow in summertime – and there was a large one of the whole family together. From the age of the children, I could tell it was taken shortly before Richard died.

Deirdre and Arnold were holding their smiling boys.

Richard and Felicity had their baby daughter and two tiny sons lined up in front of them, and, still childless at the time, Ursula and Jim stood aloof at the far side of the group.

Bella pointed at Felicity's family before I could say anything. It didn't matter. She'd reached the exact same conclusion as I had. "I've seen those children in another photograph."

THIRTY

We told the inspector to request the Tanner family's presence and then order them to come if they refused. I wasn't sure whether it was a good idea to have Neville there but, in the end, my thoughts of a selective gathering went out of the window.

I would have spoken to them in a salon where we could have sat down in comfort and thrashed out the matter more civilly, but I discovered that Percy was being spoilt by a friendly footman in the Alhambra Room and, as I took a minute to check on him, that was where our suspects found us.

"This had better not be a waste of my time," Ursula Tanner announced with a sour expression on her face that made her look as if she'd been sucking on a cyanide tablet.

"Thank you for coming," I said to her husband as much as her, but the pair were not alone.

"We feel we should be a part of any discussion you have from this point onwards," Peter announced as he bustled inside after his aunt and uncle.

Paul and Neville were right behind him and, unlike the rest of their family, they looked apologetic for the intrusion. I was about to argue that I did not require every last suspect to be present when Deirdre stuck her head into the room.

"Why have you commandeered so many of my servants?"

I wouldn't have understood her question had a line of her employees not paraded into the room after her.

"What on earth are you all doing here?" I asked, as the octagonal room became more and more crowded.

It was the butler's turn to look rueful. "My apologies, sir. I wouldn't have dreamed of intruding, however—"

"Good. They're all here." The inspector interrupted the interrupted interruption, a look of genuine pride on his face, and I realised that his conversion to a competent copper was not quite complete. "I thought you'd like me to get everyone together in one place for you to work your magic."

"Why would you ever imagine such a thing?" My voice was coated with bemusement, and the dear, mad inspector evidently realised he'd done something wrong.

"That's how your sort do this, isn't it? You bring everyone together to expose the blackguard."

"Why would I want people here who are unconnected to the crimes?"

"I... Well, I don't know. But that's the way it happens in mystery novels. I reckoned you'd approve."

It was tempting to tell the man he hadn't a brain cell in his little toe – which may well have come as a surprise to him as there was a shortage of them in his head – but I calmed myself and spoke to the Rhinefield staff.

"I'm sorry to have bothered you, but your presence is not required..." I checked my watch. "... this afternoon."

There were any number of disgruntled voices, faces and shoulders, and one of the footmen made his feelings clear on the matter. "That's not fair. We were promised a good yarn!"

"Gregory!" the butler instantly corrected him. "Mr Quin

has made himself clear on the matter. I would appreciate it if you kept such comments to yourself."

Ursula glared across at the underlings with no compassion for their situation. The inspector looked worried that he might be in trouble and, as the servants filed back out again, Nanny Yapp pushed her way into the room.

"Very well, one of you can stay." I turned to Peter's sweetheart. "Emily, you can remain here to listen and then pass the news on to your colleagues once I've finished."

Gregory the footman clearly wasn't happy with this but followed the others from the room, and Peter's jaw nearly smashed to pieces as it hit the floor. His eyes darted between me and his secret love, but there was nothing Emily could do about the situation, and so she sat down on the bench that ran around the room. With this burst of action complete, a hush fell. Including Bella, the inspector and me, there were eleven of us in the ornately decorated chamber, and just enough room for everyone to sit down with a space between each of us.

Percy decided that we had all gathered there to admire him, and so he lumbered up onto his feet and gave a quick turn, his tail wagging furiously as he did so. Nanny Yapp was the first to take an interest in him and, having a sixth sense that revealed who would treat him best, he bounded over to her. I doubted he would listen to a word I said for the next fifteen minutes as he was fussed over and petted.

Bella gestured for me to take the stage, but I was neither puppet nor puppeteer and was happy where I was. Deciding where I should start the story was hard enough without having to perform for them as well. I finally decided how I would set about it and spoke from where I sat.

"It was not easy, but we have come to understand why two people were murdered." The room practically exploded with the sound of suspect chattering to suspect (and Nanny Yapp praising Percy). "Before I reveal more, my dear friend Lady

Bella Montague would like to explain how we came to be involved in this case."

She looked a little nervous as she stood up but was not one to shy from attention. With little true reluctance, she cleared her throat, as though a teacher had asked her to make a speech at the end-of-year assembly.

"It won't be a surprise to many of you to hear that we came to the New Forest this weekend in search of information on Felicity Mortimer."

This was as much as Ursula allowed her to say before her voice cut through the room. "If you're suggesting that there is any connection between the death of Arnold Stradbrooke and what that wicked woman did fifteen years ago, then you're mistaken."

Neville looked much as if he'd had an electric shock when she said this, and he leaned forward to reply. "Don't be short-sighted, Mother. What are the odds of two members of a family being murdered without some connection between the killings? Even all that time apart, the probability must be low."

I believe that Ursula was a little startled to hear his confident response, though, to be honest, so was Neville. He straightened his posture, and I thought, *Good for you, boy! You're finally standing up for yourself.*

Bella continued as though neither of them had spoken. "Marius learnt about Felicity Mortimer this week from an old newspaper at the London Library. Since then, he's been to prison – for a visit at least. His car has been robbed. He has encountered two dead bodies and formed the very clear impression that, when Richard Mortimer died fifteen years ago, an innocent woman was locked up for a crime that never took place."

I don't know about the others, but I could have listened to Bella talk for ever. Her confidence was almost enough to make me believe she had cast her dead fiancé from her mind for a short while, though I knew in my heart this was unlikely.

Deirdre watched with a half-smile on her face, as if this was all a piece of theatre for her entertainment. Paul's gaze travelled around the room, as though considering each suspect in turn, and Peter still looked terrified that one of us would disclose his secrets.

"I won't go too deeply into the facts of the case. It's enough to tell you that, while Felicity was convicted of murdering her husband with arsenic, tests showed that there wasn't nearly enough of the poison in his body when he died to have killed him. Furthermore, due to Deirdre's suspicion of Felicity, the couple were kept apart for the week before Richard died, and a nursemaid was present at all times at the invalid's bedside."

She stopped to direct her attention to Jim, who hadn't even got a mention by this point. He was clearly disquieted by the look she gave him. His wife, meanwhile, huffed and snorted her derision at every point she heard. The biggest eruption so far was about to come.

"To say it even more succinctly, there was no way that Felicity Mortimer could have murdered her husband."

Cue Ursula's howl of derision.

"Even more alarming is what happened at the trial, which even several newspapers that were critical of her actions believed would be little more than a formality to clear her name. She was given a well-meaning but increasingly senile barrister who was paid for by someone in this family. The judge, Lord Fenwick, couldn't have been more critical of the accused, despite the fact that it was her physically violent husband who had fathered several illegitimate children without his wife's knowledge. Indeed, that very information was deemed inadmissible and, when the time came for sentencing, on the judge's lengthy recommendation, the jury found her guilty."

If you have been paying attention, little of what Bella said should come as a surprise. However, she is far better at concision than I am, and she certainly filled in some gaps for those who were not so well informed.

Of course, Nanny Yapp was one of the least informed people in the county, and her only reaction to the story so far had been to shout the odd, "Hussy!" and "Strumpet!" when Felicity's name was mentioned.

This break from my responsibilities also gave me the chance to reflect on what I would eventually have to tell them. Even as Bella spoke, little sparks exploded in my brain to help previously disconnected elements meld together. I had a good idea of who had done what to whom, but the why and how was still less fixed than I would have liked, and I was glad of the extra time.

"The furious public reaction to the trial was so strong that a man called Carleton Hobbes – an out-of-work author and actor who previously had no connection to the case – took it upon himself to direct the efforts to overturn Felicity's conviction. He devoted a year of his life to it and worked with various prominent figures, but the best that they could do was convince the Home Secretary – my friend and your neighbour, Lord Thomas Verlaine – that Felicity's death sentence should be commuted."

Bella tapped her foot as she spoke. It made me think of the repeated movements of a musician to keep time. In her case, I believe she was encouraging herself to keep going and perform to the best of her ability. Sadly for me, she wouldn't keep playing all night.

"Carleton Hobbes was the first man who was killed this week. His throat was slit and his house set on fire just before Marius could talk to him about the case. We presented the information we had gained to Lord Verlaine, but he demanded more evidence, which is why we came here, and why we were only too happy to accept Deirdre's invitation to her birthday celebrations."

"My birthday…" the grieving widow echoed in a sad whisper, and I had to wonder whether she had forgotten all about it. If things had gone to plan, she would have been preparing for her party at that moment. Instead, she was mourning her husband and having to relive the sad events of fifteen years earlier.

"We came here this morning to convince her of the danger that the killer presented to the family, but we were too late. Arnold had been murdered shortly before we arrived. However, if we are dealing with the same killer, why would he have murdered Carleton Hobbes, who had defended Felicity, and Arnold who, along with his wife, had given evidence against her?"

She paused so long that Paul – who, let's be honest, could be something of a smart Alec – thought she was asking for suggestions.

"Perhaps the killer is a maniac, and his actions were taken without sane reasoning."

"Possibly," Bella replied, too generously if you ask me. "But unless the police have found evidence to the contrary, the only people who could have murdered him are present in this room. So who amongst you could we describe as maniacal?"

It didn't help that Nanny Yapp was allowing Percy to lick her face at this moment. Everyone turned to look at her, contemplated the possibility that she was a two-time killer, and then dismissed it. The question of whether she had the means and ability to travel up to London may also have entered into their thinking.

"One of the most difficult elements of this investigation was to decipher the relationships within the family. You three boys clearly get on well. Ursula does nothing to hide her disapproval of her sister, and yet it is difficult to imagine she would murder her brother-in-law as a result. No, the motive was a lot more than disapproval or a petty feud. There had to be something to connect the different crimes we've uncovered – something that made you keep Nanny here all these years to ensure she wouldn't blurt your secret to the wrong people. A secret that, in order to conceal it, you fired all your other staff after Felicity was convicted."

She paused and swept her beguiling green eyes around the room. She paused on the beautiful young maid, Emily Smith, who looked as confident as her lover was nervous. Emily would play no part in the proceedings that afternoon, but Peter didn't know that, and he was clearly frightened of what might come next. Sitting next to him, Inspector Falk was scribbling away in his notepad while, on the other side, Paul was taking in every detail, perhaps on the off-chance he would need to contest our claims in court.

It was the older generation of the family who interested me most. Deirdre was terribly sad again – far more so than when we'd spoken to her in the garden. She looked like a woman whose party no one had bothered to attend (except for one person who was swiftly murdered). Her sister, of course, was inscrutable, and I couldn't begin to imagine what she was thinking, so I turned to Jim Tanner instead. He was a straightforward sort and wore his emotions for all to see. At that moment, I decided he was bewildered by events and perhaps a little hungry.

"That secret, which at least half of you must know, is..." She came to a sudden stop and looked at me. "...my fellow detective Marius's responsibility to reveal."

THIRTY-ONE

Bella smiled to show that she could throw me in at the deep end, just as I had her. To be fair, she had done the hard work of ensuring everyone could make sense of what came next. So now it was my turn, but I stayed sitting down, despite Falk's encouragement to take the floor.

"There was one question in particular to which I've kept returning over the last day," I said to set us on the right path from the beginning. "Why did any of this happen now?"

I wasn't expecting an answer and no one there would provide one. I saw Falk scribbling several question marks in his pad and, to be fair to the man, I'd felt just as uncertain until approximately half an hour earlier.

"I was able to visit Felicity herself in prison."

This brought the obligatory tut and turn of the eyes from Ursula that I had been expecting and a brief "Trollop!" from Nanny Yapp.

"That meeting convinced me of her innocence, and I subsequently travelled to see her barrister to obtain any pertinent files he still possessed. They contained evidence of the lack of arsenic in Richard's body, which proved that the main pillar of the prosecution's case against Felicity was void."

"If that's true, then why was she convicted?" Ursula snapped, and she sucked her cheeks in to suggest that she had already demolished my argument.

"Because you made sure that Felicity was represented by a man who was no longer at the peak of his powers. Her barrister, Noel Carpenter, may have been overwhelmed by the scientific data, or perhaps he simply forgot to include it in court, but the evidence was never presented at her trial. Even if it had been, I'm sure that the entirely prejudiced judge would have found reason to deem it inadmissible, as he did with the evidence of Richard's adultery. With these obstacles against her from the beginning, Felicity didn't stand a chance."

"She killed our brother," Deirdre insisted, but I could tell that her conviction was wavering.

"That's right, dear." These may have been the first gentle words I'd heard Ursula impart. "All we did was give justice a helping hand."

"So you admit to conspiring against her?" I replied with great satisfaction.

Ursula wouldn't look at me. She gazed up at the brightly coloured fragments of glass in the golden cupula of that exquisite room. "I admit nothing. But whatever we did, we did for the sake of the family."

I looked to Deirdre, keen to see how she would react to her sister's repeated use of the pronoun 'we'. She either didn't notice or was unflustered by the suggestion that she was involved in the plan, and I continued to lay out the evidence as I saw it.

"That is true. What you did was definitely for your family's sake." I wasn't ready to explain my thinking just yet and returned to my previous point. "It wasn't enough to interfere with the trial, though. The case was established on such shaky foundations that there was always the possibility someone would overturn the conviction. In fact, Carleton Hobbes set out to do this very thing. Our mutual friend Bertie Price-Lewis described him as a jack of all trades who rarely stayed in one job for long, but he dedicated a year of his life to helping Felicity. From what I understand, his failure to rescue her left its mark. It was one of the things I would have discussed with him on Tuesday, but he had already been murdered.

"I couldn't comprehend why this would have happened when his involvement in the case ended fourteen years ago. What had changed this week that meant Hobbes had to die? After Arnold was killed, these questions became all the more pressing. And when the answer finally came to me, I realised that Hobbes wasn't the person I'd taken him to be."

This was a significant point, and I let it sit between us for a time. "You paid him, didn't you, Ursula? You made certain that Felicity would remain in prison by hiring a man to co-ordinate and thus sabotage the efforts to quash her sentence. He'd once been an actor and possessed all the skills needed to convince Felicity that he was there to help her."

Ursula said nothing, but Bella was still a little shocked by this revelation, even though I'd told her most of what I knew before we entered the room. "How did you realise any of this?" she wondered aloud, her voice not quite her own.

"For one thing, Hobbes never went to see Felicity's barrister to look over the files of the case. It was the first thing I did, and I soon found the evidence that proved she was innocent. Why wouldn't he have done the same if he really wanted to help her?"

There were a few grunts and sighs as those who had been involved in this despicable plan came to realise that their crimes would finally be punished. As I pressed on, Jim looked more distressed than anyone.

"Once again, the question of why this happened now

becomes important. Why was Hobbes killed so soon after I learnt of Felicity's story?"

"Doesn't all this mean that...?" Paul began, but he couldn't finish his question and sat looking baffled. He certainly had a half-decent brain, as his mother had attested, but it hadn't helped him piece the case together.

"The one thing that changed this week – the thing that stirred up all the trouble – was our involvement in the case. No one knew that I was looking into Richard Mortimer's supposed murder except my mother, my editor and Carleton Hobbes, whom Bertie had called to tell him of my interest in Felicity's case. The killer had to hear about it from someone and, as I trust my mother and dear Bertie, I was left with only one option. That is why the killer got to Hobbes before we did, and how he knew to follow me after the murder and take the papers Felicity's barrister had given me."

I thought this was crackerjack stuff – I mean, real dynamite – but Emily Smith just looked bored. She smoothed her skirt over her knee and perhaps wished that she and Peter played a more central part in the tale.

Ursula had one more attempt at dismissing what I'd discovered, but her heart wasn't in it this time. "You're full of nonsense, Quin."

"And you're pack-full of something, madam, but I wouldn't like to say what it is."

She sneered at me then, but Jim's reaction was more telling. He couldn't look at me anymore. He stared at his hands and occasionally shook his head, perhaps thinking how stupid they had been to believe they could ever get away with such an audacious plan.

"I don't understand, Ursula." Deirdre spoke in the small, needy voice that she reserved for conversations with her sister.

"You never do, you stupid woman." This was Ursula speaking, not me. "That's why we had to hide the details from you."

"Is this about the children?" Deirdre's eyes were as shiny as the artificial stars above us, and her sister immediately flinched.

"Shut up, you fool. Don't say another word."

Deirdre was tired of being told what to do. She rose from the bench and launched her response across the room. "I've kept your secret just as you told me for fifteen years. I've never once questioned why I had to do so, but this is too much." She turned to me, and I felt truly sorry for her. "Are you saying that it wasn't Felicity who killed my brother? Are you saying that Ursula is to blame for—"

"No," I interrupted, to reassure her of this small mercy. "No, I don't believe that she killed Richard. I think it is highly likely that he died of his existing conditions and the long-term effects of an overly experimental attitude to toxic medicines. Though Ursula is responsible for several crimes, I don't believe that fratricide is one of them."

Deirdre didn't sit back down just yet but leaned against the nearest bronze pillar, and so Peter stood up to comfort her. Though some dismissed her as an empty-headed dimwit, she had shown more compassion than the rest of her family, and she would suffer the events of that week for a long time. While she may have had the wrong impression of Felicity, and treated her unkindly as a result, her greatest failing was surely the trust she placed in her sister and, indeed, her brother before he died.

"I don't know what the point of any of this is." Ursula started up again like a gramophone that someone had previously forgotten to wind. "I admit to wanting to see a treacherous woman placed behind bars, but you have yet to show any evidence to explain why I would go about killing people."

I leaned back on the bench and had to smile. "When did I say that you were the killer?"

THIRTY-TWO

"Carleton Hobbes was murdered because he could have revealed the plot against Felicity. Perhaps it was the knowledge of her innocence that scarred him so. Perhaps he was tired of lying and would have told me of your involvement if he hadn't been killed."

The room was silent as I put this to them. "When Arnold was subsequently murdered, we found Hobbes's phone number on a slip of paper in his right-hand trouser pocket. I had my suspicions from the first moment that something wasn't quite right about it. For one thing, it was bloodstained, but Arnold was stabbed through the heart." In case they failed to grasp my meaning, I pointed to the left side of my chest. "This suggested that the paper was placed there after he was stabbed. I suppose it's possible that, with his dying breath, he concealed it for some reason, but I imagine he had other things on his mind."

Deirdre released a pained gasp, and I reminded myself not to be so flippant.

"The implication of the paper was clear. The killer wanted me to believe that Arnold was behind the conspiracy and Hobbes's death, and that someone killed him as a result. Either way, I was open to the idea that the second victim was involved in the scheme against Felicity. His business must have suffered back in 1913 with war on the cards, and Felicity's imprisonment would give her husband's family control of his estate. Whatever Arnold's involvement was, though, I still felt that his death was designed to make him the scapegoat. If Hobbes was killed to hide the truth, then perhaps Arnold's murder, the very morning after we arrived here, and after his wife had been threatened for saying too much, was meant to divert us from the real killer."

I continued to watch Jim's reactions. It struck me that he hadn't denied anything. In fact, he'd barely made a sound since he entered the room. He was a blunt, plain-speaking man, but he hadn't come to his wife's defence or attempted to throw me out of the house for saying such things about her.

"My father did have trouble with money," Paul admitted. "He was never much of a businessman. He once told me that he almost lost everything during the war. But I don't believe he would have sanctioned murder." This was a far more honest appraisal than most I had received that weekend, and I acknowledged him with a nod.

"That may well be the reason he died." My words were sombre and cold. "When I came here, he was nervous when he heard my name, then proceeded to consume half of the drinks cabinet as the evening continued. Deirdre didn't know who I was before inviting us here, so Arnold had no reason to prevent us from coming. But I think it's fair to assume that Hobbes rang to tell him of my investigation and that Arnold learnt of Hobbes's murder and confronted the killer. I truly believe that he died because, just like Hobbes, he would no longer do what was necessary to keep the secret."

"What is this secret you keep mentioning?" Peter demanded, and his paramour looked up at him tenderly for a moment. "Mother, you apparently know as much as anyone else. Quin has clearly extracted every last dark truth our family holds, so you might as well tell us."

Deirdre still didn't have it in her to betray her cruel sister. She looked at Ursula with pity, and if there is one thing that happened there to give me cause for relief, it was the shift in power between them.

As no one else was going to say it, I took up the task. "Arnold needed money and so he went along with Ursula and her husband's plan to incriminate Felicity. She was much younger than Richard, and they viewed her as an opportunist from the start, so the three had no allegiance to her. But it wasn't money that Ursula wanted. She was desperate for something else."

Bella already knew what this was. She had helped me put the pieces together, but she still looked up at the coloured dome above our heads, as if she couldn't bear to hear what I was about to say.

"Several of you told us what a good person Ursula was. I didn't understand at first why you believed this to be the case, but it was ultimately because of the sympathy you had for her when she struggled to have children. My parents have friends who have experienced such problems, and I know that it can be a truly torturous ordeal. She no doubt deserved your compassion at the time, but there was something that didn't make sense in this account. From what I've seen in photographs around the house, Ursula was in her early twenties when she married and, working it out from the time when Felicity was sentenced, her older children are now around eighteen years old."

I turned to the Yorkshireman, who still couldn't raise his eyes to look at me. "Perhaps it's an impolite question, but how old is your wife now, Jim?" He wouldn't answer, and so I tried his son instead. "How old is your mother, Neville?"

The boy rocked back in his seat. I could see how painful this was for him, but he answered just the same. "She was forty-two on her last birthday. I don't understand how—"

There was no time for questions, and so I spoke right over him. "Even if my estimations are wide of the mark, the longest she can have waited for her first child was a few short years. This might have caused some pain and consternation, but not enough for people to talk of her as a long-suffering saint. Five years would have been quite a sentence to fail to have children, even at a young age. Seven? Now that is truly painful, but I would say that two or three years is relatively common."

Until now, Neville had maintained a far-off look, especially when I talked of the mother who had never shown him enough love in the first place. But as my point unfolded, he fixed his eyes on her, and his gaze wouldn't shift for some time.

"If you had cleared out Richard and his family's old rooms, I might never have realised what happened. You see, there's a photograph up there of the whole family shortly before he died. Peter and Paul were tiny. Ursula and Jim were yet to have offspring of their own, but it was Felicity and Richard's three children that caught my attention. One was not much more than a baby, but the two older boys, while still just toddlers, had distinct features that I recognised from another photograph I'd seen on display in the Great Hall. It was taken several years later, but there is no doubt about it. The three oldest children in a photo of Ursula and Jim's family are their nephews and niece. They went from having no children in 1913 to a full family with eight-year-old twin boys, a six-year-old girl and little Neville to round off the group five years later."

There were a lot of names and ages involved in all this and so, to make sure that even Nanny Yapp (and perhaps Percy) could understand the allegation I was making, I laid it out plainly to Ursula and Jim. "After Richard died, you plotted against your sister-in-law so that you could take possession of her children."

It was interesting to discover at this point that Peter and Paul really were in the dark on the matter. Deirdre's children hadn't a clue that their cousins were really... well, still their cousins, but not the ones they thought them to be. The older generation would have all been there to witness the change of custody – that was something that couldn't be hidden from Deirdre – but the boys grew up believing that Felicity's children were really Ursula and Jim's. The children themselves were young enough to have been tricked into thinking they never had any other parents.

"You all gave Ursula credit because she tried for years to have children and bore the pain of their absence. Though it is broody mothers that society tends to discuss, for him to agree to the plan, Jim must have felt the same urge and agony." I was filling in gaps by this point, but I was fairly sure all I'd said was true. "Perhaps that is why Ursula has always judged you so harshly, Neville; you are a living reminder of the lengths to which she'd gone to become a mother. You appeared like a miracle after she'd already made a deal with the devil."

His lip was shaking just a tiny bit, but he would not cry.

"You monsters," Peter said, still on his feet – still with his arm around Deirdre. "You sent an innocent woman to gaol only to steal her children and pass them off as your own." These facts needed no embellishment.

Ursula couldn't summon an excuse for her cruelty and egotism, and yet, what she'd done was almost understandable. She had suffered dreadfully and sought a terrible solution.

"But why?" The confusion that had raged within Paul since he'd entered the room was plain in his voice. "Why hide the fact you were their aunt? It was perfectly natural for you to take care of them after their father died and their mother was sent to prison."

"Because they wouldn't have been mine otherwise!" Ursula's voice was ripped through with emotion. "I didn't want someone else's children. I wanted my own. And they looked just like me and Richard, not that woman. I'd lived a good life and went unrewarded, whereas the hussy who made my brother so unhappy was blessed with three angels."

On cue, Nanny Yapp shouted "Hussy!" and got down from her spot on the bench to sit beside Percy.

"I have cared for those children with every ounce of my strength and love," Ursula continued. "I've done a far superior job of it than Felicity Mortimer ever could have." Her voice got louder with every sentence she spoke.

I, on the other hand, was happy to respond in my usual calm voice. "If that's true, then why don't your adopted children wish to see you any longer?"

My adversary for the weekend jerked her head back. "What are you talking about?" Still in this awkward position, she turned to her husband. "James, what is he talking about?"

Jim looked up as if he were finally aware that what we were discussing related to him. "Ya overheard our conversation, didn't ya? Ya've been listening at doors all day!"

Considering the various crimes he had committed, I thought it rich that he should criticise me for such a minor offence.

"How long have they been angry at you?" I asked, to add to the list of questions that would go unanswered.

Jim and Ursula stared at one another. They both knew that the situation in which they found themselves was inescapable, and neither could produce a response, but the fear in their eyes told me what I needed to know.

"Did they find out who their parents really were? Is that why they're so upset?"

I believe the shock of all this had got too much for Deirdre. Her sons helped her sit down as she began to whimper. Falk, meanwhile, was scribbling away, and Bella had evidently decided that she wouldn't interrupt again, though I could tell there were at least a dozen questions she wished to ask.

"I don't know how it happened," I continued, "but I believe that this discovery set everything else in motion. It's really quite sad that, had it not been for the truth coming to light, Arnold and Carleton would not have died."

Jim found his voice again, and for all of his faults, he could cling on to one small, redeeming fact: he was not a murderer. "Ya keep talking and talking, but I 'aven't heard the slightest hint of who killed 'em. Do you really even know?"

Even the nonchalant maid was gripped now, and I believe that Nanny Yapp looked up from my dog for a moment to see whether I would finally reveal the name they all wanted to hear.

I glanced around the group one last time before turning to Ursula for the final part of the story. "As we've already established, Hobbes called one or perhaps all of you to reveal the interest I'd taken in Felicity's case. I don't know whether the killer overheard the call or charmed the information out of Arnold, but it was enough to send him to London to make sure Hobbes was already dead when I wanted to speak to him. After Arnold read about it in the newspaper, and Bella and I appeared here at the house, he confronted the murderer and was killed."

"Who did it, Marius?" Peter ran his hand through his hair and looked as desperate as any of his more devious relatives.

"The revelation of the three Mortimer siblings' true parentage affected more than just them. There was someone else whose whole life changed when the truth was revealed."

"It *was* you," Paul yelled, pointing across the room at his aunt, and I must say that I really don't like it when people jump ahead like that.

"Yes," I said before things could get out of control. "I thought the same thing at first. Ursula had the most to lose and refused to speak to me today, but something didn't make sense.

Deirdre was just as likely to say the wrong thing and give the game away as her husband was to develop a conscience and tell us what he knew. And yet, your aunt was given a noose but not murdered. Part of me wanted to believe that this was Deidre's own clever stratagem for distancing herself from the crimes, but the only evidence I could find that she conspired against her sister-in-law, let alone murdered anyone, was what her nephew told us this morning."

Ursula, the previously guaranteed killer, closed her eyes just as a few heads turned to look at her son.

"Neville convinced us that, if anyone had plotted against Felicity, it had to be Deirdre because she was the only one who still talked about what happened back then. She also kept newspaper articles related to Richard's death and the subsequent trial, which he had studied at length. I assume you discovered you were an only child shortly before you started coming here to find out about the case. Isn't that right, Neville?"

The young fellow was never the most fluid speaker in his mother's presence, but his tongue deserted him altogether now.

"You threatened Deirdre rather than kill her outright because you would eventually need someone to take the blame for the murders you committed. That's why you tried to convince us she knew more about the conspiracy than she really did."

"It was you!" Falk proclaimed, now that it was evident that this was the case. His glee did not last long, and he pouted for a moment before speaking again. "Hang on a second. Why would he bother?"

"Because he'd lived in his siblings' shadows all his life," Bella confidently explained. She had unearthed the bones of the case just as quickly as I had. "Neville is a clever boy. He realised, just as Felicity's children had, that there must have been a reason for his parents to lie and keep so many secrets."

I wouldn't be distracted as I continued to address the killer.

"I don't yet know the path your supposed siblings took in their attempt to right wrongs, but you set out to stop them. Much as Bella and I did for different reasons, you sought any evidence that could incriminate your parents, and you tried to destroy it."

"That can't be," Peter put in. "Neville hates his mother."

"Does he?" I was quick to respond. "Or does he trail after her like a slave, opening doors and carrying bags in a desperate attempt to impress her? He was the one who brought the birthday presents into the house last night, and he would have known where they were left. As you yourself attested, he's also a boy scout, and must be a dab hand at tying knots. I can't say for certain that they teach young fellows to produce nooses, but I imagine he has a better understanding of how to make one than I would."

"You're wrong," Ursula said with tears now glistening in her eyes. "How could a son of mine do any of this?"

"Because you deprived him of love and raised him to feel bad about the world." You may be surprised to know that this wasn't me speaking. It was the woman's own sister. "You waited for a child of your own all that time and then convinced yourself he was a disappointment."

"That's definitely part of it," I said and gestured to Inspector Falk to prepare for the arrest. "Neville went to such cruel and vicious lengths because, despite all of that, he loved his parents and wanted to prove himself. He believed that, if he stopped Felicity's children from uncovering what really happened to their mother, then Ursula would have to love him back."

"No... You're wrong. You must be." The heartless woman's hands shook as the reality of the grief and destruction she had enabled became apparent. Perhaps I'm being unfair, and Jim Tanner was equally to blame, but it was hard to draw that conclusion from what I'd seen.

Her husband wouldn't move to reassure her. He had his

head in his hands as the fact that he had raised a killer was shared with his family. As for Neville himself, the seemingly shy, studious adolescent showed no emotion. He was neither happy to have executed his plan nor ashamed of the violence it had required. I wasn't expecting a plea for forgiveness, and I didn't get one, but he did have something to say.

"There's one part you got wrong, Marius. Arnold wasn't supposed to die. He was a good uncle to me." He sat a little straighter, his back lined up perfectly with the ornately tiled wall behind him. His voice was just as jolly as if he'd been discussing a favourite book with us. If anything, I think he was happy to get the chance to explain himself. "Uncle Arnold realised from my questions that I knew more than I was supposed to about Aunt Felicity, and he eventually confided in me. He actually said that it was a relief to be able to share what he and my parents had done to get rid of her."

It was unsettling to hear this, but no one interrupted. "I wouldn't have started down this path if, just as you did, my supposed siblings hadn't come across an old family photo in the attic at home. They were furious with our parents, which shows what ungrateful brats they are." His lip curled then, much as his mother's often did, and I had no doubt where he got his less savoury instincts.

"How did you know about Hobbes?" I asked when he needed prompting.

"He telephoned to tell Arnold that you were sticking your nose in our business. He said that he couldn't lie any longer. He had never forgiven himself for the part he played and finally wished to ease his conscience. Poor old Arnold got all het up about it, so I decided to accompany my cousins to London the next day to resolve the problem. After it was done, Marius, I followed you about town in the hope I might kill you too. The chance sadly never arose, but I did manage to pinch the papers you'd obtained. I spent a small fortune on taxis that day, I can tell you!"

"You swine!" Peter screamed, and you can imagine how I felt about this.

His brother raised his hand to silence him. "Let him speak." Paul gritted his teeth and forced the words from his mouth. "I need to know why he killed our father."

Neville looked at his cousins with a bemused expression, but he kept on with his story. "I went to see Arnold in his room this morning. I thought he would be proud or at least grateful, but the way he looked at me was horribly judgemental." He stared into space for a moment, and I realised that this twisted little boy couldn't comprehend why someone would disapprove of his terrible act. "He said he couldn't believe that I was responsible for Hobbes's murder until he saw the noose last night. That was when he decided to tell the police everything that he and my parents had done. I didn't want to kill him, but what else could I do?"

"You could have let him tell them!" Peter flared up, and Paul moved to stop him from punching the monster, who continued the story with a half-smile.

"No, no. That wouldn't do at all. But there was a knife on his nightstand. He tended to leave such things lying about after he'd been hunting, and so I took it, and I stabbed him. In a perfect world, I would have done more to tie him to Hobbes's death, but that couldn't be helped. I knew I would have the chance to push you towards Auntie Dreary at some point, so I wasn't too concerned."

Perhaps the most frightening thing that week was hearing this calm, confident appraisal of his acts. There was no remorse in him – no sorrow – even as he came to reckon with the punishment that now awaited.

"On the day Hobbes was killed," Paul said, not wanting for emotion as he made sense of his cousin's treachery, "you said you were going to a bookshop whilst we visited friends at the Rag. You came back looking very pleased with yourself after you'd murdered a man."

I finally got up from my seat, but not to drive my point home. Bella was crying. Silent tears rolled from her cheeks, and I went to comfort her.

"This isn't possible!" Ursula still couldn't accept what was happening, but I felt it was the punishment rather than the crime that had inspired this response.

"Yes, it is," I whispered, before finding my voice and a new train of thought. "But then, this really shouldn't come as a surprise to you. You evidently knew there was something wrong with Neville. When I listened at your door this morning, Jim was trying to convince you to tell the police about your son, wasn't he?"

No reply came back to me, but I didn't need one. "You said that it would destroy your family. I assumed he was talking about confessing to your part in Felicity's imprisonment, but that wasn't it. You avoided speaking to us because you were afraid we'd get the truth about Neville from you."

With every point I expressed, another came into focus in my mind. "Is that why you made him read works by classic philosophers? In the hope he might pick up the morality that you failed to teach him? The real question is whether you treated your only child differently from your other wards because you saw something wicked in him, or you were the one who put it there in the first place."

Silence followed in my wake, and it was clear that the sad story was complete. As Falk moved to escort his three suspects to the nearest police station, Neville had one last thing to say.

"Marius was right, Mother. I did it for you." He stopped then, a look of regret plain to see. "I'm so sorry I let you down. I thought that I finally had the chance to show my worth, but I made a mess of things as I always have."

Falk secured the boy's wrists with handcuffs, and Neville continued to stare at his mother, perhaps hoping it wasn't too late – perhaps still believing that she might offer some kind utterance after all he'd done.

Ursula Tanner's face had turned scarlet. Her pupils had shrunk to the size of pin pricks, and she could no longer look at anyone there. Falk called one of the constables in from the hall, and she was ushered outside without a word of dissent.

THIRTY-THREE

"It's a remarkable story," Lord Verlaine told us in his office a few days later. We'd just presented him with the evidence that would secure the annulment of Felicity Mortimer's unjust sentence. "It's amazing that the Tanners could pull the strings so effectively. Noel Carpenter is a dear old fellow and would have tried his best for his client even in his twilight years, but to think that they went so far as to organise a campaign to have her pardoned just so that they could sabotage it…"

He was apparently quite impressed by what we had done in such a short time and stroked the hair at the back of his neck. "You know, I met Hobbes on more than one occasion. He came here demanding that I free Felicity from prison, and yet he never mentioned the limited amount of arsenic in her husband's body, nor presented much of a case to sway my thinking. It was all for show."

"We can only assume that he kept anything worth sharing to himself." Bella was happy to do the talking for both of us, for the moment at least. "That's what Arnold Stradbrooke and the Tanners paid him to do."

"Then I must congratulate you." Verlaine tapped one arm

of his chair. "I can only imagine the lengths to which you went to uncover what really occurred."

"Will it take long to release her from prison?" My companion was not one to lose sight of her objective. "I'm aware that the wheels of justice turn slowly."

His face brightened, and he rolled his chair a little closer to his desk. "You will be happy to know that I have been greasing them ever since I first heard the reports of the arrests at Rhinefield House. You'll be less happy to know that it can take some time to convene the Court of Appeal. If I could simply quash her sentence and release her, I would, but this is the only way to clear her name entirely."

"I'm sure you'll do whatever you can to expedite the process."

"I truly will." He hid his lips in his mouth for a few moments before changing tack. "I'm terribly sorry that my wife wasn't well enough to see you during your stay in Hampshire. The timing couldn't have been worse, but I am hopeful that we can entertain you both at Littleton Place in the future. As I'm sure you remember, Letitia is normally a most gracious hostess."

"Thank you." Bella still wouldn't be distracted. "But what about Felicity? Now that her innocence has been proved, how long will it take before she can walk free?"

He looked at her with affection, as if she were a cheeky young girl. "I hope that everything will be processed within a few days and that her appeal will be heard within weeks. My only regret is that this didn't come to light sooner."

"Are you sure?" I asked, and I think that my voice bursting into the conversation surprised them both.

"I beg your pardon?" he replied quite neutrally.

"Are you sure that you would have wanted this to be resolved any quicker? After all, we told you last week of the scientific evidence that disproved the case against Felicity, but you still insisted that we go to the New Forest to find proof of the conspiracy against her."

He put his hands on the edge of his desk and held them there tightly. "What exactly are you implying?"

"Nothing, yet, but give me a moment and I'll get to it." I'm not so cruel that I'd gone into that office without telling Bella what I was going to say. She knew what was coming and had prepared herself accordingly. "There were too many unlikely outcomes stacked against Felicity for someone high up not to have been involved. The choice of an uncompromising and misogynistic judge was key to her conviction. That and the subsequent dismissal of relevant evidence that left her barrister hamstrung from the start were your doing, weren't they?"

I'd noticed a portrait of Lord Verlaine on one wall as we came into the building, and he now did a perfect imitation of the slightly stunned expression he sported in it.

"I imagine that you had a word with Lord Fenwick to make sure he advised the jury to find her guilty. He was such a fierce old traditionalist. All you had to tell him was that Felicity was a modern, independent woman who had failed to obey her husband, and he did the rest."

"You might as well admit the truth, Uncle Thomas." Bella was perfectly calm and showed no sign of apprehension or doubt. "We know what happened."

"I found it strange that the name of Felicity's lover wasn't mentioned in the trial." I delivered more evidence in case he still needed convincing. "The letter that she wrote was to you, wasn't it? You told us you'd known her when she lived in London. Was it then or while her spiteful and adulterous husband was in his sickbed on the estate next to yours in Hampshire that the pair of you fell in love?" Sometimes rhetorical questions are an awful lot of fun. "The nanny at Rhinefield House intercepted one of the missives and, when the Tanners wished to influence Felicity's trial, they blackmailed you into going along with their plan."

"I saved her life!" he immediately responded. "That odious judge gave her a death sentence and, even though Mortimer's family told me not to, I made sure it was reduced."

"Felicity's children were stolen away from her, and she has spent fifteen years in gaol," I countered. "You put your reputation ahead of her welfare."

"I had no choice!"

Bella scoffed just a little. "That's balderdash; you compromised your position as the senior arbiter of justice for the whole country. You hoped that your family wouldn't find out about the feelings you had for another woman, and so you sent your lover to prison. The worst part of it now is that, judging by her inability to face us this weekend, your wife evidently found out somehow anyway. All that pain and suffering and the death of two men could have been avoided."

An important fact that we were yet to mention was that the information we now held on Lord Verlaine was far more damaging than the disclosure of the affair he'd conducted. He had conspired to pervert the course of justice, and we could destroy him if we so wished.

He must have known this, as he said nothing for the best part of a minute. Even when he eventually spoke, he looked as though he'd been tapped on the head with a sledgehammer. "What happens now?"

I looked at Bella, as I felt the choice of what we did next should be hers.

She left him to endure another ten seconds of silent agony before revealing his sentence. "Once Felicity is free, you will retire from the government and spend the rest of your life being a kind and devoted husband to your beloved Letitia. Marius has already visited Felicity in prison to tell her the good and bad news. She wants nothing more to do with you, and if you ever contact her again, we will know."

A strange thing happened then. Lord Verlaine cleared his throat, straightened his tie and would make no further reference to what we had just discussed. "Felicity Mortimer will leave Holloway Prison before the month is out. You have my word on that."

Bella glanced over at me and, presumably happy with the result of our visit, rose to leave. "Thank you for your time, Lord Verlaine." She had become just as formal as he was.

"It's always nice to see you, Bella. Please send my regards to your parents."

He shook hands with us both and pointed to the door. When it closed behind us, I was half tempted to spy through the keyhole to watch his mask slip as reality hit him, but Bella powered past the secretary and out into the hall.

We would not have to speak to Verlaine again, but he exerted the necessary influence and fulfilled his side of the bargain.

Bella was occupied for much of the next week. She had Gilbert's funeral to arrange and who knows what other painful tasks to complete. But the time finally came for Felicity's appeal to be heard and, the following day, we were there at the prison to welcome her back to the world.

"Isn't it odd that I've never met the woman, and yet I'm anxious for her to be free?" Bella asked me as we stood on Camden Road, waiting to catch a glimpse of the famous prisoner.

"I wouldn't say that was odd in the slightest," I told her. "You're a caring person with functioning morals."

She offered me a sad sort of smile in return, but there were no huffs or sighs or even digs at my expense. She had not recovered from Gilbert's death after a few short weeks, but I had begun to see spots of her hope and lightness emerge once more, and that was worth celebrating.

"I must say that I still find Neville's duplicity somewhat frightening," she said, to avoid talking of things that neither of us wished to discuss. "He seemed like a nice young man, and I had such sympathy for him because of his loveless upbringing."

"Yes, but it wasn't quite unfathomable to me at least. I had noticed a certain duality to his behaviour." I moved on the spot to keep warm. Although the sun was out, it was a cold day, and winter would soon descend upon London. "He was one person in front of his parents and quite another with his cousins. It put the hint of an idea in my head that, having lived his life in that manner, it wouldn't be difficult to hide a more violent side from us."

She shivered then, and I doubt it was the cold that caused it. Death has touched us both in so many ways this year, and I admit that even I struggled to comprehend how a boy like Neville Stradbrooke could commit such evil acts.

Bella frowned as she switched to a slightly less unsavoury but still quite despicable element of the case. "It's amazing that his parents hid their lies for so long."

"Inspector Falk sent me a report on some of the missing pieces of the story. He may not be the finest detective I've ever met, but he is quite competent with a pencil and paper."

She smiled at this. "Oh, yes? What did he say?"

"Aside from the less interesting formalities of who was where at the time of the first killing, he revealed that Ursula Tanner has confessed to her involvement. It turns out that she moved the family to Yorkshire for several years after Felicity was imprisoned. That's why no one noticed her suddenly having a large family, and why Peter and Paul never questioned anything. The children were too young to remember their real parents years later, and Nanny Yapp was the only person still living at Rhinefield House who could have given away the secret."

To my surprise, she responded with more than a little compassion in her voice. "Imagine how desperate the Tanners must have been even to conceive of such a plan. It's all so sad."

It bore mentioning how sad it was that they hadn't considered another mother's misery in their plotting, but I was distracted by a crowd who had just arrived at the gates across the road. They were all holding white roses and had apparently come to celebrate Felicity's release. They joined a large pack of journalists and photographers who had been waiting for some time.

Bella was not as easily distracted as I was. "Does anyone know what has happened to Felicity's children?"

"After they discovered the photograph in the attic that Neville mentioned, they ran away from home and haven't spoken to their adopted parents since." I cleared my throat, as I hoped I was about to impress her. "As it happens, there's something I haven't told you about them."

Before I could continue, someone turned up to see us.

"I thought I'd find you here," Chief Inspector Darrington said in his usual commanding voice.

We both knew what his presence meant, and I was frightened for how Bella might react. In fact, I was afraid that whatever progress she'd made could be undone in an instant.

"I was going to send a message via Inspector Lovebrook, but I was passing through the area this morning and decided to stop by." Whether it was his intention or not, he could be quite intimidating, and we stood there waiting for his disclosure. "You've done some wonderful work over the last few weeks."

He stood with an uncharacteristic grin on his face, and I was about to ask him whether this was all he wanted to say, when there was a clang of metal, and a call went up from the crowd.

"She's coming out!" one of the reporters predicted, and then the gate swung inwards in front of the turreted stone gatehouse.

Felicity appeared in the weak sunlight, not blinking, but clearly overwhelmed to be free at last. There was quite a kerfuffle as the crowd closed in, and two warders ran to her aid. They helped clear a path and, as they did so, she caught sight of us standing on the periphery of the action. I believe that she would have come to see us, but then a voice cut through the tumult, and she turned away.

"We're sorry," a young girl declared. She couldn't have been more than sixteen, but something about her face was most familiar.

"We mean it, Mother," a broad fellow a couple of years older stepped forward to agree. "If we'd known anything, we would have come to find you earlier. But as soon as we worked it out, we tried our very best to help you."

It was uncanny how quickly the scene fell still. All of those hardened journalists and every admirer of the long-suffering prisoner stopped to listen to what she would say.

A second brawny youngster moved closer, and Felicity studied these three individuals whom she hadn't set eyes on in fifteen years. Eva, the youngest, looked a little like her, whereas the burly twin boys were the very spit of Richard Mortimer.

"You must believe us, Mother," the girl said. "I don't think we ever truly forgot you. I never felt that the woman who raised us was someone I could love, but it was only this year we discovered why."

Felicity was spellbound by the sight before her. She couldn't speak. She could barely move, in fact, but she managed to shuffle closer and extended her arms to embrace them. It wasn't just the reunited family who cried then. Felicity's supporters threw their flowers, but with tearful exuberance this time. Even one of the wardens looked misty-eyed, and I admit that I felt something in my throat too.

If you ever find yourself dwelling on stories of great injustice like Felicity's, it can make you want to give up on the human race entirely. However, the look on her face as she kissed her three children was enough to restore my faith in fellow men. The joy that flowed through them was indescribable. She managed to put her arms around her immense sons, and the huddle of four put their heads together as if they'd been doing it their whole lives.

Even as camera bulbs flashed, and the reporters went back to shouting questions over one another's heads, the three Mortimer children led her to a black Alvis 12/50 that was parked nearby.

"None of that matters anymore," I heard her tell the stockier of the two boys before he climbed into the car. And the very last thing that she did before she followed him inside the vehicle was to smile across at Bella and me. It was only half a second, and her face was soon obscured by the rush of people who passed in front of us, but it was all we needed by way of thanks.

"Was it them?" Bella put to me before Darrington requested a little context.

"Was it who?"

"Have you followed the case?" I asked, and he nodded his head in a manner which suggested this was a silly question. "So then you'll know that I first came across a report about Felicity Mortimer in a pile of newspapers at the London Library. I'd wondered for some time whether it was more than just chance that helped me find it, and this confirms my theory."

When he was unable or unmotivated to fill in the missing information, I explained myself. "There were two boys squabbling in the library that day. I thought it strange, but didn't consider it too carefully as, when I returned to my desk, there was Felicity's face looking back at me. The boys must have made a scene so that their sister could place it in the pile for me to find. They must have been watching me there all morning and formulated a plan. She'd already followed me across London the night before. She had her hair hidden in a flat cap, and I thought she must have been connected to Lucien Pike, so I did my best to lose her in Charing Cross."

"They must have read about our case in Torquay and decided that we could help them," Bella guessed, and a similar thought had already crossed my mind.

"It's a shame they didn't just knock on the front door and hire us."

"It's an unusual way of going about things." The chief inspector looked puzzled for a moment, then shrugged and shifted his perspective. "I suppose that they are rather young to know what to do, though."

"Or have any money to pay us," Bella pointed out. "Especially after they ran away from home. But at least they achieved the right result in the end."

We watched the car slowly pulling away, and the persistent newsmen darting out of its path. When it was nothing but a black dot half a mile down Camden Road, Darrington spoke again.

"And now to business." He rolled back his shoulders so that he was even more upright and correct than normal. "I would have told you before, but I didn't want to distract you. My men discovered something on..." He looked for a suitable expression. "... the other case. We knew that Gilbert Baines worked for Hargreaves Bank, through whom he was previously assigned to oversee the investments of a successful actor."

"Is that significant?" Bella looked anxious again, and I moved closer to remind her that I was there if she needed me.

"Not in itself, but after that he started working for a man by the name of Brian Grimage."

A bell started ringing in my head at this moment, but it was no louder than one you might hear over the door of a corner shop, and I didn't think anything of it.

"Yes, I remember," Bella replied. "He was ever so excited when the work began back in May. I believe that Grimage made his money in mining or oil or some such thing."

"That agrees with the information we discovered in your fiancé's office, but there is one problem." Darrington had a dour manner that suited this kind of report. He held us in suspense for a moment as the journalists packed up their cameras and wandered off in the direction of the Holloway Road tube station. "You see, there is only one person in Britain with the name Brian Grimage, and he—"

"Was murdered last year," I interrupted, as the bell in my head had become quite deafening. "He was an actor in an adaptation of my novel that never opened to the public because people kept getting killed. That was where you and I first met, Chief Inspector."

"You are correct, Mr Quin. I should probably have recognised his name immediately, but I've been a friend of Lord Edgington for a very long time, and a policeman even longer, so I'm afraid to say that I've investigated rather a lot of murders over the years."

I could see that his jovial tone did nothing to set Bella's mind at ease, and she pressed him for more information. "What does any of this have to do with Gilbert's death?"

Darrington ruffled his moustache and fell serious again. "Gilbert's client was clearly using a false name, so we showed his secretary a photograph of the person we believe killed him." His pause was shorter this time, but it served the same purpose. "She identified him as one Brian Grimage."

I was slightly less amazed by this than Bella was, and I managed to reply. "You mean to say that, for the last six months, Lucien Pike – the man who kidnapped my father, hired us to betray our country, and then left our friend's dead body in my flat – has been paying Gilbert for financial advice?"

"That's about the size of it, yes."

I felt a great pain in my stomach and could hardly bring myself to ask anything more. "But why would he do such a thing?"

"Well..." Darrington clicked his heels together but would need a little longer to reply. "I was hoping you could tell me."

I don't know whether it was the shock she now felt or a need to consider the possibilities, but Bella still wouldn't reply, and so it fell to me to form a conclusion. "It might sound unlikely, but perhaps this was all just a coincidence and Pike knew nothing of our connection to the man he employed. It's quite possible that Gilbert discovered something that he shouldn't have about the source of his client's wealth and was killed because of it."

Bella suddenly reached out to grip my arm for support. "I don't believe that for a second. So far in our dealings with him, Pike is always several steps ahead." She gazed into the distance, and I could practically feel the fear flowing through her once more. "He ingratiated himself in Gilbert's life and then killed him to see how we would react. Just as cats toy with mice before biting their heads off, he's enjoying himself."

I put my hand on her back and pulled her closer. "In which case, the most important question remains unanswered: why us?"

A LETTER FROM THE AUTHOR

Many thanks for reading *Arsenic and Old Lies*, I hope you were glued to the book as Marius and Bella raced to unmask the killer. If you'd like to join other readers in accessing free novellas and hearing all about my new releases, you can sign up to my readers' club!

benedictbrown.net/benedict-brown-readers-club

If you enjoyed this book and could spare a few moments to leave a review, that would be hugely appreciated. Even a short comment can make all the difference in encouraging a reader to discover my books for the first time.

Becoming a writer was my dream for two decades as I scribbled away without an audience, so to finally be able to do this as my job for the last few years is out of this world. One of my favourite things about my work is hearing from you lovely people who all approach my books in different ways, so feel free to get in touch via my website.

Thanks again for being part of my story– Marius, Bella and I have so many more adventures still to come.

Benedict

benedictbrown.net

facebook.com/benedictbrownauthor

ABOUT THIS BOOK

A warning up front: the next two chapters are full of spoilers. I would not recommend consuming them if you haven't already devoured the book!

This is not the first time I've used my writing as a form of wish fulfilment. Despite the happy ending to Felicity's story, the inspiration for the book was not so lucky. Florence Maybrick never saw her children again after she was released from jail, and I think that was what immediately struck me when I learnt of her story. I was determined to write/right that wrong here, and it fired my imagination for how such a resolution could come about.

And now that you know that sad fact, let me jump back to tell you more about her. She was actually born to a wealthy family in Alabama and met her husband, James Maybrick, on the ship over to the UK when she emigrated with her thrice-married (twice-widowed) socialite mother in 1880. As in this book, Florence was twenty-three years younger than her cotton merchant husband, and they were married within a year. He was not a perfect husband; in addition to being a hypochondriac, who consumed all manner of medicines including arsenic and strychnine, he was physically abusive, had many affairs and fathered five children in addition to his three with Florence. Florence herself took lovers and, when James found out about one of them, he throttled her and gave her a black eye.

Florence was already considering divorce before this point and, as James's will left her little, there wasn't a great reason for her to stay in the marriage, or kill him, for that matter. However, shortly after their argument, James consumed a load of strychnine – along with countless other unprescribed medicines – and fell ill. Much of the rest of the story follows the one I have laid out in this book. Florence's in-laws took against her and kept her away from James for the week before he died. Weeks before then, she really was seen soaking flypapers to extract arsenic but, that being said, there was a load of poison in James's medicine she could have used if she wanted to kill him. One small difference in the two tales is that, in real life, it was James's brothers who were particularly suspicious of his wife, but when you consider that she is thought to have had an affair with one of them, and the other is a potential Jack the Ripper suspect (as is James, for that matter!) they don't sound like the most easy-going and impartial types.

It was that pesky nanny (Alice Yapp) who really did for poor Florence, though. She regularly accused her of being unsympathetic to her sick husband by withholding those toxic medicines, and she was the one who intercepted the letter to Florence's lover (a local businessman). A week before he died, her in-laws tested James for poison, and the results came back negative. So even if she had designs on killing him, she failed, and he soon deteriorated and died anyway. Police tests found arsenic everywhere in the house, but less than a quarter of a lethal dose was discovered in James's body. Despite this, Florence was arrested and taken to prison.

Were the crime to occur today, you would have to hope that the evidence wouldn't even allow it to reach court, as there was nowhere near enough to prove that Florence was a killer. However, Victorian society disapproved of independent women who spent time with men other than their abusive husbands (and worst of all, she was from the Colonies!), so she didn't really stand a chance. A large portion of the press took against her, and at the end of the initial public inquest, the all-male jury took just thirty-five minutes to convict her.

This meant that a criminal trial was necessary, which presented the same witnesses and evidence. If anything, this worked in Florence's favour as, by this time, new evidence had been discovered which, for example, ruled out the possibility that one particular bottle of poison Florence had handled was given to her husband. There was also the testimony of a doctor whom Florence had asked to reduce her husband's excessive use of medicine. So things might have gone differently for her had it not been for Virginia Woolf's uncle... Wait, what?

That's right, the malicious judge, who spent twelve hours damningly summing up the case, was the paternal uncle of the author of *Mrs Dalloway* and *To the Lighthouse*. James Fitzpatrick Stephen was a very conservative, traditional man who, by 1888, was close to the end of his career. He had already had a stroke and been criticised for bias and even anti-Semitism in previous cases. His mental acuity was also reportedly in decline (as opposed to Florence's barrister's, as in my story). When the verdict came in, Justice Stephen had no hesitation in condemning Florence Maybrick to death, but this led to a backlash against the sentence, or "minor riots" as one newspaper at the time described it.

The Home Secretary at the time did not like bowing to public pressure and continued to believe that Florence had intended to kill her husband. Despite the influence of many leading scientists and public figures, it was only on the night before Florence was due to be hanged that he requested that Queen Victoria commute her sentence to life imprisonment. So that's what happened. She spent the next fifteen years in jail, despite appeals for her release by family, famous supporters and the US government. If the British authorities had pardoned her or even overturned her sentence, it would have meant that they accepted responsibility for the miscarriage of justice, and so it wasn't until 1903, when the Victorian age was over and (largely) done with, that Florence was finally freed.

What I found particularly interesting when I looked for articles about her from the twenties was that she was still headline news over two decades later. In an article from 1929, it talks of a visit she made to the UK, having returned to the US, where she saw out her days. In it, she still protests her innocence, and it is revealed that she was coming to try to see her children, an ambition which, as I've already mentioned, she failed to realise. In another from 1925, there is an account of a man who, nearly forty years after the fact, suddenly remembered Florence faking her credentials in order to buy "enough arsenic to kill a regiment" shortly before her husband died. It's amazing that, not only was she still famous enough for this to be reported, some in the press were still trying to paint her as the killer when, no matter what her intentions might have been, James Maybrick did not die of arsenic poisoning.

Another article I found describes the reaction to the death sentence of Florence's legal counsel, Baron Russell of Killowen. He always believed her innocent and, immediately after the trial had finished, he turned to his colleagues "and said, with ashen face and a voice choken with emotion: 'My boys, what is your view of this verdict?' They made no reply, and he answered: 'Mark what I say. It is the most dangerous verdict that has ever been recorded in my experience.'"

The same article described the continuing attempts to correct this mistake, but Florence was never pardoned and died as a convicted murderer despite the fact that, and I think this bears repeating, a week before he died, James Maybrick took eight doses of medicine including prussic acid, arsenic and cocaine. He was also known to have boasted of his ability to take strong drugs, which he had done for years, and even consumed arsenic as an aphrodisiac. Did no one stop to think, *Perhaps it's the years of drug abuse that finally killed him rather than a vengeful wife who would not gain from his death and spent the last week of his life at arm's length?*

Florence Maybrick's story is a fascinating one with all sorts of twists and eccentricities. I really recommend the two-part overview of the case on the *Shedunnit* podcast, which I always find hugely informative and inspirational. I thoroughly enjoy the murder mystery book group they run, too, which has introduced me to some brilliant classic detective fiction from the golden age of murder mysteries and beyond.

Another interesting thing that I only discovered when writing this chapter was that at least one of Florence's children really did go to live with their father's family. In real life, the three children were initially adopted by James's brother's doctor, but the girl lived for some time with her paternal uncle (a composer/singer/Ripper suspect) on the Isle of Wight. So who knows what was ultimately behind the family's callous treatment of the very much wronged woman?

That basically explains why I was inspired to write this book and where my ideas came from but, as tends to be the case, there were a lot of other ingredients thrown in the mix. A trial, whether taking place a hundred and forty years ago or today, is meant to establish facts and prove the accused guilty or innocent to certain fixed standards. Florence's clearly did not do that.

If you'd like my personal opinion, I don't think there's any real evidence that she wanted to murder her husband. She would have been much better off getting a divorce, and she certainly didn't gain financially from his death – she eventually inherited £150,000 from her wealthy American family and would have been better off going to them for help if she needed money. Perhaps most significant, though, was the fact that she risked losing her children, and I think that would have stopped her from going through with this dreadful plan. It would be nice to believe that such miscarriages of justice could not happen in our supposedly more enlightened age, but they definitely still do. Over the last couple of years, one particularly clear example of this has received a lot of press in Britain.

Andrew Malkinson was convicted way back in 2004 of the violent physical and sexual assault of a woman in Greater Manchester. He was found guilty despite the absence of a single shred of forensic evidence. Malkinson was also taller, hairier and more heavily tattooed than the description of the attacker that the victim gave to the police. He denied any involvement and was sentenced to a minimum of six and a half years in prison. He would have got out after this time, but he continued to maintain his innocence and ended up spending sixteen years in prison as a result.

There are several neat similarities to the Maybrick case, not least the fact that both were convicted on a 10–2 majority jury verdict, and that issues with the scientific evidence were known soon after the trial. In Malkinson's case, several governmental and police agencies were tasked with examining discrepancies, including the identification of another man's DNA at the crime scene, and for a decade and a half, the investigations failed to piece together the truth. It's easy to conclude that, just like in Florence's time, this happened because of a lack of willingness to accept that the police, courts and government had been at fault in the first place.

Andrew Malkinson was released in 2020 and, three years later, his sentence was quashed after the real attacker was arrested. That culprit's DNA had been identified back in 2007, but no one had acted on the evidence, and so an innocent man spent another thirteen years in jail. Since then, Malkinson has campaigned for reform, a full inquiry was launched into his case, and the BBC made an excellent documentary about him (coincidentally called *The Wrong Man* – the working title of this book was *The Wronged Woman*). As of early 2025, he is still waiting for the bulk of the compensation that he is was awarded for the life that was taken from him.

Shifting mood quite a bit, my character Richard Mortimer was based somewhat on a curious chap called John Bennett, who was a successful watchmaker, merchant and Lord Lieutenant of the City of London at the time of the Maybrick trial. He was an eccentric man who wore a flamboyant black velvet suit as he rode about London on a white steed. It sounds as though he was a real figure of ridicule and, as he occupied any number of ceremonial roles through his life, it's easy to imagine that he was elected to them just to see what chaos he could cause.

In fact, several of the characters (or at least their traits) in this book were inspired by real people. I think that my otherwise fictional Home Secretary was influenced by the case of Marcus Einfeld, a hugely respected judge from Australia. Einfeld was the first president of the Human Rights and Equal Opportunities Commission in his home country and was a very successful barrister, but in 2006 he contested a $77 speeding fine after being caught going just six miles an hour over the limit. He claimed that a friend from America had been driving, and the fine was cleared, but a journalist discovered that the woman to whom he supposedly lent his car had actually been dead some time before.

Perhaps if he'd held his hands up at this point, things wouldn't have gone so badly for him, but he fabricated the existence of another woman with the same name who had also, or so he said, subsequently died. His false statements caught the attention of the wider press and eventually the police, and he served two years in prison for perjury and perverting the course of justice, all because of a $77 fine. He was disbarred as a lawyer, his status as a judge was withdrawn and his reputation was destroyed, despite all the good work he'd done in his career.

One last real-life influence, whose admirable qualities greatly contrast with many characters in this book, is a man called Noel Carpenter. Noel was also a lawyer (or solicitor as we'd call them in the UK), and he was a popular and greatly admired figure in my small town in South London. He volunteered for the Crusaders organisation and ran various clubs for young people, including chess and the one in which he taught me to play table tennis – even when I knew him in his sixties, he was a real wiz with the racket. When I was sixteen, I went for work experience in Noel's firm. My father was a magistrate and had worked with the law throughout his career and, until I realised just how hard I'd have to work at school, I wanted to be a solicitor myself. I then thought, *Nah, I'm too lazy. I'll be a writer instead.* (That might sound like a joke, but that's basically how it happened.)

Noel was an incredibly kind and charitable person who was truly loved in our community. Sadly, just like my dad, he suffered from Alzheimer's in later life. I hope that his namesake in this book is a tribute to the humanity of both of those wonderful men who had such an impact on my childhood. As I was reading his scene for the first time, my nearly two-year-old Osian woke up from his nap, and I held him on my shoulder. After five quiet minutes there, he suddenly pointed to a photograph I have of Dad in my office and said "Grandpa." It was the first time he'd said the word without just repeating it, and it sent a little shiver through me. Once more, that sounds like I made it up, but I swear it's true!

With regards to Noel's speech and mannerisms in this book, they are based on my father in the last year of his life. Until then, he had been at home with Mum, but he began to become physically aggressive, even while largely maintaining his usual kind personality, and there was no way she could look after him any longer. He entered a local home and received excellent care. What was particularly interesting was that he became far more docile and sweet as, once he got used to living there, he had everything he needed. He was always excited for Mum's daily visits and would talk about the nice lady who came to visit him and would even check the visitors' book looking for her signature.

He also adored listening to music and I remember one day, when Dad was still at home, I woke up to him losing his temper. To calm him down, I put on one of his favourite Frank Sinatra records and he started swaying to it. He was so moved by the song that he asked whether he was allowed to keep it and reached out his hand to try to touch the music. This was my experience of time with a person suffering from Alzheimer's: a continuous mix of the painful and the precious.

In the home, he reacted differently towards my family than he did to other visitors, so I'm certain he still knew and loved us even if he couldn't assign the right name to the right person. Mum was "the lovely lady" and he sometimes called me (and probably my two brothers) "the boy from the garden". He was forever trying to entertain us right up to the time he died. I know that some people who have experience of loved ones with dementia might not find that the scene I have included here matches with what they witnessed. I know this because mum's twin sister was diagnosed with Alzheimer's the same year as Dad and died the same year as Dad, fifteen years after their diagnoses. In that time, their conditions couldn't have been more different. Auntie Val was unable to speak or even open her eyes for years before she died, whereas Dad was still smiling and communicating with staff on his last day, when the pneumonia he'd contracted got too much for him. I hope I have at least treated the subject sensitively and not upset anyone with the depiction.

There is one last name inspiration that people might have spotted. Carleton Hobbs (without an E in the surname) was a well-known British actor who played Sherlock Holmes on a long-running radio adaptation in the fifties and sixties. Funnily enough, his career on radio started in 1925 (the same year as my first Lord Edgington book is set) when he played a character called Hastings (though not the one from the Poirot books).

Okay, that's all the real people who influenced this book. What about the setting?

It's amazing that I haven't set a book in Rhinefield House before, as it may well have inspired my love of stately homes more than anywhere else. In the late eighties, Auntie Val's husband Uncle Aubrey (he of the James Dean good looks, who I believe I have mentioned in another of these chapters somewhere) planned a trip for our two families to the New Forest. I was about seven years old, and had to sit in the boot of our Peugeot 505 estate all the way to Hampshire because... Well, I don't actually remember why, but I do know that it wasn't strictly legal even then, and I thought it was brilliant to be hidden there amongst the suitcases.

The hotel we stayed at that week was unlike anything I'd experienced before, or for at least twenty years after. We played golf and tennis, went swimming in an outdoor pool, had breakfast in the hotel and cycled our bikes around the beautiful forest. Let me tell you that I did not have a luxurious childhood, and this whole experience was pretty mind-blowing. But the most amazing thing of all was the nineteenth-century building which still houses the hotel. Rhinefield House mixes Jacobethan, Gothic, Renaissance and Tudor styles to create something really remarkable.

There was originally a hunting lodge on the site that was built for Charles II back in the seventeenth century. The land was still owned by the Crown in the 1880s when Miss Mabel Walker leased it to build a manor house. She was the heiress to a coal mining fortune and invested a large part of it in creating somewhere unique to live. The gardens were particularly impressive at the time, and the designer went on to apply this style to several other famous stately homes, including Luton Hoo. Among other features, it includes the incredibly long pond that Bella and Marius discuss the case beside, a maze, a croquet lawn and an open-air theatre. When the house was turned into a hotel in the late twentieth century, gardeners used the original designs to restore the dilapidated site to its past glory.

Walker and her husband travelled to Spain on their honeymoon, and Mr Walker liked the Alhambra palace so much that his wife decided to recreate it as a room in their house as his Christmas present – which would have taken some wrapping. I don't remember the Alhambra Room from my childhood visit, but we ate in there two decades later when I went back with my wife to celebrate our first wedding anniversary. Even though I've been to the real Alhambra in Granada, the former smoking room, now restaurant, really is memorable and worth looking up online. Even better, of course, if you're planning a trip to the beautiful New Forest, you really should stop for afternoon tea or a few nights' rest.

My only other memory of Rhinefield House as a child was seeing an episode of *Inspector Morse* that was filmed there, but I never forgot that special holiday. The reason it took me until my thirtieth detective novel to reach out to the owners and ask whether I could set a book there might be the biggest mystery yet.

HISTORICAL RESEARCH

This time around, I spent so long reading about Florence Maybrick that there wasn't a great deal of time to go off topic as I often do. Who am I kidding? Of course I did!

One feature of this book, though, is that a lot of my background reading was focused on particular places that crop up in the story. This one possibly surpasses even *The Tangled Treasure Trail* for the sheer number of locations the characters visit. Let's start off with Charing Cross, which is just a walk away from Marius's flat.

A common piece of trivia in Britain is that Charing Cross is the point from which distances on street signs to London are measured. However, this isn't strictly true. Distances aren't measured to the famous railway station, or the recreation of the Eleanor Cross outside, but two hundred metres away at a crossroads beside Trafalgar Square where the original cross once stood. For the last three hundred and fifty years, the spot has been marked by a statue of Charles I on a horse. So now you know!

The, let's be honest, kind of ugly railway station, was thankfully expanded upwards in the late nineteenth century, which gave it the beautiful French Renaissance style hotel that still stands above the large concourse and railway tracks. I'm not going to lie; there are prettier stations in London, but it is a good place to lose a tail if you're being followed.

I like to say that you can stick a pin anywhere on a map of London and find a thousand different amazing stories there, which is pretty much what I did when choosing the location of Marius's meeting with his nemesis, the rival crime writer, Carmine Fortescue. I was playing around on Google Maps looking for any lesser-known spot in the centre that would fit with where the rest of the action was taking place, and I came across St John's Square.

There really is no better argument for London as a city of history and culture than this experiment. Though it isn't actually a square by most people's standards, it has some pretty amazing stories to tell. In terms of landmarks, it's really only St John's Gate that remains to visit, but its history dates back to 1504 when the twelfth century Clerkenwell Priory needed a swanky entrance. It belonged to the religious military order the Knights of the Order of St John, who, being Catholic, would be banned by Henry VIII, reinstated by Queen Mary, and then banned again until the Victorian era.

In the meantime, the gatehouse served as the home of the painter William Hogarth, whose father turned it into a famous coffee house. A couple of decades later, it became a printing house for *The Gentleman's Magazine*. This influential monthly periodical summarised interesting and diverse topics for its readers and featured a picture of the gatehouse on its cover for nearly two hundred years. It also employed important writers like Samuel Johnson and Jonathan Swift, and it was the first publication to take the word *magazine*, the French origin of which meant storehouse (hence its continuing military connotation), and apply it to a periodical aimed at a non-academic audience.

By the nineteenth century, the gatehouse was used as a hospital, which was a taste of things to come as the Order of St John is now best known for its connection to first aid through the St John Ambulance Service, which, to this day, trains volunteers, runs hospitals and provides medical care at public events. The gatehouse was bought back by the order in the late nineteenth century and remains in their possession today. There is now a museum there, dedicated to the history of their organisation. And I got all that from clicking in a random spot on Google Maps.

The scene with the odious Mr Fortescue was inspired by someone far more interesting. Agatha Christie was more involved in her research than this internet link-clicker. Her husband was the Egyptologist Max Mallowan, and she spent years on digs with him. The experience greatly influenced several of her novels, not to mention her travel and non-fiction writing. One famous story goes that, when enquiring of a fellow archaeologist, "Who is the world's leading authority on Mesopotamian pottery?" The answer came back, "You are, Agatha." So I rather like the idea of a mystery novelist becoming an expert on poisons. Of course, Christie was also an expert on poisons, but that didn't just come from her research. She trained in a hospital dispensary during the First World War, which I believe I previously mentioned as it happened in Torquay, where the previous Marius Quin book was set.

Sticking with books, let's head to the library. The London Library, which is next door to Marius's flat on St James's Square, has been mentioned throughout the series, but this was the first time Marius spent any length of time inside. A lot of what I've mentioned about it is true: small entrance which gives onto a warren of buildings? Tick! Frequented by almost every famous name in London from Dickens and Thackeray (who were founder members) through to Charles Darwin, John Stuart Mill, Alfred Lord Tennyson, E. M. Forster, T. S. Eliot,

Winston Churchill, right up to today with names like Tom Stoppard, Tim Rice and (the first female president of the library) Helena Bonham Carter involved? Also tick.

It came into existence after author Thomas Carlyle was annoyed at having to fight for a seat or perch on ladders in the library of the British Museum. He cajoled his friends and influential acquaintances into opening a lending library that was open to all who could afford it. It quickly became an established feature of the literary world and has attracted patronage from British princes, kings, queens and their mothers. Times haven't always been easy for the London Library and, in 1944, 16,000 books, including most of the biography section, were lost when a German bomb destroyed one wing of the building. Thirteen years later, money was so short that members held a charity auction to save the library. T. S. Eliot donated a manuscript of his most famous work (no, not *Old Possum's Book of Practical Cats!* – *The Waste Land*) which sold for £2,800. Items related to Lawrence of Arabia made £3,800. And one hundred and seventy inscribed books by the criminally underrated John Masefield made just £200.

What I really love about the history of this incredible institution is the way in which its space has been used. Starting with just one building, the library has been able to buy neighbouring ones piecemeal and cleverly link them together. Whenever space is short, they build a room in a lightwell, tack an annexe onto the side of a wall somewhere or shuffle around the floorplan to fit in more books. It's a bit like a never-ending Lego model, with the limitation that they are having to build in one of the most expensive parts of Britain, surrounded by historic buildings. It really is a testament to the project and the love people have for it that it is still here a hundred and eighty-four years after it opened.

In contrast, for this book I decided that Marius should visit some restaurants that aren't around anymore. Until now, I've generally used London restaurants that were there in the twenties and still exist today, but I was interested to dig deeper and find out about some that are long closed. I felt like an Edwardian toff as I dug into guidebooks for wealthy travellers from the era and pictured myself marvelling at the incredible interiors of the palatial dining rooms.

Verrey's is believed to have been the first French restaurant in London. It was opened in 1825 by a Swiss restaurateur, but by the end of the century it was in the hands of two French brothers called the Monsieurs Krehl. The place was well known for its desserts – including their trademark pistachio ices and the other tasty dishes that Bertie mentions in this book. It was also famous as a meeting point for rich foreign travellers. In the 1899 book *Dinners and Diners* by food critic Lieutenant Colonel Newnham-Davis, he devotes a chapter to the restaurant. He goes into great detail about his meal there with a rich American sheathed in white fur and says, "we settled down to our table in the dining-room, with its silver arches to the roof; caught and reflected a hundred times by the mirrors, and its suave dark-green panels, which formed an excellent background to the cream-coloured miracle of a dress that Mrs. Washington was wearing..." Doesn't sound bad, does it?

Another important venue at the time this book is set was French chef Marcel Boulestin's eponymously named restaurant. He was born in France and, having failed with his first novel, became a ghostwriter for the mononymous author Willy (first husband of the mononymous author, Colette). Boulestin was a great anglophile and moved to London in 1906. Whilst there, he continued his literary and journalistic career, became a familiar figure among the rich theatregoers of the day and opened a pioneering and popular interior design shop. He served as an English interpreter in the war but, when it was over, his reopened shop failed. It sounds as though times were hard for the thirty-five-year-old when he accepted a commission to write the book that would make him famous. *Simple French Cooking for English Homes* was a huge success at a time when interest in cooking was low.

His new career as a food writer led to the opportunity to cook for Virginia Woolf, train her cook, and then open his own restaurant, which first appeared in 1925 in Leicester Square before Restaurant Boulestin made its mark in Covent Garden two years later. It built a great reputation for itself and was the most expensive restaurant in London. Despite this, Boulestin's standards were so high that it didn't actually make any money, and he relied on his publishing work for income. He went on to become one of the world's first TV chefs for the BBC's experimental broadcasts in the late thirties, and his restaurant remained open until 1994, fifty-one years after he died. But what I love about him most is something that we have in common. No, I am not a great chef, nor have I ever opened a famous restaurant, but I have got my French family to eat a bunch of English food that they might otherwise have turned their noses up at. Like Boulestin, I have introduced my in-laws to mint sauce on lamb, mince pies at Christmas and afternoon tea whenever they come to London – incidentally, those are the main three foods (plus mature cheddar cheese, of course) that I have promoted to them, and also the three mentioned in the article I read on him.

Staying with swankiness, I read up once more on the tradition of young ladies being presented as debutantes at court. The tradition was started by Elizabeth I, way back in the sixteenth century, as a sort of matchmaking service for rich families. It continued until 1958 in Britain, and it was our dear Queen Elizabeth II who did away with the practice, as the long-established class barriers had apparently blurred, and the pesky nouveau riche had invaded high society. Her sister, the always outspoken Princess Margaret, said, "We had to put a stop to it. Every tart in London was getting in."

I've never been to a ball of any description – I now realise somewhat sadly. School discos were a pretty torturous affair during my teenage years, and I would have been better off staying at home playing a parlour game (how's that for a segue?). Every time I've had to mention one of these popular Victorian entertainments in my books, I've looked up old guides from the time which explain the rules. I promise I've read them carefully and tried to understand them, but they are so complicated that, most of the time, I have no idea what you're supposed to do.

To put this across, I lifted a sentence directly from 1854's *Book of Parlour Games*, and what Peter tells us is a direct quote. It explains how to play "Hot Cockles" by saying that "A Penitent, chosen by chance, or by his own choice, hides his face upon a lady's lap, which lady serves as Confessor, and places herself in an armchair in the midst of the company..." before continuing in a similar manner for another two paragraphs. I think it would take an evening just to work out what you're supposed to do. These old books are full of brilliantly named diversions and Hot Cockles, The Simpleton, the Bull's Foot, an Epistle with a Double Meaning, the Voyage to Corinth and the Nun's Kiss are all games that the Victorians would have enjoyed (or otherwise).

I wrote this book at the end of 2024 whilst at home in Spain, so there are quite a few places I haven't visited except through Google Street View and online 3D tours. One that I *have* been to is the Charles Dickens Museum at 48 Doughty Street near King's Cross. Dickens only actually lived there for a couple of years just after his marriage, but that doesn't take anything away from it, not least because it is the only one of his London houses which still stands. It's also important because it was there that he finished his first novel and wrote *Oliver Twist* and *Nicholas Nickleby*.

The building was almost demolished in 1923 but was saved by a charitable foundation which was able to raise the money to buy the house. It was turned into a museum two years later and is still open to the public today. In fact, the museum has spent the last hundred years adding to its collection of Dickens's property. You can explore the different rooms where he lived with his wife and first three children and see everything from his manuscripts to his writing desk and his wife's jewellery.

Somewhat grimly, you can also see the tombstone of the illustrator Robert Seymour. Seymour was the first illustrator for Dickens's *The Pickwick Papers*, which was a massive success and launched the author's career. It was originally conceived of as a series of illustrations with brief anecdotes to showcase Seymour's light, humorous work in a monthly periodical. However, Dickens took over the project, and it soon became a longer text with the odd illustration.

Seymour suffered with his mental health and was evidently unhappy to be sidelined on a project that he had helped think up. He argued with Dickens over one of the images for the second edition of the magazine and, the following day, was found dead at home with a bullet wound to his head. Dickens would strongly deny that the ideas in his first novel were influenced by Seymour, but it's unlikely that the book would have come to exist without him getting the ball rolling. Grimly (again), as he had killed himself, his family received no money for the illustrations he had completed. On a lighter note, if you'd like to see some of his often ornate and beautiful drawings, I recommend *The Book of Christmas* by Thomas K. Hervey, which can be read online for free.

I was going to talk to you about Newgate prison, but that last section was already sad enough. What I can say is that Florence Maybrick, who was actually imprisoned in Woking and then Aylesbury prison, did not complain of mistreatment by the guards themselves. However, for the first nine months there, she was kept in solitary confinement, and she wrote in her autobiography of the dehumanising and traumatising effect it had on her. When she was finally released, she toured England and America, campaigning for prison reform and once more arguing her innocence of the crime for which she was never pardoned. The name of her autobiography was *If I Did It: Confessions of the Killer*. No, hang on a second. That was O. J. Simpson. It was called *Mrs. Maybrick's Own Story: My Fifteen Lost Years*.

Another point on the map I chose was the spot which holds (or rather held as of a couple of years ago) the Hardy Tree. The churchyard of St Pancras Old Church has many literary and artistic connections. It gets a mention in *A Tale of Two Cities*. Mary Wollstonecraft and her husband have a tomb there – at which their daughter Mary Shelley (of *Mary Shelley's Frankenstein* fame) met with poet Percy Bysshe Shelley to plan their elopement. Architect John Soane designed his own tomb, which is thought to have inspired the shape of the classic red British phone box. The author of what is commonly considered to be the first influential vampire story, John William Polidori, is buried there, but my favourite literary connection is to Thomas Hardy.

As a young man, he worked as an architect and was put in charge of clearing a part of the churchyard for the expansion of a railway line. This meant removing old graves, and either he or one of his workmen placed the no longer needed tombstones around an ash tree in a sort of starburst formation. A brief estimate suggests there are still about eighty of them there, though sadly the tree itself fell down in 2022 due to sickness. It was over two hundred and fifty years old. Curiously, a memorial to those missing graves was later paid for by England's then wealthiest woman, Angela Burdett-Coutts. I will go into her story at a later date as, if I stick to my current plan, the next Marius book will be set in Holly Village, a unique and beautiful housing development which is considered the first gated community.

I love the little coincidences I find when I research my books, and another that cropped up this time was down to the fact that, quite at random, I chose the name Tanner for Ursula and Jim. While preparing this chapter, however, I discovered that an architect who worked on the garden at Rhinefield House and another who worked on the Royal Courts of Justice were both Tanners. Perhaps it's a common name, but it still made me smile. The same can be said for various names and places (especially William Hogarth and the Royal Courts of Justice themselves) that popped up wherever I looked.

As always, we will finish with some food and a song. I did not have to reach for my copy of Mrs Beeton this time, as all the dishes mentioned were suitable for the location where they were served. I found a real menu from Verrey's French restaurant which I include here so that, when he records the audiobook, my dear friend George Blagden has to practise his best French.

Petite marmite.
Oeufs à la Russe.
Soufflé de filets de sole à la Verrey.
Noisettes d'agneau à la Princesse.
Petits pois à la Française.
Pommes Mirelle.
Aiguillettes de caneton à l'Orange.
Salade Vénétienne.
Pouding Saxon.

For Rhinefield House, I used local dishes that are well known in the New Forest and Hampshire and also consulted the current menus of the Rhinefield House restaurant. Dishes like Hampshire venison, chalk stream trout, Tunworth English Camembert, and roast sirloin of Hampshire beef all sound mouthwatering, and they even have a Paris–Brest on the dessert menu, which reminds me...

A Paris–Brest is a choux pastry in the form of a wheel filled with praline cream. It was created in 1910 to celebrate the seven hundred and fifty mile Paris-to-Brest-and-back-again cycle ride. It soon became popular with competitors because it loaded them up with calories for the challenge – though it's hard to imagine modern pro-cyclists filling their face with fancy desserts.

As for the song, well there's only one and, to be perfectly honest, I only added it at the end when I realised there wasn't a hint of musicality in this book. It's only a snippet, too, but it has some history. "Sally in our Alley" was written way back in 1725 by Henry Carey, the poet and dramatist who gave the English language the phrase "namby-pamby" in one of his poems and was one of the first people to sing "God Save the King" as part of the Patriotic movement of the eighteenth century (even if he didn't write it, as his son claimed). More impressively, his song, which Deirdre sings, went on to be arranged by no less than both Ludwig van Beethoven and Benjamin Britten, and it had a musical and Gracie Fields film named after it. That really isn't bad going for a song that features the lines,

> There is no lady in the land
> Is half so sweet as Sally;
> She is the darling of my heart,
> And she lives in our alley.

Right, enough blathering. I have other books to write. Marius and Bella will be back in time for Christmas. Bye bye for now!

WORDS AND REFERENCES

gallows humour – black humour. At the time, the German expression *Galgenhumor* seems to have been just as common, and this is where the phrase originates.

money-maker – a bestseller, this term dates right back to 1850.

shoeblack – shoeshine, which is the US term.

leaders – the British term for editorials in the newspaper.

Great Wen – a nickname for London dating back to the 1820s. A wen is another word for a cyst and the term was coined to criticise the swelling capital city that was invading the countryside around it. Just imagine how the guy who thought it up would feel if he visited now.

prattle-box – another word for a chatterbox.

shoeing horn – in terms of food, this is a rather blunt

metaphor for a dish which eases you into your next dish. So an appetiser, basically.

entremets – a dish that's eaten with a main course, or a dessert. Take your pick.

Worshipful Company of Clockmakers – a livery company (a bit like a guild) dating back to the seventeenth century, which still exists today.

drunk as a drowned mouse – not my poetic turn of phrase. It's apparently common enough to get an entry in the dictionary.

shellac – resin (lac) dissolved in alcohol and shaped to make a brittle plasticky sort of material that was used to make gramophone records. It dates back to 1713.

cod's head – one of the million different terms you can find for "idiot".

topiarian – the adjective of topiary.

lunkhead – one of the million different terms you can find for "idiot".

shāh māt – another possibility is that the phrase originally comes from Persian and meant *the king is helpless*, but Carmine Fortescue isn't the type of person who is worried about nuances or accuracy.

knight of the quill – a posh, sometimes tongue in cheek term, for a writer.

photogenique – can you guess what it means? It entered the language in 1923, whereas photogenic appeared a year earlier but seems to have been more American than British.

get an iggri on – get a move on. A word that came from British troops in Egypt. Their Australian colleagues nicknamed a particular spot Iggri (apparently the Egyptian Arabic word for hurry up!), because it was so dangerous, you had to move quickly through it.

tha knows – "you know" in Yorkshire dialect.

Dashing White Sergeant – a Scottish country dance.

gawby – Yorkshire dialect and another one of the million different terms you can find for "idiot".

barrack – as a verb it means to cajole and pressure, but I was interested to discover that it didn't originate in the military but comes from Australia before the English adopted it to mean 'to brag, to be boastful of one's fighting powers'.

bureau plat – a writing desk decorated in a French style.

wires crossed – I should have probably realised before that this expression meaning to have things confused originated in telephony, when operators would patch one line onto another.

palaver – in British English, this can mean a lot of bother or commotion. I don't normally go out of my way to explain differences between UK and US English, but my early readers were so convinced I was wrong, I felt that I should.

Rag, the – the nickname for the Army & Navy Club, one of the fanciest in London. It is something of an ironic moniker and comes from a time when a member complained of the food being served and compared it to a local dive gambling hall by saying it was "a rag and famish affair". The name stuck and is still used around a hundred and eighty-five years later.

CHARACTER LIST

Old Favourites

Marius Quin – he's there on the cover! You must know him by now!

Lady Bella Montague – Marius's former girlfriend, sleuthing partner and close friend.

Gilbert Baines – Bella's fiancé. A dull banker who was murdered in the last book.

Lucien Pike – a shadowy individual who has been messing with Marius and Bella and appears to have murdered Gilbert.

Chief Inspector James Darrington – hardworking senior police officer with friends in high and clandestine places.

Inspector Valentine Lovebrook – a happy-go-lucky officer who befriended Marius & Co. in the first book of the series.

Bertrand Price Lewis – Marius's larger than life editor.

Marius's Mum – Marius's Mum.

Carmine Fortescue – Marius's rival mystery writer and a bit of a know-it-all!

New Favourites

Felicity Mortimer – imprisoned for the murder of her husband fifteen years earlier.

Deirdre/Dreary Stradbrooke – Felicity's sister-in-law who took against her when her ill brother was living in Rhinefield House.

Arnold Stradbrooke – old-moneyed and traditional husband of Deirdre.

Peter and Paul Stradbrooke – two little birds who— No, wait. They're Arnold and Deirdre's sons. Peter is the impetuous one, Paul a bit dreamy but supposedly smart.

Jim Tanner – a Yorkshireman who has made a fortune in coal.

Ursula Tanner – his wife, Deirdre's sister. She's a nasty one!

Neville Tanner – their fourteen-year-old son who is clearly afraid of his overbearing mother.

Nanny Yapp – the former nanny of the Stradbrooke household, who still lives with them.

Lord Verlaine – the Home Secretary.

Carleton Hobbes – a friend of Marius's editor, Bertie, who helped Felicity try to overturn her sentence.

Noel Carpenter – Felicity's barrister. We also meet his wife, Millicent.

Inspector Falk – he's an inspector. He's not a particularly good one, but he is an inspector.

ACKNOWLEDGEMENTS

I must always start this section by thanking my brilliant editor, Emily. She and her very nice fiancé should be married by the time this book comes out. I'm sure she's been busier than ever over the last months and still had to put up with me missing a deadline and springing an uncommissioned book on her. So thank you very much as always, Emily. I hope the wedding goes fantastically and you and Josh have a long, happy life ahead of you!

Thanks must go to the current owners of Rhinefield House for allowing me to use the image on the cover and the name in the book. I have such happy memories of my childhood holiday there and it's nice to have spent the last few months wandering its halls. Thanks to my always helpful legal expert (former judge, my mother's cousin and the inspiration for Bertie in these books), Rhodri Price Lewis KC.

I must thank my brilliant ARC readers, who chip away at each book to make it ten times better (especially Joe and Kathleen Martin for keeping me honest even when I don't want to be). My kids and wife for forcing me to take breaks and play games. Osian and Amelie (and Marion, too, of course) are true wonders, and they inspire me every day.

And, of course, thank you also to every person who has read this book. I couldn't do it without you.